THE PLAYER

'How about a split deal, then?'

The slim blonde straightened again, frowning and shaking her head as she turned back towards him.

'I don't follow . . .'

'You win the best of five games, I give you fifty quid. But if you happen to lose, I'm going to expect some extra special attention from that mouth of yours.'

'Excuse me?'

'Down on your knees in the gents' toilets. For as long as it takes until I come in your throat.' Carter smiled, watching her face pale at his description. 'How does that sound to you?'

'Perverted.'

His eyes never left her face. 'But you haven't slapped me yet.'

'Are we talking cash?'

'Naturally.'

THE PLAYER

Cat Scarlett

This book is a work of fiction.
In real life, make sure you practise safe, sane and
consensual sex.

First published in 2004 by
Nexus
Thames Wharf Studios
Rainville Road
London W6 9HA

Copyright © Cat Scarlett 2004

The right of Cat Scarlett to be identified as the Author of
this Work has been asserted by her in accordance with the
Copyright, Designs and Patents Act 1988.

www.nexus-books.co.uk

Typeset by TW Typesetting, Plymouth, Devon

Printed and bound by
Clays Ltd, St Ives PLC

ISBN 0 352 33894 6

You'll notice that we have introduced a set of symbols onto our book jackets, so that you can tell at a glance what fetishes each of our brand new novels contains. Here's the key – enjoy!

cp (traditional)

cp (modern)

spanking

restraint/bondage

rope bondage/hojojutsu

latex/rubber/leather/enclosure

fem dom

willing captivity

medical

period setting

uniforms

sex rituals

One

Carter picked up his pint and wandered idly down the pool hall, his face expressionless. Beneath that cool exterior, his heart was thudding with a sudden nervous excitement. He kept walking though, eyes fixed on the shadowy player at the far end of the hall.

If you're looking for action, the bartender had said, check out the kid on table seven. The shots he had seen from the bar had made him stiffen instinctively, beginning to frown – though a few good shots did not make a player, he reminded himself. Could this be the one he had been searching for all these months? The hairs were rising on the back of his neck but he found himself grimacing all the same, tensed for one more disappointment. He had only wandered in here on a whim. It seemed too good to be true, finding the final player to complete his tour in this grubby backstreet club. He no longer possessed that sort of luck.

Yet as Carter drew nearer, the slim girl in faded green jeans and tight T-shirt bent over the baize for another shot and he drew a sharp breath. His body tingled as if at an electric shock. He had not been mistaken. There was real accuracy behind that cue arm; a raw talent that might be worth bringing out and polishing.

'You practising on your own?'

1

She glanced up from the table and straightened, eyes narrowing on his clean shirt and neatly laundered jeans as she took two cautious steps backwards and leant on her cue. Presumably clocking him as a married man, he thought cynically, though she could not have been more wrong. Pure icy blue, those eyes, and short cropped hair the colour of wheat. At first glance, standing at the bar, he had thought it was a boy slamming the balls into the pockets. But her figure was not so boyish close up. Slim-hipped and with smallish breasts, but curved enough in the right places to be feminine. She was not wearing a bra and he could see the tantalising shape of her nipples through the thin material of her T-shirt.

'What's it to you?'

'No need to bite my head off,' he replied mildly, putting his pint down on a side table. 'I'm just looking for a game.'

'Friendly?'

He shook his head. 'I'm more of a betting man, myself.'

'How much?'

'Do we have to play for money?' he asked, choosing a cue from the nearby wall rack. They were all pretty bad, he realised, but it hardly mattered on this occasion.

'What's the alternative?'

He shot her a wry look. 'Don't you have an imagination?'

'Sorry, I'm not interested in that sort of arrangement.' She turned away from him with a shrug, bending back to the pool table as though the matter was closed.

'Perhaps you ought to try one of the girls on the street instead. I believe their price is quite reasonable.'

Carter guessed his suggestion had disappointed her. Perhaps she was too conventional for what he was offering. Appraisingly, he allowed his eyes to move down over the raised backside, noticing how her legs were spread slightly apart as she took another shot. For someone who was not interested, it was one hell of an inviting pose. He took another step closer and lowered his voice this time so no one else in the pool hall could hear them. Her initial reaction had worried him, but there was still a chance she might accept if he handled this properly.

'What's the matter? You a lesbian?'

'No.'

'So what's wrong?'

She laughed briefly, slamming a ball down towards the far pocket so hard it rattled twice before dropping. 'I'm just trying to make a living here.'

'How about a split deal, then?'

The slim blonde straightened again, frowning and shaking her head as she turned back towards him.

'I don't follow . . .'

'You win the best of five games, I give you fifty quid. But if you happen to lose, I'm going to expect some extra special attention from that mouth of yours.'

'Excuse me?'

'Down on your knees in the gents' toilets. For as long as it takes until I come in your throat.' Carter smiled, watching her face pale at his description. 'How does that sound to you?'

'Perverted.'

His eyes never left her face. 'But you haven't slapped me yet.'

'Are we talking cash?'

'Naturally.'

'How can I be sure you've got that much on you?'

The voice was crisp and competent but he suspected she must be bluffing now, her cheeks a little too flushed as she faced him out. He took a bulging leather wallet from his back pocket and threw it down on the faded green baize of the pool table. He saw her blue eyes focus on the wallet for a moment, then move slowly back to his face. What was she thinking? The girl had bitten her lower lip so hard, there was a bright bead of blood on it. She was breathing quite heavily too, her chest rising and falling under the thin T-shirt. That was when he realised how tempted she was by the offer. Was she ready to trade that warm supple mouth on the strength of her pool skills? Perhaps the girl was more experienced than he had supposed.

Carter imagined this petite blonde dropping to her knees in front of him and felt the beginnings of an erection press uncomfortably against the front of his jeans. That reaction startled him and he spoke hurriedly to hide his surprise.

'Take a look in the wallet. I'm good for it.'

'Fifty's a bit shallow,' she muttered. 'Perhaps a hundred . . .'

'Done,' he said smartly.

She licked her lips, clearly taken aback by his ready agreement to double the stakes, then nodded. 'OK then.'

'Let's get this straight before we shake on it. So there's no argument later. You win, I give you a cool hundred in cash. But if I win, you get down on your knees and blow me. Is that clear?'

'Crystal.'

He held out his hand. 'You need a witness?'

'I'll trust you.'

'But I may not trust you.'

She smiled then, almost confident again, neat white teeth showing behind the torn lip. 'You'll need to trust me if you win.'

'Why's that?' Unable to resist her provocative charm, Carter found himself smiling back. 'You don't bite, do you?'

'Only when I lose.'

Carter found himself mesmerised by the way her tongue emerged as she murmured that, slipping gently across her lip and probing the slight tear left by her teeth. The discomfort in his jeans grew steadily and he knew there was no way she was going to win this match. He badly needed to push her down onto her knees, bury himself between those moist lips and plumb the depths of her throat until he came. His erection was almost straining at the zip now, so embarrassingly obvious that Carter found himself shrinking back into the shadows around the table to hide it. But his urgent need for relief could not be ignored for long. Even if it meant cheating whenever her back was turned, he would have to make sure that she lost this match.

'I'll try to remember that,' he said unsteadily.

But the girl had turned her back on him and did not seem to be listening. With a practised air, she positioned the balls in their triangle and aligned them with a long-faded mark on the cloth beneath. Her hands moved swiftly and without hesitation. There was a genuine confidence to this one, he realised, watching closely as she rolled the white towards the far end of the table and picked up her cue again. It was no act. This girl believed she could win and was clearly not afraid to take the risk of such a stake, even when sexual humiliation must lie ahead if he beat her.

She held up a small coin. 'Heads or tails?'

'What's your name first?'

'Roz.'

He extended his hand. 'I'm Carter. Heads, please.'

They shook hands in a perfunctory manner and Roz tossed the coin, catching it deftly on the back of her hand and glancing down almost in the same movement.

'It's heads.' Her disappointment at losing the toss was palpable, but she kept her chin up. The girl had guts, he had to give her that. 'You want me to break?'

'I don't think so, sweetheart,' he murmured, shifting to the head of the table.

Staring along his cue at the tightly clustered pack ahead, Carter felt a sudden tremor of uncertainty. He might have pulled harder tricks out of the bag on previous occasions, and in rather more threatening surroundings than this pleasantly smoky backstreet club, but there was no absolute guarantee that he would beat this girl. Roz was no novice, that was obvious. In spite of her sexy looks and figure, this blonde had the eyes of a striking snake. What if his attempts at cheating, however well practised, happened to fail on this occasion? She seemed so confident, as though one poor shot on his part might place her in a winning position. Even amongst strangers in an unfamiliar pool hall, he did not want to end up out of pocket and looking foolish.

Carter split the pack with a deliberately exaggerated crack and stepped back to watch the balls fly to every corner of the table. He wiped a damp palm on his jeans, noting to his satisfaction that several balls had already gone down. It was an excellent opener, and there was every possibility that he would follow it up with a swift smooth kill. So stop sweating, damn it. He had to take control of this game before he lost an excellent opportunity to recruit a new player to the tour. Not to mention empty his aching balls into her beautiful mouth.

There was something pleasantly cruel about leading Roz into the gents' toilets after the last game, turning to stand in the middle of the small tiled room and watching her expression as he unzipped his flies without further ceremony and pointed to the floor.

The tiles were damp with a mixture of water and splashed urine, the familiar smell just short of offensive. The girl would not have to work down there for very long, Carter thought wryly. He had been stiff for some minutes now, knowing the match must be in his pocket and only waiting for that last black to roll down before he demanded the soft wetness of her mouth on his penis. Roz had been taken by surprise by his constant good luck – that much was obvious. But she had not seen the way he kept nudging the white past awkward balls to set himself up for an easier shot, his quick moves restricted to whenever she glanced away from the table or turned to take a sip from her drink.

His conscience was troubling him though. Naturally he would have preferred to beat her in a fair fashion, and he was not such a bad player that he needed to cheat in order to get the right result, but this had been too important a win to leave to chance. He was being paid to handle a troupe of eight female players and if there were still only seven at tonight's tournament, his position as tour manager would begin to look decidedly shaky. If he could only persuade her to join the tour, Roz would complete the minimum number of players. So a little nudge here and a tweak there had been entirely in order. He could always apologise at some point in the future if necessary. But not until she had sucked his cock and preferably accepted the proposition he would make as soon as she had fulfilled her part of the bargain.

'Down on your knees.'

Roz seemed shaken. 'Right here? But someone might come in.'

'So what if they do?'

His laconic reply left the blonde speechless. Without bothering to protest any longer, she sank to her knees on the damp tiled floor of the gents' toilets and stared disconsolately at his exposed crotch, mere inches from her eye-level. Her breasts looked firm and high as they pushed against the thin T-shirt.

He briefly considered asking her to strip first, then realised he could not wait that long. Not only was he uncomfortably rigid now but it was getting late and he would have to make his way back to the hotel soon to check that all the preparations for tonight's tournament were going smoothly. Eager to watch the girl at work, Carter nudged his penis firmly towards her mouth.

'You lost, so you suck,' he reminded her. 'That was the deal.'

'I know,' she said miserably.

'Listen sweetheart. I'm not going to let you walk away here without payment. I want what's due to me.'

Reluctantly, her hands came up and fumbled with his underpants, releasing him further so the full length sprang out against her face, hot and darkly flushed. The veins bulged at the surface, tense with blood. He felt a familiar twinge in his balls and considered holding her head and forcing himself deep into her throat. But he was enjoying the moment too much to hurry the pace.

His hand rested lightly on her short blonde hair, using only the minimum of pressure to encourage her forward. Now her head was tilting slowly back to reveal a pale smooth-skinned throat, poised to accommodate him. There was a look of dismay on her face which aroused him even further. Although he had grown accustomed to being surrounded by submissive women on the tour, it was rather exciting when a woman had to be coerced like this.

Then he groaned, pulling her closer as her lips parted at last and she took him in. Sweet Jesus, what a mouth. The warm, moist tightness enclosing his shaft was almost too much for him and Carter had to take a few short panting breaths to keep himself under control. This girl was beautiful and talented and his exclusive property for the next few minutes. It would be a waste to spoil such a pleasurable experience by shooting his load too soon.

Carter was suddenly torn, wanting to swear at the blonde, call her a whore as she sucked. But there was something so alluringly innocent about the way her head bobbed at the end of his cock, cheeks blown out by his length in her mouth, the earnest way her eyes had shut tight as she worked. He liked the illusion that she was a novice, that he was teaching her something new. To call her a whore would ruin that illusion, he thought hazily, watching her through half-closed eyes. Then he stopped thinking as her hands moved up to cup his balls in such an erotically submissive fashion, kneeling there like a concubine at his feet, that his penis slipped quite naturally further down her throat and he encouraged it with a jerk of his hips. It was clearly not what she had expected.

Roz gagged on his length but Carter did not bother to pull back. In his imagination, this was her punishment for daring to outplay him on the table. It was a physical act of invasion, claiming the territory as his own, showing her who was in charge here, and he loved it. The sensation was exquisite and brutal at the same time, and he knew it would not be long before he came.

'Come on. Suck it right in.' His hands tangled in her hair, jerking her back and forth on his penis with

9

an uncompromisingly urgent rhythm. 'You know what's going to happen next? I'm going to spunk in your throat and you're going to swallow it all.'

Her muffled grunt sounded like a mixture of horror and despair yet Roz obeyed him and sucked harder, increasing his rigidity until his cock felt almost numb with it.

He suddenly imagined withdrawing from her throat and dragging those tight green jeans to her knees, turning the blonde over so that he could enter her from behind. The thought of her body writhing helplessly beneath his on the damp floor of the men's urinals nearly had him climaxing in spasms; but he controlled it with an effort, concentrating instead on sexually explicit graffiti scrawled in red biro above the nearest stall. 'Mike sucks cock,' it read, 'Fletcher takes it up the arse.'

He screwed up his eyes and gradually allowed himself to enjoy the sensation of that constantly working mouth, impaling the girl with each thrust of his hips so that she had no chance of escape until he was satisfied. If she joined the tour, he thought with dim realisation, he would not be able to do this again. Except on special occasions, it was forbidden for any of the tour staff to have sex with the players, and that included him as the manager. So this might be his only chance to experience the pleasure of her lips wrapped so obediently around his flesh.

'You love this, don't you?' he muttered, pulling back slightly so her tongue could lick along the intensely sensitive underside of his penis. His skin prickled, a clear signal that orgasm was imminent, and the hairs were standing up on the back of his neck.

Her face was flushed now. He bent his knees and reached down to grab at her T-shirt, yanking it up so he could see the high breasts with their small pinkish nipples. Holding her in position by the hair, his free hand sought one of those nipples and squeezed it like a teat. He did not bother with gentleness; he could tell by the kittenish little noises she was making under her breath that she was as aroused by this act of humiliation as he was. The skin of her nipple puckered and came alive under his rough fingers, quickly erect.

'Touch yourself down there,' he ordered her hurriedly. 'Unzip your jeans so I can see you.'

He had half expected the young blonde to resist but to his surprise she did as she was told, hands struggling to slip past the tight crotch of her jeans and locate her clitoris. He could see a fine crop of gingerish hairs peeking out from the jeans and her fingers working down there, rubbing back and forth with the same urgency he felt himself. The flush on her face had deepened as he continued to clench her nipple with a vicelike grip. Seconds later, he heard Roz groan audibly against the penis in her mouth and her hips began to buck like a mating animal's.

The little bitch was coming, he thought with amazement, and before he had even finished too. He must be hurting her and yet she was still able to climax. It was clear that this fresh-faced kid had the potential to be something really special on the tour, a genuine submissive whose angelic body and face cried out to be defiled. The realisation that he had discovered a possible future star of the pool tour – and even witnessed the bitch pleasuring herself as she sucked his cock – proved too much for Carter. He felt his balls clench in uncontrollable excitement and then he too was coming, forcing his penis back inside her mouth so he could pump his full load into the blonde.

'Christ, you hot little slut,' he grunted, dragging her up by the hair until he was buried up to the hilt

11

in her throat. She twisted against him like a butterfly on a pin. His come spurted again and again, the hot glorious release intensely satisfying. 'Go on, take it all. I want to watch you swallow every drop.'

Carter loved that moment at the end, when you pull out afterwards and see the whitish viscous fluid still lingering on her lips or dribbling out of the corner of her mouth where she was not able to swallow fast enough. It was an integral part of the ritual for him, an indication that the girl had gone beyond submission and into the far reaches of humiliation. So when he saw Roz kneeling there before him like an exhausted sprinter, wiping the mingled saliva and sperm from her chin with the back of her hand, his pleasure was complete.

He helped Roz to stand, noting with amusement that her legs were actually trembling. Whether that was from her ordeal though, or the aftermath of her own orgasm, he could not be sure. 'You OK?'

She was staring, eyes wide. 'I . . . think so.'

'Good,' he said.

'Is it finished now?'

'Yes, and it was excellent. Much better than I expected.'

There were tears in her eyes but the girl lifted her chin, not giving in to them, and faced him with reasonable composure as she zipped up her jeans.

'You don't think much of me, do you?' Her voice shook slightly

'I didn't realise you'd be so . . . experienced.'

Her eyes flashed angrily. 'I'm not a child, you know.'

'How old are you?' he asked curiously, tidying himself up with hands which were not quite steady.

'Twenty.'

He was surprised. 'You look much younger.'

'So people keep telling me. But I've been round the block a few times and I'm no innocent.'

'Sucked plenty of cock, have you?' he replied, his tone deliberately insulting, and was amused to see her blush a fiery red. She might be twenty, and old enough to be out on her own in a place like this, but it did not take much to embarrass her.

'Mind your own business,' Roz snapped, and turned to wash her hands and face at the sink. She checked her reflection in the mirror as she washed with an apparent lack of self-consciousness, every movement careful and unhurried. Carter watched her as he tucked his shirt back into his trousers, his eyes narrowed thoughtfully on her back. He could see why she was such a good pool player. Her physical co-ordination seemed perfect, her entire body a well-organised machine as she moved to the hand-drier and made herself presentable once more.

That physical co-ordination had its uses in a few other departments too, he thought, reflecting with admiration on how she had managed to achieve her own orgasm whilst sucking eagerly on his shaft. That was one skill which would be highly prized by his boss, McNaughton, whose appetite for beautiful and accomplished players was notorious. The more he considered it, in fact, the more certain he became that this girl should join the pool tour as their eighth player.

'OK, I've got another proposition to put to you,' Carter said casually, coming up behind her as the hand-drier finished and straightening her T-shirt which had ridden up at the back. 'If you're interested in broadening your horizons, it would be worth your time to hear me out.'

She turned to look at him, her face wary.

'Whatever it is, I'm not interested. What I just did, that was a one-off.'

'So you didn't enjoy it?'

Her face was still red as she shrugged. 'That's not the point.'

'It's precisely the point.'

'Look, it was a deal.'

He nodded, understanding her. 'So is this. A very special deal . . . and one you shouldn't turn down without thinking about it.'

'I only do deals when it's to do with pool.'

'Well, that's perfect. Because this is to do with pool. An all-female pool tour to be accurate. During the season, they play exhibition matches for wealthy private clients. I've only got seven players at the moment, but I need eight for a proper tournament. One of our best players dropped out last month and it's been hell trying to find a good enough replacement. Most of the girls I've seen recently don't have the first idea how to hold a cue, let alone play a decent game of pool.' He smiled, still watching her face as he tried to gauge her reaction. 'But here you are . . . and you're sexy too, which helps.'

She frowned, but she was listening with interest. 'What's being sexy got to do with it?'

'Part of this particular deal is that you have sex after every match,' he said, his eyes on her face. 'With the men in the audience.'

'Christ.'

'Not just straightforward sex, either.'

Her face had paled now. 'I don't understand.'

'I won't insult your intelligence by lying to you, Roz. These men pay an obscene amount of money just to get through the door and they like to play around a bit before they get off.' He remembered how she had responded to having her nipple so painfully twisted and did not bother trying to hide the truth. 'They tend to whet their appetites first with a little bondage and corporal punishment.'

'Corporal punishment?'

'I thought you'd been round the block a few times? You know what I'm talking about. Whips, canes, that sort of thing.'

Roz bit her lip, staring at him. 'But which way round? I mean, do we hit them or do they hit us?'

He gave her an ironic smile. 'What do you think?'

'Oh.'

'Would that be a major problem?'

She was a difficult player to read, he thought, realising how little her emotions showed in her face, both on and off the table. The petite blonde seemed calm enough, in spite of her increased pallor and a certain nervousness in the way she spoke. But he was sure there must be more going on below the surface that she was determined not to show him.

'I don't know. Maybe.'

'That's what you said about giving me a blow job. But you went through with it in the end, didn't you?'

'You beat me. I didn't have a choice.'

He shook his head. 'Everybody has a choice.'

Those clear blue eyes focused on his face and he felt an odd frisson of arousal, wishing he had time to stay and take advantage of more than just her mouth. But it was getting late and he had to get back to the hotel. Whenever he left it too late to show up at a venue, the arrangements always seemed to fall apart.

'So,' he said, meeting her gaze, 'are you interested or not? There's a good living to be made on the tour, and the best players always get a bonus at the end of the season.'

'I'll think about it.'

'Don't think too long. We'll be moving on after

15

tonight and there's no guarantee you'll be able to catch up with us.'

'It doesn't sound like my sort of thing.'

'You prefer this? Hanging round a fly-bitten back-street pool hall, scratching a living as a hustler?'

'That's my choice.'

'Then your choice is worthless,' he said bluntly and reached out to grab her. As she protested, struggling against his hands in sudden panic, he unzipped her green jeans and pulled them down to reveal her bare backside. The smooth white skin looked alluring and he was tempted to investigate further, but he knew his options were limited at the moment. Instead, he drew a pen from his pocket and bent to write the hotel address in a loose scrawl across her buttocks.

'Keep still, would you? You can reach me at this address tonight if you change your mind.'

'Fuck you,' Roz swore angrily, pulling away.

'Another time, sweetheart,' he replied without hesitation, reaching for the door and leaving her standing alone in the men's toilets. 'When you've learnt to ask me nicely, perhaps.'

By the time Carter reached the darkened car park, his head was already buzzing with the memory of what he had just done to her in there and the knowledge that he wanted to do it again. Only much harder next time and with a few added twists. Swiftly turning his car in the direction of the hotel venue for that night, he checked his watch and put his foot down on the accelerator. There was no denying it, he would be disappointed if this new blonde failed to turn up at the tournament tonight. He would particularly enjoy supervising her personal training, able to watch her face change as she took the cane and the tawse for the very first time.

He smiled to himself, his hands tightening on the wheel as he imagined marking that pale flawless skin. Carter had the impression that Roz would make an eager and highly rewarding pupil.

Two

Roz climbed up the rusty fire escape to her bedroom window, dragged the window open and slid one leg cautiously over the sill. It was a narrow aperture, even for a girl of her slender figure, but somehow she managed to haul herself inside without too much of a struggle and dropped quietly to the floor.

She hesitated for a long moment, listening for any sounds from the stairs or the other flats below her, but there was nothing. The flat was in darkness. Back on her feet, Roz negotiated her way across the sparsely decorated room and felt along the wall for the light switch. It would have been easier to use the main stairs, but her slimeball of a landlord, Peters, had been after her for rent arrears since last month, and she had not particularly wanted to bump into him on her way home.

When the light came on, Roz gasped in horror at the sight of her landlord lying stretched out on her mattress.

'What the hell . . .?'

At her cry, Peters sat up and stared back at her, blinking at the sudden light. His creased shirt was unbuttoned halfway down his chest and the fly of his jeans was already open. She could see greying pubic hairs and a glimpse of his semi-erect penis, purplish and stub-nosed, as the landlord swung his legs off the bed without bothering to hide his arousal. Shuddering with distaste, Roz could only guess at what the bastard had been doing there in her bed.

She backed away, her eyes slowly lifting from his penis to his face. He had cornered her before like this, but she had always managed to wriggle out of the situation. But as he came closer, Roz saw the cruelty in his eyes and knew there would be little chance of escape this time. From the thick bulging penis now nudging out of his fly, she guessed that Peters had not come up here to collect his money. The vile little man had even tried to make himself look attractive. His coarse black hair had been slicked back with some sort of noxious-smelling oil and, to judge by the reddened skin, he had clearly trimmed his chin stubble in the past few hours.

'I've been waiting all evening, Roz. You owe me three months' rent and I'm tired of your excuses.'

'I'll get the money for you tomorrow.'

Peters laughed unpleasantly, approaching her with both hands holding up the sagging material of his jeans.

'Forget about the money. It's not important. I'm a reasonable man, Roz, and you're a very sexy girl. And you could really be hot, if you'd quit wearing those old boots and jeans and put on a short skirt for once. High heels too.' His voice became dreamy. 'I'd really like to see you in high heels. Black stilettos and a short leather skirt.'

'You've got no chance . . .'

'Don't be so quick to say no.' He came closer, almost within touching distance. She could smell his greasy hair oil and her stomach turned. 'If you do what you're told, you won't ever have to worry about the rent again.'

'I'm not playing the whore for you, Peters.'

The landlord stopped a few inches from her body, his face darkening with anger. 'That's an ugly thing to say. It wouldn't be like that. A few of my friends, that's all I'd expect, and only two or three nights a week. Just enough to pay off your rent.'

'And you?'

He smiled again, cheekily, like a schoolboy caught reading a dirty magazine under the covers. He stroked a finger down her cheek, his eyes on the fullness of her mouth. 'Naturally, I would expect a little . . . extra . . . for myself.'

Roz licked her lips, her mouth dry as she watched his face. She was remembering the man she had met in the pool hall, and his offer of 'incredible' money. She had not liked the thought of leaving this place behind, squalid though it might be at times, and putting herself in the power of a bunch of strangers who liked to play kinky games of pool. But perhaps it was not such a bad idea after all.

'Extra?'

His hands fumbled with his fly, soon widening the gap and allowing his thickening penis to flop out into his palm.

'You've got cold eyes, Roz. Cold eyes but such a hot mouth. I've always wondered how it would feel to push you down onto your knees,' Peters muttered, his breathing starting to quicken as he fingered himself to a full erection. 'And force that hot little mouth of yours to suck me. Suck me all the way until you choke on my come.'

His hands came down on her shoulders and suddenly she felt an unbearable pressure almost crushing her bones. Giving way beneath it, Roz stumbled to her knees and found his hand tilting her chin back to widen her throat. Her eyes were closed but the lids stung with unexpected tears of anger and humiliation. Peters was going to force her to suck his penis. He was going to shove it past her protesting lips and into the depths of her throat – and there was absolutely nothing she could do about it.

But as the bulbous purple-tipped head began to nudge against her chin, pre-come dribbling muskily from its gaping slit, a daringly outrageous idea flashed through her mind. It might not work, of course, but she had nothing to lose.

She reached up to clutch at his hips, pulling him even closer in spite of the fact that his proximity made her flesh creep, and tried to make her voice sound inviting.

'What's your hurry? You don't want to come straight away, do you? After all, there's plenty of time . . .' Her head tilted backwards now, Roz forced herself to run her tongue lovingly across the oozing slit, cleaning the pre-come from his penis. The smell of his unwashed genitals made her gag but she fought the impulse to be sick, pretending it was merely a shudder of delight at his arousal and hoping he would not notice the difference. 'For something special.'

His hand grasped her hair. There was suspicion in his tone as he attempted to read her expression.

'Special?'

'That's right.' She fingered the thick leather belt, loosened but still looped around his jeans, and lowered her voice to an inviting purr. 'For instance, have you ever been ridden? Ridden hard?'

'Ridden?' Peters licked his lips as he realised what she was insinuating, eyes narrowing with greed and lust. 'That sounds more like it. I wouldn't mind having a girl on top – tits bouncing in my face, lazy slut doing all the hard work for once. So that's what you fancy?'

'Maybe.'

'Christ, I had you down as one of these man-hating dykes. But you're a hot little whore underneath, aren't you?' With a harsh laugh, he dragged her up from the floor and gestured towards the bed. 'Hurry up and get your clothes off, then. I'm going to enjoy watching you work up a sweat on my cock.'

'No, not yet!'

'Come on, you little tease –'

'Hold on a minute. I want to tie you up first.' She sucked one finger in a provocative fashion, watching his face. 'Tie you to the bed with that leather belt of yours. Not your feet, just your wrists. It's much more exciting for the man if he can't move his hands.'

'You've done this before?' Peters demanded, incredulous.

'Dozens of times.'

'Christ,' he repeated blankly, but he was clearly enticed by the idea. No doubt he had thought this would be a rape, Roz thought ironically, forcing the pool-playing dyke onto her back so he could use her properly, but his eyes were popping out of his head as he watched her casually yank off her top and stand there bra-less before him. Her high tits swung temptingly as she bent to release his belt and he did not stop her. Instead, his gaze riveted to the dusky pink nipples already stiffening in the cool air, Peters dragged his own shirt and jeans off without further hesitation.

Disentangling his grubby underpants from the erection pressing out of the front slit, he threw them on the floor too. It was in a breathless daze that he allowed Roz to push him back onto the bed. His head sank unprotestingly into the soft white pillows.

Before he could change his mind, she had grabbed both his wrists and pulled them above his head, fastening them together behind one of the old-fashioned iron rods of the bedstead. But to draw the leather belt tight enough to ensure he could not move, she had to jump up and straddle his body, close enough to be seized and held if he got his hands free. But Peters seemed stupidly oblivious to the danger he was in. Far from struggling, he was staring up at her naked breasts and the slightly rounded curve of her stomach. Then his eyes dropped lower and his erection grew even more rigid, jerking towards her body even as she finished tying his hands and climbed hurriedly off the bed. He seemed almost on the verge of orgasm again; pre-come was dribbling from the end of his penis.

No doubt he thought she was actually going to ride him now, to slave and struggle for his pleasure, sweat breaking out on her skin as the bitch slid up and down on his cock until he had taken his money's worth of her body. More than his money's worth, Roz thought angrily, remembering how he had intended his friends to enjoy her as well. Night after night they would have come up to this dark room on the third floor and forced her to take them all, again and again, in every spunk-filled hole, probably telling each other the slut loved every minute of it, that she was gagging for that sort of treatment.

Roz stepped back and unzipped her jeans, sliding them off her hips with a tight little smile. She was naked underneath. From his panting breaths and the way his penis kept jerking, she guessed the sight of her exposed triangle of hair must be driving him crazy.

'You want this cunt?' she whispered, fingering herself.

'Uhuh.'

'You want to spunk into this cunt?'

23

He grunted hoarsely again and nodded, raising his hips in what she assumed was a mute invitation to climb on top.

'But if I sit on your cock ... if I let you spunk inside me ... you might make too much noise,' she said, with mock hesitancy. 'And I really wouldn't like that, it might put me off my rhythm.'

Peters was staring at her in disbelief now, his rigid penis straining upwards in sheer frustration.

'What?'

Roz sighed. 'Time to say goodbye, I'm afraid.'

'Just get on my cock, you stupid bitch, and let me do the business. Or I'll see you in court for the fucking arrears. Do you hear what I'm saying?'

'I certainly do.' She bit her lip, glancing around the room as if searching for something, and then stooped for his underpants. She sniffed at them, making a disgusted face, then scrumpled them up into a ball and came quietly towards him. 'Would you mind opening a little wider?'

Peters struggled angrily as she bent forwards over his prone body to stuff the underpants into his mouth. Her tits were brushing his chest as she pushed the gag further in, moist open cunt pressed down into his stomach like a split fruit; his cock twitched uncontrollably, swollen and purple-headed, almost ready to burst. From his urgent expression, it was obvious Peters wanted her to straddle his cock before it was too late and he split his load over the bedclothes and his own thighs. But all he seemed able to manage were a few violent kicks in the air and some incomprehensible grunts from behind the gag of his underpants.

'Sorry, Mr Peters,' Roz murmured, sliding to the floor and throwing an empty suitcase onto the bed. 'But I can't understand a word you're saying.'

The landlord watched in horror, the realisation slowly dawning in his eyes that she was not going to have sex with him at all. Against a background of furious noises as he struggled to get free, Roz packed her clothes and her few personal possessions lying about the room. Dragging a midriff top down over her tits, she wriggled into some low-slung denim shorts and a pair of red leather boots. Her face was cool and unmoved as she checked her reflection in the mirror, ignoring his writhing body behind her. Peters was yanking at the leather belt around his wrists now, no doubt trying to work himself free from the iron bedstead. But it had been tied far too tightly. His panicked eyes followed her about the room instead, presumably hopeful that this was a joke, that she was still planning to untie his hands and ride him as promised.

Staring down at him for a moment, Roz bent to slip his penis into her mouth again, generously bathing the head in warm saliva and running her tongue back and forth over the swollen glans, before picking up her case and switching off the light. That quick little suck would at least give the man something to think about while he lay there alone in the dark.

'Sweet dreams, Peters.'

Outside in the corridor, Roz glanced down at her watch and made some swift calculations. There was still plenty of time to get to that hotel. But was it the right thing to do? For a start, she had never played pool against her own sex before. Men, yes. Probably thousands of men in hundreds of different pool halls and dingy backstreet clubs. But she had never lifted a cue against another girl and she had no regrets about that.

It threw her a little, she realised with a shock, the idea of competing against another version of herself.

25

Her nerves jumped at the thought of losing to a girl. She did not mind losing to a man – though it rarely happened – but the possibility that she might lose to a member of her own sex left a bad taste in her mouth. Women pool players, for Christ's sake! What women pool players? She had seen other girls playing pool sometimes, out in the clubs with their boyfriends squeezing their backsides over the table, and had laughed with contempt. They could barely hold the cue properly, let alone pot a ball. But Carter had said these girls on the tour had real talent. That they might be as good as her on the table . . . better, even.

The suggestion that any woman could be better at pool than her made Roz angry. Very angry. Her teeth came together in a firm snap and she narrowed her eyes on her watch again. Time was ticking. But how the hell was she meant to find this hotel if she could not even read the address, since the bastard had written it on her backside?

Without bothering to knock, she pushed open the door into Susie's apartment next door. It was never locked.

'Honey, could you look at my arse for a second? Oh, shit . . . sorry. I didn't realise you were busy.'

Her next-door neighbour was lying sprawled out naked on the bed, fingers trapped like meat-hooks between her legs. But she sat up without any sign of embarrassment at having been caught masturbating and gave her a slow-burning smile across the room. Susie was a natural blonde with huge breasts and a tiny waist who looked every inch the fuckable Barbie doll-type, yet somehow she had grown up to prefer women to men.

'No problem, I was getting lonely anyway,' she said, putting her juice-slick fingers to her mouth and slowly licking them clean. 'Come in and let me see your gorgeous arse then. I didn't think you were that way inclined, sweetie, or I would have offered to kiss it a long time ago.'

'Sorry, it's not what you think. I just need you to tell me what this says,' Roz said, slipping the jeans off her hips and turning to present her bare bottom to the other girl. Bending forward with one hand resting on her knee, she hoped the writing had not rubbed off while she had been changing clothes. 'Some bastard wrote his address there and I can't read it myself.'

'Oh baby, your arse is superb. Couldn't I just . . .?'

'The address,' Roz reminded her curtly.

Sighing and clearly disappointed by her straight refusal, Susie read the address of the London hotel off her backside while Roz noted it down on the back of her hand in biro. A much more practical place to write an address, she thought wryly, straightening up with some relief as Susie finished. Though she realised the impact might have been lost if Carter had taken a more pedestrian approach to advertising his pool tour. This way at least his offer of a job had stuck in her mind.

'So what's all this about?' Susie asked curiously.

'That's not important. But I'm going to be out of town for a while. It's getting a bit tricky here. Peters is in my room right now, tied to the bed. Could you wait half an hour, then go in and pretend to find him? That should give me long enough to get away.'

'Tied to the bed?'

'Sleazy bastard thought I'd suck him and half the neighbourhood off in return for waiving the rent.'

Susie shuddered. 'Ugh, that man makes my skin crawl. Can't I leave him there until tomorrow? It would serve him right.'

'Thirty minutes and no more. You promise?'

'Yeah, whatever.' With obvious reluctance, Susie watched her hoist her jeans up onto her hips and refasten them, fingers slipping down again into the exposed flesh between her thighs. Her voice dropped to a soft feline purr. 'Now you're sure I can't tempt you to a licking-out? I can smell your hot cunt from here. Not even for a minute or two, you cruel bitch? Come and let me kiss you goodbye, at least.'

Roz hesitated, then went back to the bed and bent over Susie's naked body. Normally she would have said no. But this was an attractive girl offering to kiss her, not some ugly bastard who just wanted to pimp her out to his friends every night. Sighing at the contrast between this and her encounter with Peters, she let her mouth meet Susie's and did not recoil when that sharp little tongue darted inside and rubbed against her lips and tongue.

They had been friends for nearly six months now, ever since the day Roz had moved into the bedsit next door. Though she had known from the start that Susie liked taking women to bed, she had never felt tempted to join her before. But when Susie's hands wandered over her stomach in the midriff top and gently traced the outline of her breasts, Roz was amazed to feel her nipples hardening under the contact. Her gasp must have alerted Susie, who drew back to stare up knowingly into her flushed face.

'Good, huh?'

'I'm not sure . . . maybe.'

'What's up, sweetie?' Susie smiled, pushing the midriff top higher and cupping her friend's exposed breasts. 'You sound a little out of breath.'

'Look, I really ought to go.'

'What's your rush?' That knowing look again. 'Peters is tied up next door – you said so yourself.

He's going nowhere. Why bother running off so fast? Lie down on the bed and let me take those tight jeans off.'

Roz moaned and closed her eyes as clever fingers stroked her breasts; she thought her nipples would explode with pleasure.

'I can't, Susie. I need to be somewhere. That address, the hotel . . .' She was stammering now, betraying her weakness. Perhaps it was true there was a trace of lesbianism in all women, Roz thought hazily, feeling her body sink down into the soft covers of Susie's bed. The hard dry facts. They were what she needed to hold onto here. 'It's important. I can't stay here any more. That hotel is my only . . .'

'Shhh. Kiss me.'

Their mouths met once more, the cheap mattress sagged under their weight and Roz felt her jeans being unfastened. One hand forced its way under the tight denim and stroked her exposed belly, making her jerk in reaction. Then those fingers slipped lower, brushing the wisps of pubic hair until they reached the lips of her vagina. Much to her shame they were already moist and puffy with sexual excitement, opening without any difficulty to Susie's fingers. It did not take long for her jeans to be yanked right down to her thighs, leaving her open and helpless under the blonde's insistent caress. Roz gasped and arched her back in sudden pleasure. It was the first time a woman had ever touched her there but she guessed it would not be the last, it felt so good. Her clitoris was being manipulated by an expert, the sensitive inner lips quickly soaked with her own juices as Susie's fingers moved back and forth across the taut bud.

Her head fell back and she groaned. 'Please . . . oh, God . . . Susie . . .'

'What do you want?'

Roz knew her face was burning. 'I don't know . . .'

'This?' One of those clever fingers penetrated her sex, spreading the lips apart and pushing inside. 'Or something thicker?'

She did not reply, could not find the strength to reply, yet that was not important. Somehow, Susie seemed able to understand the message in her restless shifting hips without any further need for words. Her probing fingers withdrew for a moment and Roz lay there on the bed in a dazed silence, heart beating violently as she listened to her friend rummaging in the bedside drawers. Then Susie swung back into place, above her body this time, opening her mouth to oil a long black dildo with saliva.

'Is this thick enough?'

Roz stared up, dry-mouthed, at the large thick phallus slipping in and out between Susie's lips. For a moment she considered pushing the girl off and running straight down the stairs but curiosity made her stay where she was. She had never seen anything like it before in her life. Just above Susie's fingers were two massive black balls, complete with veins, moulded into the stem of the dildo. Beyond them, the phallus stretched about nine inches, ending in a realistically swollen black glans with a thin slit, so wet and shiny from Susie's mouth it could have been oozing pre-come.

'Bloody hell.'

'What's the matter? Are you worried I might hurt you?' The blonde smiled, licking her lips as she leant forward over the half-undressed body beneath her. 'You ought to be, sweetheart. Can you imagine this inside you?'

Susie's hand slipped upwards so she could see the base more clearly. Roz gasped at what she saw, shaking her head and trying to scramble backwards on the bed. Below the moulded scrotum was a ring of black latex spikes, thick and cruel, presumably intended to grind viciously against the woman's labia as the phallus plunged in and out of her body. There was no way she wanted to accommodate that torturous device inside her.

But Susie's thighs clamped down hard on either side of her body and she could not move.

'Where do you think you're going?'

Roz took a deep shuddering breath, looking up to meet her friend's eyes. There was a pleading note in her voice. 'Not with that, Susie. For pity's sake, it's fucking enormous . . . and what about those spikes? You could really damage me with that thing.'

'Only if you struggle.'

'Which I would,' Roz said faintly.

'Really?'

Susie gave another knowing little smile, slipping one hand between Roz's thighs to stroke the fleshy bud of her clitoris. That gesture and the breathy groan that followed demonstrated to them both that Roz was lying. She felt a sting of embarrassment but was helpless to prevent her physical reaction. Hot colour flooded her face as Susie's fingers moved swiftly, expertly, bringing her back to the verge of orgasm with the minimum of effort. No longer able to resist, Roz slumped back on the bed in mute invitation, allowing her trapped thighs to fall limply apart against the prison of Susie's body. Closing her mind to the pleasure was like trying to fight a tidal wave. Her whole body trembled with a mixture of fear and excitement at what was about to happen; she was aching for release, but knew it would be denied until she had taken that cruel-looking dildo inside her.

Moving to one side for a moment, Susie firmly pushed her thighs apart and drew the knees up for easier access. Resettling herself between them on the bed, she licked around the rounded base of the dildo to lubricate it. Roz closed her eyes, growing hot in the face and moving her head from side to side on the creased sheets. Once again, fingers prised open her vaginal lips – though this time without any attempt at gentleness – and seconds later she felt the large false glans of the phallus pressing against her. It felt too huge to enter and she drew a sharp breath, staring up at Susie in alarm.

'Please, it won't fit. You'll tear me.'

'Shut up and lie still.'

Her knees were pushed even higher up towards her body, her thighs automatically dropping further apart. She lay there on her back with the girl between her thighs, her belly aching with the need for penetration. Like a battering-ram, the dildo pressed relentlessly against the entrance to her cunt, this time forcing it to open. Inexorably her lips peeled back to let the phallus enter, making her twist and moan under her breath. It felt as though her sex were on fire. Yet even the pain was good. Somehow this was what she had needed, after that sordid time on her knees in the men's bathroom, sucking Carter's penis until it had exploded into her throat. It had left a moist longing between her legs that had not gone away, and which Peters could never have assuaged, not even if he had fucked her for hours. It was the sort of longing which craved intense one-to-one contact, not some sleazy five or ten minutes of sweat and sperm.

Had she wanted Carter to fuck her properly? That was the only explanation for her almost constant state of arousal since meeting him that afternoon. She closed her eyes in agonised pleasure as the dildo reached its full length inside her, stretching her tight muscular walls, and began to withdraw. She should have offered him her body instead of merely sucking him off. It was such a pity to have wasted his spunk in her mouth when she could have taken it in her cunt or arse. The thought sent her temperature soaring. She tried to imagine how it would have felt to bend over the wash-basins for his penis, hands gripping the slippery enamel while he pumped his thick meat inside her, and felt a familiar surge of heat stir down in her belly. She was close to orgasm. So close that her whole body was alight with it.

The blonde shifted position, head bent low between her thighs, and suddenly the phallus was joined by an eager little tongue. Each time that swollen head forced its way back inside her, Susie accompanied its forward thrust with a run of her tongue along the inner flesh towards her clitoris. There she licked and sucked and probed, still working the dildo back and forth in a pumping action right next to her face. Roz threw back her head to scream, grasping the blonde's hair and dragging her closer as she came repeatedly in Susie's mouth. It was as if someone had thrown a switch in the back of her head and she was being electrocuted. Everything blacked out for a few wild incredible seconds. Her knees jerked into spasm. Had she actually stopped breathing? The orgasm burnt through her body like wildfire, pulsing across her clitoris and up her tensed belly towards her breasts, where the nipples had stiffened to ticking bombs.

The phallus was rammed home once, twice, three times, intensifying the orgasm until she thought her nervous system would short-circuit. It was too much, far too much. She was going to die. Roz cried out in a high unfamiliar voice, pushing the girl away. The dildo was abruptly withdrawn and Susie lifted her head to stare down at her in astonishment. Streams of hot juice poured from her cunt as it was unplugged, dripping down the crack of her arse and soaking into the sheets beneath her like sperm.

'My god, what was that?'

For a moment, Roz merely lay there too dazed to speak, staring up into the pale blur that was Susie's face. Then her vision stopped swimming and she managed to struggle up onto one elbow, gazing down at the wet patch spreading darkly across the sheets.

'What was what?' Roz groaned breathlessly. 'I came and the bed got a bit wet. Is that a problem?'

Susie raised her eyebrows, rocking back on her heels. 'That is not normal, sweetheart. Look at all the mess you made. Jesus, you come like a man. No one ever tell you that before?'

'No.'

Still staring at her, Susie slipped the dildo into her mouth, licking it clean with a thoughtful air. Then she removed it, shrugging delicately.

'I thought at first it might be urine. That you'd pissed yourself when you came. But that's pussy juice, one hundred per cent. I'd know the taste blindfold. You're one horny little fuck, do you know that?'

Susie leant back on the crumpled sheets with a shuddering sigh, her naked breasts still taut with arousal. She seemed oblivious to the damp stains beneath her. Using the fingers of both hands, she reached down to pull apart the glistening folds of her own pussy.

'Now it's my turn.' Her voice hardened, striking out like a whip. 'So get your head down here, bitch, and bring me off with your tongue!'

Three

The two blondes were squabbling again. It was never certain to anyone on the tour how these things started. But the two Scandinavian girls, similar in height, build and colouring, always seemed to be at each other's throats. Kizzy had grabbed at Bianca's see-through bodice and ripped the thin material. Squealing with fury, Bianca slapped her violently around the face and then pushed her to the floor, fingers tangled in the other blonde's voluminous hair as she slammed her head against the deep-pile carpet. Beyond their struggling bodies the floor-to-ceiling windows of the hotel suite looked out across central London at night, lit up now with flashing neon.

Carter sat on the white leather sofa, holding a mobile phone to his ear and watching the two girls with a distracted expression. Kizzy was spitting venom into her enemy's face, her muscular legs under that tiny skirt locking about Bianca's back and squeezing. Yet they were obviously both enjoying their struggle. Bianca was mewling like a cat and Kizzy's flushed face looked exactly as it did when she was being fucked in the arse – pained but ecstatic.

He knew with one part of his mind that he ought to interfere, maybe pack the two Nordic blondes off to separate rooms until their tempers had cooled down, but he was too preoccupied to spare them more than a sigh of irritation.

'No, it's got to be champagne,' he interrupted, barely listening to the hotel manager on the other end of the phone. 'Just sort it, OK? There's some very important people waiting for us downstairs. Now find them two dozen bottles of champagne or you can kiss this fucking contract goodbye.' He hung up without another word, shaking his head in disbelief at the man's incompetence. 'Jesus, I thought this was supposed to be a five-star hotel.'

Some of the others girls had crowded around the fighting pair now, either urging them on with malicious expressions or trying to pull Bianca away from the howling Kizzy. Not that they would have had much success, he thought wryly. The two girls were completely focused on each other.

With her free hand, Kizzy suddenly managed to claw at Bianca's breasts, making the girl gasp and writhe away. Seizing the advantage, Kizzy leapt across her rival and pinned her to the floor on her back. One fierce hand yanked at the crop of white-blonde hair, ripping at the roots until Bianca yelped like a wounded animal and stared around at the watching crowd of girls as if begging one of them to help her. But not one of them moved. The older blonde was too cold and distant to have made any friends on the tour.

Clipping the mobile back onto his belt, Carter sat watching the scene for a few more minutes before making his decision. His face registered little emotion as he listened to their agonised panting breaths and let his gaze move slowly over the long slender legs and rounded buttocks of the Scandinavian blonde on top.

It was not the first time he had thought about punishing Kizzy himself rather than letting one of the minders do the honours. Briefly he let his imagination roam wild, considering how the tall blonde would look held down across that white leather sofa, head pushed down and buttocks forced up, sobbing helplessly as the cane bit into that soft flesh. Then Kizzy straddled Bianca with a wild cry, gripping her throat, and the tiny skirt rode up almost to the narrow curve of her waist. Unable to tear his eyes away, Carter realised that the bulge in his suit trousers was becoming uncomfortable.

Some of the other girls were looking at him curiously, no doubt wondering why he had not yet intervened. He ought to step in and stop the fight before one of these girls ended up too damaged to play tonight. But his eyes were still lingering thoughtfully on Kizzy's exposed backside in the minuscule silver thong. The young blonde had not been marked by any of their clients for some weeks and the skin on her buttocks was temptingly smooth and unblemished. He would be well within his rights to take up a cane and mark the girl himself.

Tonight was not a good time for self-indulgence though, Carter reminded himself reluctantly. Play was due to start in less than an hour and the arrangements for this evening's matches had already been messed up enough. He could not afford to lose clients by making them wait any longer while he took his own satisfaction up here.

'OK, that's enough,' he said curtly.

He clicked his fingers and one of the minders came forward with a whip, a large burly man in an Italian suit, his eyes on Carter's face. At his nod, the minder jerked back the whip and laid it viciously across the shoulders of the watching girls. There was a loud screeching as the girls realised what was happening and then they scattered in hysterics, struggling to get out of his reach.

Kizzy and Bianca, still rolling on the floor, paid little attention to the minder standing above them, legs apart for balance as he raised the whip for a second time. There was a smile on the man's face as he flayed his whip across Kizzy's back and listened with obvious pleasure to her high-pitched scream. Seconds later, an angry-looking mark had sprung up less than an inch beneath the fastening of her silver bra top. Kizzy glanced over her shoulder in sudden fear and scrambled to her feet before he could lash out again, blonde hair falling down her back too late to protect her pale-gold skin.

With those long, tanned legs she was almost as tall as the man wielding the whip, Carter noticed, once again feeling the sharp tug of arousal. It was a pity he did not have time to enjoy her body properly. Perhaps later, when the matches were finished and all the clients had been satisfied, he could summon her to his room for a private punishment session.

It might be true that neither Carter nor any of the minders were allowed to have sex with the players during their match season – that pleasure was generally reserved for the clients – but there were ways to get around that rule. Most of the girls on the tour had given it up to him at one time or another, he thought drily, rule or no rule. But he had never had Kizzy, and the mere thought of forcing the blonde down on her knees to suck was almost too much for his self-control.

His whip still raised menacingly over one shoulder, the minder was looking at Carter for the signal either to stop or continue. He hesitated, then reluctantly gave the nod for him to stop as the hotel phone began to ring shrilly. It had been fun watching the young blonde squirm for a few minutes but there was no time for a serious beating now.

Irritated by the interruption, Carter picked up the phone and spoke sharply into the receiver.

'Carter here. What is it now?'

The receptionist seemed overly intimidated by his tone. Perhaps the manager had warned her to be careful with him. Carter remembered the woman from checking in, that pleasing Devon accent. Late twenties and probably married. Mousey shoulder-length hair, a little too thin for his liking, but with firm breasts under her uniform and a promisingly full lipsticked mouth.

'I'm sorry, sir.' Her voice almost trembled. 'I know you gave strict instructions not to be disturbed, but there's a young lady at Reception who says she's expected.'

He frowned. 'Did she give a name?'

'Roz.'

Surprised at her reply, he did not answer immediately. That cool-eyed little blonde from the pool hall, he thought suddenly. So she had changed her mind after all.

'OK, I'll meet her in the bar in ten minutes.'

Carter congratulated himself for having recruited the blonde so successfully. Now they would have eight players again, they could go back to charging their clients the full price.

'Just don't let her go anywhere, OK? Organise a drink for her, some food, whatever she wants. Put it on my bill.'

'Very good, sir.'

'You're a long way from home. That's a West Country accent, isn't it?'

'Yes, sir.'

'I thought so. You've got a beautiful voice.'

'Thank you.'

He smiled at her hesitancy. 'What's your name?'

'Sylvia.'

'I'm going to need a bottle of Jack Daniel's and a couple of beef sandwiches in the penthouse suite at about three in the morning. Think you can arrange that for me, Sylvia?'

'Yes, sir.'

His groin tightened. He liked the way she said that, so sweetly, so submissively. Yes, sir. It was a pity some of the pool players did not treat him with the same respect, Carter thought wryly. But he could scarcely be the big bad wolf to them as well as the father figure.

'Make sure you bring it up here in person though.'

'I'm not sure that's –'

'In person, remember. And you'd better make that three beef sandwiches. I'm always starving after a tournament.'

Carter put the phone down without waiting for a reply and smiled to himself. It was unlikely she would risk offending him by not turning up, which meant he had a pleasant night to look forward to after the players had finished. The receptionist might have looked married but that did not mean she would refuse the sort of bonus he could offer her. Not with that mouth, anyway. Even if he could not have Kizzy, he would at least have some relief for his aching groin tonight.

He left the girls to finish getting dressed and knocked at the door to Paula's room. Widely regarded as the best player on the tour, she also had an unofficial status amongst the others as top dog. In light of that, she enjoyed a semi-private room at most venues, shared with her French girlfriend and fellow pool player, Cherie. It had been made clear to both of them on joining the tour that they would need to make themselves available to male as well as female clients. Cherie had resisted at first and been threatened with termination of her contract, but Paula had persuaded her it was far better on the tour than going back to hustling in pool halls.

Greedy and sensual by nature, Paula displayed no qualms about pleasing the clients in whatever manner they preferred. She was a small-boned Welsh girl with jet-black hair, small high breasts and a permanent sneer in her voice. That superior attitude had annoyed some of the other girls when she and Cherie first joined on the tour, but Paula's talent on the table and her excited reaction to the clients' demands had persuaded Carter to keep her on.

By contrast, her girlfriend Cherie had quite a sweet temperament and a restless searching sexuality which had gradually accustomed itself to the reality of satisfying a man. Wide-eyed and deceptively fragile-looking, Cherie often surprised the clients by being able to take more punishment than the stronger English girls. Indeed, Carter had enjoyed the young Parisienne himself on several occasions and knew that the sight of a cane slicing across her beautiful olive skin was unforgettable.

'Paula, I've got to do something downstairs,' he said briefly, glancing round the door at the two girls. 'Make sure the others get ready on time. You've got about fifteen minutes before the first match is due to start.'

The Welsh girl nodded without looking up at him, leaning over her dressing table while Cherie stood behind to fasten the tight bodice of her leather outfit. 'Which room are we using?'

'The Roseman Suite on the seventh floor. Take the private lift at the end of the corridor.'

'Who's playing first?' Cherie asked huskily, turning to give him one of her flickering smiles. 'Not me again, I hope. I haven't even had time to put my own clothes on.'

'So I see,' he murmured, admiring her firm buttocks and smooth-skinned thighs as she bent to pick up her skirt.

Paula sounded impatient. 'I told you, Cherie. It's me and Kizzy to play first. Then you play that bitch Lauren and you'd better beat her this time. I'm sick of meeting her in the final.'

Without replying, Cherie shrugged into a tiny sequin-studded halter top and tied the two straps behind her neck. But there was an oddly mulish look in her eyes that he had not seen before as she glanced across at Paula. No doubt she was growing tired of her girlfriend's demanding ways, he thought wryly, slipping out of the room and making his way down to the hotel lobby.

He would not be surprised if that relationship exploded at some point in the future. He only prayed it would not happen in the middle of a tournament when there were clients present. That could prove disastrous to the reputation of the tour.

Roz was waiting for him in the bar, just as he had hoped. She was wearing jeans and the slender aluminium cue case that he remembered from the pool hall was by her side. He had half expected her to have changed her mind and disappeared before he got down to her, but Roz turned as he entered the bar and he could see cold determination in her face. Some fear there as well, perhaps. That did not particularly worry him though. She did not seem the sort of girl to allow fear to influence her decisions.

'So you came in the end. I'm glad,' he said, shaking her hand.

'What happens now?'

'You come straight upstairs with me. I'll find you something more suitable to wear.' He saw the frown in her eyes and shrugged, gesturing to her jeans and midriff top. 'You can't compete in that, I'm afraid. The clients expect something a little more exotic from our players.'

'Something easier to remove, you mean?'

He deliberately ignored her sharp-edged comment. 'When you're ready, I'll take you down to the Roseman Suite. That's where the matches are being played. You'll be drawn against Bianca tonight. She would have walked it into the next round without a game, but since you're here now –'

'Who's the number one?'

'I beg your pardon?'

She looked impatient. 'Your best player. Who is it?'

'Paula, I suppose.'

'Then she's the one I have to beat,' Roz said flatly.

She turned to finish her drink and pick up her aluminium cue case. Her eyes seemed even colder than they had been in the pool hall. They walked together back to the lift and he pressed the button for the penthouse, his eyes on her face. She was truly formidable, he thought, feeling the first uncomfortable stirrings of apprehension as he tried to imagine how the other girls would react to her fanaticism.

'So is this Paula in my half of the draw?'

'I don't know.'

She stared at him, meeting his eyes properly for the first time. 'You don't know? Who did the draw then?'

'I did,' Carter said calmly. 'But it's not that important, who plays who. That's not what this tour is about.'

Much to his surprise, the girl threw back her head and laughed. The high breasts shifted under her top and his eyes riveted to them. His mouth was suddenly dry as he remembered how Roz had sunk so submissively to her knees in the men's toilets and opened her mouth for him. Now her throat muscles clenched and relaxed as she laughed, strong under the pale skin. She must have used the same muscles on him, he realised with an unexpected surge of hunger, milking his penis into her throat with incredible strength. It was almost animalistic, the way she used her body to express her moods. He was aroused now and the knowledge irritated him. He could not enjoy her properly yet, not before she had been broken in.

'What's so funny?' he snapped.

'Nothing, forget it,' she said drily, following him out of the lift. 'But I don't imagine your best players think the draw is unimportant.'

Carter remembered Paula's comments about Lauren, the jealousy between those two girls being legendary, and was unable to deny the truth of what Roz had said. But his face revealed nothing as he unlocked the door to the penthouse suite and motioned her inside.

'There should be a clothes rack somewhere around here,' he said curtly. 'What size are you?'

The lounge was hectic with girls everywhere, cram-med together like kids onto the white leather sofa or sprawling barefoot on the carpet as they waited to play. Paula and Kizzy were nowhere in evidence, he noted with some relief, aware that the Welsh girl might have clashed with their new addition to the tour. Paula always liked to assert her dominance over new players as soon as they arrived, usually by causing a scene and forcing him to punish them both. But the fact that she was not here meant the tournament must have kicked off at the correct time. On most occasions he would have been downstairs before the matches even began, greeting the clients and checking they were comfortable, though he knew that one of the other minders would have done that in his absence. It had seemed more important to collect their new player from the bar and ensure she was ready to play.

He found the clothes rack and flicked through it while she stood silently beside him, eyeing the other girls with a detached coolness which surprised him. Most new players seemed nervous when they first met the rest of the tour, if not terrified. But Roz behaved more like predator than prey, her slender body poised as he handed her various items from the rack and ordered her to strip.

Shedding her own clothes without any sign of inhibition, Roz soon wriggled into the skintight PVC skirt and bra top. The shiny black material stretched taut across her breasts and the tops of her thighs. Lastly, she slipped her feet into the precariously high black heels he had handed her and fastened the ankle clasps.

'How do I look?'

Carter examined her with deliberate nonchalance. He had found her attractive in the pool hall. In tight PVC and heels though, she was easily the hottest player on the tour. But to admit that in front of the other girls might be dangerous.

'You'll pass,' he shrugged. 'Come on, I'll take you down early so you can get a feel for the place.'

'I need five minutes.'

'What for?'

'To prepare myself.' She fixed him with a cold eye when he laughed. 'It doesn't matter where, I just need to be alone for five minutes before I go down to play. Where's the nearest loo?'

'Through the blue door.'

* * *

With the door safely bolted against intruders, Roz stared at herself in the bathroom mirror. She was almost unrecognisable. The make-up had felt strange enough – the lipstick taste on her teeth and that sweeping mascara thickening her lashes. But was she expected to wear this sort of outfit every time she played? The skirt was so tight she could hardly breathe and it was barely long enough to cover her groin. The audience would be able to see everything whenever she bent over the table. Which was presumably the point. Not that she really cared about any of that. She was here to play pool and win.

She hitched up her skirt and peered at her bare pussy in the mirror. The fleshy little slit showed pink between dark hairs. Holding her breath as if afraid someone outside the door might realise what she was doing, she reached down and ran a finger across the exposed lips. It was not going to be an easy thing to do in here. The marble-tiled bathroom was so immaculate, she could not imagine even going to the toilet in case she dirtied something. But there was nowhere else to prepare herself for the match.

It might be an unconventional way to approach the game, Roz thought, but she had discovered long ago that masturbation sharpened her senses before going to the table. She always felt a thousand times more alive after an orgasm, the blood pumping freely round her body and all her nerve-endings tingling. In fact, it had only taken a few spectacular performances to persuade her to incorporate it into her usual pre-match routine. Now she regularly masturbated to orgasm before the break-off shot and sometimes even fingered herself in between games when possible. And if there was a risk that she might be caught with her jeans down and several fingers stuck in her wet gash, the thrill of the forbidden merely seemed to increase her ability to play.

Her mind went straight back to the men's toilets where she had knelt to suck Carter off, honouring their agreement. Only this time he did not come in her mouth and make her swallow it. Fingers working in her sex, the other hand stretching those soft lips wide enough to let herself in and out without effort, she imagined Carter changing his mind about a blow job and pushing her onto all fours instead. That was what she secretly wished he had done. After pulling down her jeans until they strained at the white skin of her mid-thighs, she imagined his fingers spreading her lips apart without even checking she was lubricated. Then she pictured him forcing his penis into the tight channel of her sex.

She would have bucked and cried aloud as the man entered her, but his other hand clamped down over her mouth and she was silenced. In her imagination, he was already moving inside her to a brutal rhythm. Short staccato thrusts that wrung moans of pleasure and humiliation from her throat. Her fingers jerking now to the same rhythm, in and out of her soaking pussy, she felt her own arousal begin to build and went back to that lurid picture in her mind.

Not satisfied with her sex, Carter pulled out and she felt that large cockhead pushing against the tight ring of her anus. Her mouth gaped wide, tasting the thick salty flesh of his hand, and Roz found herself crying out wordlessly as the pain increased. His fingers worked between her legs, using the slop of pussy juice as a lubricant before pressing himself into the narrower opening of her anus. The penetration was no easier though, even with lubricant. Her whole body stiffened and tried to pull away but he caught her by the hips, dragging her backwards onto the full length of his penis. It felt huge and swollen as it stretched the muscular walls of her rectum and slid home, right up to the hilt.

Her mouth freed at last, she began to pant and moan as she felt those large balls press down against the mound of her vagina. He was fully inside her anus now, pushing more smoothly in and out as he began to build up a steady rhythm. It did not take long for the pain to disappear. Her head was buzzing with pleasure as she rocked with him, aware of the wet tiled floor of the men's toilets under her hands and knees, the sheer ignominy of her position as she took this man's penis right up her bottom.

Roz whimpered, teetering on the verge of orgasm. Her five minutes alone in the bathroom must be nearly up. But her sex was so steamy and dripping with juice, she could no longer achieve a satisfactory amount of friction. Hurriedly pushing one finger past the tight sphincter of her anus, she simulated the thrusts of a man's penis into her bottom, knowing it would soon push her over the edge.

The sheer rudeness of what she was doing started her gasping, clutching fiercely at herself as her finger popped free of her slippery anus. Instinctively, Roz lifted the soiled finger to her mouth and sucked it clean before shoving it back inside her pussy for one last moment of ecstasy. Suddenly she could taste the pungent aroma of her own back passage. Urged on by the realisation of how filthy she was being, her fingers moved urgently, rubbing back and forth across her erect clitoris until it hurt.

Then the dam broke inside her body and Roz fell to her knees, jerking and moaning as she orgasmed, a sticky puddle forming slowly beneath her on the marble-tiled bathroom floor.

Somebody knocked impatiently at the door. 'Are you ready yet? Your match is due to start soon.'

It was Carter, she realised, her head still spinning from the violence of her orgasm.

'Hang on. I'll be out in a second.'

Staggering to her feet, Roz quickly washed her hands under the hot tap, hoping it would not be too obvious from her flushed cheeks and wild eyes what she had been doing in here. Then she tugged her short PVC skirt back into position, adjusted the shiny bra top to keep her nipples safely inside, and unlocked the door.

He held out her cue. 'You'll need this.'

'Thanks,' she said huskily.

From the look on his face, it was clear Carter had his suspicions about her method of match preparation. Perhaps she had made too much noise, she thought, with a little twinge of embarrassment. But he did not comment, merely pulled her towards the lift and jabbed the button for the seventh floor.

'You may be interested to learn that Paula won her first match,' he muttered. 'And yes, she is in the other half of the draw.'

'You said there are eight players altogether.'

He nodded. 'Including you, yes.'

'So if I win twice tonight, I should meet her in the final?'

'Theoretically.'

Roz slid one hand caressingly down her cue case, loving the cool glide of the aluminium beneath her fingers.

'I can't wait,' she said softly.

Four

The Roseman suite was a large high-ceilinged room with red carpets and thick black curtains running along the far wall, presumably to cover the windows and protect their clients from being seen. As they entered the room, Roz noticed the two burly minders on the door and realised how exclusive this gathering must be. Menacing in their black suits and expressionless faces, the two men waved them through easily enough but they were clearly on the door to prevent anyone entering without an invitation.

Inside, the atmosphere was curiously hushed. The pool table itself had been set out in the centre of the room on a raised platform. On every side, seats had been placed for the spectators. The audience was almost entirely male, Roz could not help noticing. Right at the front, watching every shot with avid attention, were middle-aged men in expensive-looking business suits. There were a few younger men in some of the back rows, their clothes rather less formal and one or two of them smoking as they watched. In amongst the men was a small handful of women, most following the game with pale intense expressions but some looking away, their heads lowered as if in shame.

Standing back from the pool table was an olive-skinned young woman in a tiny sequinned top. The girl she was playing seemed a few years older, probably in her early twenties, her skin much paler and with her long brown hair coiled on top of her head in an elegant bun. The scarlet rubber corset she was wearing emphasised her hour-glass figure, hips curving voluptuously below a narrow waist and her firm breasts jutting out invitingly from the shiny rubber. It was a little difficult to see the state of play from that distance. But by the look of dismay on the olive-skinned girl's face, it seemed likely she was losing.

With some reluctance, Roz tore her eyes away from the match. Her high heels sank into the luxurious carpet as Carter led her across the back of the room and told her to wait by a narrow aisle until she was summoned to play. In spite of that tremendous orgasm, she was still feeling nervous. But it was not a problem. These little twists and knottings in her stomach were perfectly normal, she reassured herself silently. In fact, it was rare for her to play well when her nerves were not on edge like this.

There was a sudden burst of applause from the watching men, and she craned her neck to see the olive-skinned girl jerkily shake hands with her opponent and walk away from the table. She must have lost her match, Roz thought without much sympathy. But the torment was not over for the loser yet.

Grabbed by a middle-aged businessman, the olive-skinned girl's skirt was pushed to her waist and she was simply lowered onto the man's lap without any preliminaries, her shocked expression indicating that she had just been penetrated. The girl in the rubber corset did not escape such treatment either. Dragged away from the pool table by two young men, she was already sucking enthusiastically on one of their penises while the other prepared to enter her from behind.

Roz began to wonder when her turn would come, feeling an entire row of male eyes turn towards her as she waited alone at the back of the room. But just as one of the older men had stood up and begun heading purposefully in her direction, Carter appeared on the raised platform to announce the next match and the man fell back, a look of almost comic disappointment on his face as he fumbled to refasten his trousers.

'Gentlemen, please!' Carter's voice echoed around the room as most of the men fell silent again, some leaning forward eagerly. 'Tonight's tournament continues with an old Nordic favourite of the tour, Beautiful Bianca, coming up against our new player from right here in London, Randy Roz!'

Deafened by the applause which followed that introduction, Roz quickly made her way along the narrow aisle and stepped up onto the raised platform. From the other side of the room she could see Bianca approaching the table more showily in a little dress of silver netting which concealed absolutely nothing and stopped just below the front curve of her thong. For a moment, Roz wondered whether she looked as sexy and available as the tall blonde, then guessed she must do by some of those hungry stares emanating from men in the front row, their hands dropping urgently to their laps as the applause died away.

It had been a long time since she had played a match like this, on public display with a large audience, and she could feel her heart racing as she slid open her aluminium case to screw the two parts of her cue together. To make matters worse, Roz was suddenly and horribly aware of the moisture seeping from her freshly come pussy. The men in the front row might actually be able to see it trickling down her inner thigh, she thought, unable to stop herself flushing with embarrassment. It was bad enough to know that she would be expected to make herself sexually available to these men after the match without displaying her own wantonness to the whole world beforehand.

But it was impossible to clean herself up here, she realised, right in front of everyone. She would just have to hope her still-tingling pussy stopped dripping juice as the game wore on.

Bianca stepped forward to shake hands and an odd hum of expectation came from the audience. The reason was soon obvious when the Nordic blonde won the coin toss and elected to break, bending forward over the table in clear view of those lucky men seated behind her. With her legs wide apart for balance, the silver netting of her dress rose steeply up her buttocks as she lowered herself to the white ball, openly displaying the full pink flesh of her shaven pussy. Roz even caught a glimpse of the girl's crinkled bottom hole, lewdly winking above the wide-spread thighs, before the white ball smacked into the pack and Bianca was quickly straightening up, her dress sliding back over those pale gold buttocks.

None of the balls had gone down at that opening shot, which meant that Roz could delay the inevitable no longer. It was now her own turn to bend over the pool table and expose herself to the watching men, face burning with embarrassment as she teetered towards the white ball on ridiculously high heels.

She felt cool air on her bottom as she bent, spreading her legs wide for balance just as the other girl had done. Before the match started, Roz had naively imagined herself being unable to go through with it at the last moment. But now that she was here, it was a fiercely exciting sensation, realising how many men must have their eyes fixed on her pussy as she lowered herself to the shot. The shiny PVC skirt tautened across her backside, rising irrevocably until everything down there was on full show.

Recalling how Bianca had looked when hitting the ball, she could guess what they must be able to see. Moist sex lips, a little puffy from their recent orgasm and no doubt still streaked with juice, peeping out from curly straw-coloured hair. Then the humiliating exposure of her bottom hole, hopefully not too dirty, the tiny brown star clenching as her muscles tensed for the shot.

The rudeness of it all was almost enough to put her off the game. But much to her relief, she potted that first ball cleanly, hearing a murmur of pleasure as she moved around the table to her next shot and bent over for another group of eagerly watching men.

Her first round match did not last long. It took her less than fifteen minutes to dispatch the Scandinavian girl, who retreated in tears through the crowds only to be seized by a man near the back who pushed her head down into his crotch. Roz had almost reached the door herself when a man and a woman caught up with her and dragged her back. In spite of her protests, a pair of hands moved straight up her skirt to finger her aching sex until she came, her cries muffled as the man's penis was shoved unceremoniously into her face for sucking.

She was still licking and stroking some other swollen cock in the audience when she heard her name being announced again and looked up in dismay to see Carter gesturing her back to the table. The time had simply flown by while she was being asked to satisfy man after man and now it must be time for the semi-finals.

Rubbing her sore knees, Roz grabbed her cue case and hobbled back up onto the platform. Her hair was now in disarray and her lipstick had been obliterated by long periods of sucking, but she was still ready to play. Her new opponent was the cool brunette in red rubber she had seen at the table earlier. Belatedly recalling that the girl was a pretty impressive player, Roz took a few long swallows of the iced water provided and made an effort to clear her head. She had come here to play pool, she reminded herself sternly, not lose herself in the pleasures of giving head.

That pre-match orgasm in the bathroom had certainly helped her performance. Even under the pressure of this exposed situation, Roz found herself playing tremendous pool. Every ball she struck flew sweetly across the baize and into the pockets, never so much as touching the sides. Gasps of admiration from the men spurred her on to play even riskier shots, aware that she had a golden touch that evening and seemed incapable of missing. The brunette in the shiny rubber corset stood to one side of the table and watched in helpless silence, losing the match without having been given much of a chance to salvage anything from the debris.

'Don't move from the table,' Carter discreetly warned her as the applause died away. 'You're in the final now and Paula's on her way here to try and beat you.'

'She doesn't stand a chance,' Roz whispered back.

The audience never wasted any time in relieving their frustrations, she thought, shocked at their rapacity. The poor brunette had already been snatched by several pairs of demanding hands. All that was visible of her body was a rubber-clad bottom in the front row as she was pushed over the back of a chair into a woman's lap and ordered to lick. The woman's shapely legs were stretched out on either side of the girl's helpless body, twitching and jerking with pleasure, the woman beginning to moan noisily as her orgasm approached. As Roz watched, startled to find herself aroused by such scenes of debauchery, a man in his sixties moved towards their writhing bodies and carefully inserted a finger beneath the rubber corset. From the brunette's agonised yelp, it was obvious that he had penetrated her bottom. Clearly satisfied with her response, the man undid the stud fastenings between her legs and had soon replaced that finger with his erect penis.

Then Roz stopped watching because Carter had announced Paula's arrival and the atmosphere changed dramatically. Within seconds of her entry an awed hush had descended over the room, heads swinging like magnets towards the reigning champion. Men unzipped their trousers almost like a salute as she passed by, hips swaying and a dirty smile on her face, and began playing with themselves openly. It was clear that Roz would have a battle on her hands if she wanted to beat this girl.

Paula was shorter than she had expected, but her body was perfectly proportioned, small breasts swelling over the top of a tight bustier like some eighteenth-century whore, her hips encased in smooth leather, a skirt which halted just short of her buttocks. The sliver of black leather underneath was a thong slipped neatly between the cheeks of her bottom, which must have been on show to every man in the room as she climbed onto the platform and executed a little curtsey. She slipped her cue onto the baize with the briefest of sideways glances at Roz and turned back to the audience, though in that tiny second all her hostility and desire to win had been made abundantly clear.

Between her teeth, Paula was holding a thin white cane. With an experienced flourish, Carter came forward and signalled the black-haired girl to her knees before the audience.

'Give it to me, bitch!'

Like a well-trained dog, Paula strained her upper body towards Carter and allowed him to release the cane from her teeth. The men in the audience gave a gasp of anticipation as she was ordered to bend over the pool table and present her bottom. Paula seemed unconcerned by her impending punishment, making every movement of her lithe frame count as she settled herself gracefully over the baize and pulled the leather skirt slowly above her backside. The tight pale buttocks gleamed with some sort of oil, making the contours seem even more desirable.

Roz looked on, astonished. This was not what she had expected when she reached the final. She had to hand it to the other girl though. Paula knew how to make an audience beg for more. The sheer showmanship of her performance might be impressive, she thought drily, but how much of Paula's winning streak was based on intimidating the opposition with this pre-match spectacle and how much on actual talent? Of course, it had been made painfully clear to her by Carter that the game itself should take second place to satisfying the punters, but Roz had her pride to consider. She would not have come here if there had been nothing but filthy antics on the agenda. Before everything else, she was a player. And that was something she would never allow herself to forget, however much cock she had to suck.

Standing to one side, so as not to block the clients' view, Carter raised the cane high above the girl's exposed buttocks.

'Have you been naughty since your last match, Paula?'

'Yes, sir,' she admitted.

'What have you done wrong?'

'I fingered myself.'

The cane swept down in a sharp white arc and Paula hissed loudly, almost rising from her position. But from the gritted teeth and fixed stare, it was plain she did not intend to ruin the show by refusing to continue. Instead, her fists unclenched on the baize and she took a deep shuddering breath.

'What do you say, Paula?'

'Thank you, sir.'

The cane was lifted above her buttocks once again and held there, a cruel smile on Carter's face.

'What else have you done wrong?'

'I . . .' The girl was stammering now, a tell-tale flush in her cheeks. 'I licked out my girlfriend without permission, sir.'

The cane sliced into her fleshy buttocks for a second time and she shrieked with genuine pain, only held down by Carter's hand.

'I'm waiting for an apology.'

'I'm sorry, sir,' she moaned, writhing beneath his grip. 'I won't ever do it again. I promise.'

The marks on her skin were already beginning to show, throbbing violent-looking lines which overlaid paler and older marks from what must have been previous punishments. Lowering the cane one last time, Carter put his whole strength into the blow. The girl's body jerked in agony and her eyes clamped shut, a rasping cry issuing from deep in her throat. Yet she did not move from her subservient position until Carter had smoothed the tiny leather skirt over her red-striped buttocks and ordered her to rise.

'Do you want to play some pool now?'

'Yes please, sir.'

'And who's going to win tonight?'

'I am,' she said with deliberate emphasis, her dark

eyes skewing sideways to where Roz stood silent and motionless, watching the proceedings.

Carter seemed amused. 'Roz is new here. She doesn't know the rules yet. You'd better tell her how we punish the loser.'

'We make her suck,' Paula said with a sudden vicious smile. 'And suck, and suck, and suck.'

'And what happens to the winner?'

'Oh, first I get beaten. Then I get fucked. In my mouth, in my cunt and in my arse.'

The audience burst into spontaneous applause, clearly appreciating that mental image. Paula looked down at them all for a moment with a provocative smile, tongue running greedily across her lips, then she took up her pool cue and gestured to Carter to toss the coin. The dark-haired girl's eyes were like flint as she and Roz came together to shake hands, palms touching with contemptuous speed. Suddenly everything had changed on the platform. The show was over and the game was on.

The other girls had been reasonably good players, but it was soon plain that Paula was in a different league. Her eyes narrowed to a single purpose as soon as she got to the table. Her shot selection was cunning and intelligent. She missed almost nothing. And when she did fail to pot a ball, she rarely left Roz anything better than a poor half chance. No wonder she was their top player, Roz thought tensely, battling hard not to lose the first game. But it was impossible to stop Paula winning. The other girl had got the run of the cloth long before Roz and knocked too many balls down early on. All Roz could hope for now was to come back in the second game and stop the bitch taking the match.

Thinking tactically at last, Roz played a slow and cagey game once the balls had been set up again. She constantly tied the dark-haired girl up on the back cushion and left her as little room for manoeuvre as possible. It was not long before Paula's frustration began to show, fingers drumming impatiently on that tiny leather skirt between shots and her face tight as she waited to get back to the table. She was clearly unused to players who did not falter at the sight of her incredible potting power. But Roz had been around the pool halls too long not to know how to trip up a fast potter. And once the dark-haired girl was rattled enough to leave her a few good openings, she began potting balls in earnest.

The last game lasted less than five minutes. Paula, determined not to be shown up, had smashed the pack all over the place on her break-off shot. But nothing had gone down. So Roz had come to the table with cold sharp eyes and lowered herself to pot that crucial ball in the absolute knowledge that she would not be leaving the table until the match was hers. Her breathing became tense and shallow as she swung around the baize, spreading her legs as wide as they would go, loving the gasps from the audience as her sex lips pouted between her thighs. They would be swollen and soaking with the sheer excitement of the game by now, and no doubt perfectly visible to every man in the room.

Roz got down to pot the black, heart thumping and her mouth dry, and heard a hoarse whisper at her back.

'Sink that and you're dead!'

But she paid no attention to that warning from the furious Paula, audible to no one but herself. It was the sort of attitude she had encountered many times before in the pool halls, beating a player who thought they were invincible. Players like that deserved nothing but her contempt, Roz thought, making absolutely sure she put the black away before rising to shake the other girl's hand.

'And tonight's winner is Randy Roz!' Carter's voice rang out and the entire room of spectators erupted into rapturous applause. She was surprised by that reaction, having expected them to prefer their usual champion. But as Paula was dragged away, howling bitterly at her defeat, and pressed down onto her knees to suck a row of eagerly waiting men, Roz suddenly realised that she had no idea what sort of treatment to expect as the winner. She stood there with her arms by her sides, trembling with anticipation, as a crowd of hungry-eyed men pushed to the front of the room. She might have stamped her authority on the tour but what would be the price of that victory?

'Quick, up on the table,' Carter ordered her brusquely. 'Our clients need to see what they're about to enjoy.'

He helped her up onto the pool table, one leg swinging awkwardly and exposing her moist pussy as she clambered first to her knees and then to her feet, staring down at the sea of faces below her. Unused to balancing in such high heels, her position felt dangerously precarious. But the last thing she wanted was for Carter to think she could not handle this situation. She had nowhere else to go at the moment. It was this life or no life at all.

'Turn around and bend over,' he instructed her, watching from below as she obeyed. 'Spread your legs a little wider.'

Head dangling helplessly between her knees, Roz tried not to peer through her curtain of hair at the men who pressed close against the table. The prospect of what would follow this display was too nerve-racking. Instead, she focused hard on Carter's voice.

'Now grasp your ankles and hold that position.'

Her body arched even further as she felt down along her leg for each ankle and held them firmly, her hamstrings stretching and burning with discomfort. From the ripple of approval which ran through the watching crowd, Roz guessed with a flush of humiliation that her lower body was now on display. The bright ceiling light, suspended high above the table, illuminated her like a public exhibit. With her legs spread so painfully wide, the men below must have been able to savour every inch of her gaping sex and exposed bottom hole. No doubt they had already noticed the tell-tale dampness on those inner lips.

Roz was astonished by her own lack of self-control. The very fact that she was being displayed like this to a roomful of men, like some sex slave up for auction, had actually aroused her.

Under the hot lights, Carter had climbed onto the pool table beside her and released her PVC skirt so that it fell in a glistening black puddle around her heels. His fingers searched unerringly for her pussy lips and stretched them wide, the damp flesh tingling under his touch.

'Look at that, ladies and gentlemen! Dripping with juice and ready for anything.' His voice sounded triumphant as he dragged her sex lips even further apart and displayed them to the audience, two or three fingers forcing themselves up inside her protesting body. 'I knew it as soon as I saw her. The girl's a born player.'

Then his hands dropped away and she remained bent over there in a tense silence, naked buttocks thrust high in the air and wondering what on earth would happen next. Seconds later, she yelped in sudden excruciating pain as a cruel heat burnt across her bottom. Carter must have hit her with something!

Turning her head ever so slightly, Roz watched him raise a thin white cane above her exposed body and remembered how he had used it to cane Paula before the match. So this was to be her reward for winning the competition tonight. She was not particularly impressed by their performance incentives on this tour, she thought grimly, but had no time to complain. The cane descended again in a vicious white blur and she screamed this time, reaching up instinctively to clasp her sore backside.

Tears had sprung unbidden into her eyes. Roz blinked them away fiercely, ordering herself not to cry. But as the cane came down a third and fourth time, she found it almost impossible to stop herself, her chest tight with the effort of holding back the pained salty tears she longed to shed. The knowledge that Paula was out there in the audience somewhere, though, kept her teeth gritted and her resolve strong. There was no way she was going to let the former champion of the tour see her crying, not after she had taken her own beating – apart from the odd yelp – with apparent nonchalance.

When the caning was over, Carter helped her down from the table with a solicitous hand.

'Are you OK?' he whispered.

Unshed tears burning behind her eyes, she raised her chin and gave him a tight little smile.

'Never better.'

He nodded abruptly, even though it was clear he did not believe her, and raised his voice for the benefit of the whole room. 'You can take that bra top off now, slut. I think the audience wants to see your tits.'

A great roar from the floor greeted that order and Roz soon found herself fumbling with the catch to her PVC bra top, letting the shiny material slip to the floor and standing there completely naked. Carter took her arm and led her about along the narrow aisles, displaying her pale slender body to the audience like a prize animal. Her face flushed with embarrassment, she tried not to meet anyone's eyes but stared straight ahead above the crowd. Perhaps this torment would be over soon, she kept telling herself. But she gradually realised that her ordeal had only just begun. Wherever she moved through the long rows of seats, hands reached out to trail across her bare thighs and breasts, growing ever more audacious as the crowd about her thickened. Soon she could feel rough fingers prising her buttocks apart or slipping between her thighs to locate the moist entrance to her sex.

Roz cried out in shock and alarm, turning to ask Carter for help, but he had disappeared. She stood alone and naked in a crowd of dark-suited men, their eyes narrowed on her body.

'Please,' she murmured, shaking her head as they pressed closer. 'I only came here to play pool.'

But her sex was already dripping warm juices in anticipation and one of the more aggressive-looking men gave a grunt of satisfaction as he shoved a couple of fingers up there, immediately discovering how well lubricated she was.

'This dirty little bitch is begging for it,' he shouted, lifting his juice-slick fingers to show the other men how excited she had become.

'Come on then.' Another man grabbed at her breasts, squeezing them with large calloused fingers. 'Help me push her down on the floor. I want to do it doggy-style.'

'No, sit her on my lap first,' insisted another, unzipping his fly to reveal an obscenely swollen and purple-headed penis which he handled with great care as though it were about to spray semen everywhere. 'This won't take long, I promise.'

Lifted on high by many determined hands, she cried out for them to slow down. But it was absolutely no use. They had sensed her readiness to be fucked and would not stop now until they were fully satisfied. In spite of her protests, she was lowered onto the man's lap, her thighs pressed apart to straddle his body and the muscular walls of her pussy stretched as his swollen penis impaled her. Facing away from his grasping hands on her hips, she was forced up and down on his penis in a fast urgent rhythm.

Roz tried to fight her growing excitement but failed miserably, her moans and whimpers only too audible as the cock inside her grew fatter and more tensely rigid. Fingers felt for her erect nipples and pinched them repeatedly, the men listening to her gasps of pain with apparent pleasure. Then another man, heavier set and balding, pulled one of the chairs forward and knelt up on it, pushing her head towards his proffered penis. Her mouth and throat were soon filled with his bloated thickness, his large balls pressed sweatily against her chin.

The man inside her suddenly tensed and yelled out, forcing her right down on his penis as it began to pump his ejaculation into her belly. This act seemed to inspire the man thrusting himself in and out of her throat. He too gave a hoarse strangled cry and shoved his entire length past her tonsils, causing her to gag as his salty come spurted into her mouth and down her throat.

'Me next,' grated a foreign-sounding voice to her right. The man looked Arabic, and his sturdy cock already protruding from the folds of his expensive-looking trousers. 'Turn her towards me.'

Face flushed and blonde hair dishevelled, Roz found herself lifted away from the other man's wilting penis and straight onto the Arab's lap. His fingers quickly located her gaping wet hole, keeping it spread wide for his own entrance. Her cry was one of humiliated pleasure as that solid column of flesh slid up into her sex and began to thrust back and forth without even the slightest attempt at gentleness. She ought not to be enjoying this barbaric treatment but she could not help herself. His dark eyes locked with hers and she felt an orgasm begin to build inside her. The expensive pinstriped material of his suit rubbed against her breasts as she rose and fell, her nipples tightening with inexorable excitement.

'You play well,' he murmured, watching with an enigmatic smile as the first waves of her orgasm hit. 'And fuck well too.'

She groaned and writhed uncontrollably on his rigid penis, heat spreading through her body and leaving a trail of reddish blotches across her face and chest. Breathless and aching for more, she leant forward and put her tongue inside his mouth in a moist invitation for him to come. She thought at first he had not understood, but then he tightened his grip on her hips and emptied himself fully into her pussy. Mere seconds later he withdrew, pulling her sweating body away from his lap and handing her back to the crowd of onlookers. He had made no sound as he came, she realised, except that his breathing had quickened slightly. Removing a white handkerchief from the breast pocket of his jacket, the Arab wiped every trace of her juices and hair from his penis before zipping himself up again.

Then she could not see him any more. Another man had taken her head and pressed it down into his crotch, so that she soon found herself sucking obediently on his penis while another man knelt between her legs and penetrated her from behind. The others crowded round to watch, some stroking her body and others merely rubbing and squeezing their cocks, one dark-haired woman's hand slipping over her buttocks until the slender fingers had found the tiny puckered entrance to her rectum and slid inside.

Dizzy and confused, Roz lost count of the number of times a man had spunked in her throat or filled her sex with his come. The fucking seemed to go for ever and ever, even though she knew in her logical mind that it could not have been more than an hour since Carter had abandoned her to this audience of voracious males. By the time the tour manager reappeared at her side, her jaw ached from sucking and her vagina was gaping like an old woman's from the sheer number of cocks which had stretched it. The crowd was dispersed quite easily though, most of the men having been satisfied in one way or another by then, leaving only Roz and Paula down on their knees on the stained and sodden carpet.

When Carter helped her back to her feet, Roz stumbled and could hardly walk, gallons of excess sperm running down her inner thighs as she made her way to the nearest chair and sat down.

'So,' he said quietly, kneeling to check her body for bruising or marks. 'That was your first win. How did you enjoy it?'

'It was . . . unusual.'

His eyes flashed ironically to her face, leaving her in no doubt that her excitement and arousal were plain to see.

'You didn't come?'

Roz winced as his fingers parted the lips between her legs and pressed the inner flesh speculatively.

'Maybe once or twice,' she lied unconvincingly, knowing perfectly well that she had orgasmed with almost every man.

Paula came crawling towards them on her hands and knees, her make-up completely ruined, her face spattered with sperm. It hung from her hair in thin sticky white streamers, larger blobs dripping from her nose and eyebrows. Stripped to nothing but a damp-crotched thong, her small breasts flushed with exertion, she seemed far less intimidating than when she had first entered the Roseman suite earlier that evening. It was clear from her furious expression that she was not used to taking second place in these competitions.

'I should have won tonight, Carter. That evil bitch must have cheated,' the girl hissed venomously. 'I'm covered in spunk now. I look like a cheap whore. What are you going to do about it?'

Carter grinned and reached up to start unbuttoning his shirt. For a crazy moment, Roz thought he intended to fuck one or both of them and waited in silent anticipation of his next move. Her pussy stung from the countless men who had already stretched it but she was still aroused enough to crave more. The tour manager merely shrugged out of his white shirt though and threw it carelessly towards Paula.

'Better clean yourself up before the other girls see you.'

Ignoring Paula's gasp of outrage, Roz stood up and followed Carter rather shakily to the door. Her legs were like rubber and she had never felt sleepier in her life.

'So what happens now?' she asked, examining his body with a mild flicker of interest as Carter preceded her along the hotel corridor. He was fitter and more muscular than she had realised earlier at the pool hall. 'Is it OK if I sleep here tonight? I can't go back to that bedsit again.'

'Fallen out with your landlord?'

'Something like that.'

Carter was smiling as he pressed the button for the lift back up to the penthouse suite.

'You can sleep with one of the other girls tonight, there are plenty of beds. And when we get back to our home base tomorrow, I'll sort you out some permanent quarters.'

'So I can stay?'

He turned to glance down over her pale naked body, slick with sweat and spunk. 'You're our new champion, sweetheart. That means you're part of the tour now, whether you like it or not.'

Five

'So what do you think?'

Roz stared out at the impressive cityscape laid before her, towering glass office blocks and sky-scrapers catching the last rays of the sun. She could not remember which floor they were on here but the journey up in the mirrored private lift had taken several minutes. The tower block itself was vast. She had already counted twenty rooms at least on this floor, which seemed to be reserved entirely for the girls and their entourage. Each room had been decorated in an over-lavish style with iron-framed beds covered in black silk sheets in the bedrooms and huge leather sofas in the living rooms. The plush deep-pile carpet encouraged a hushed atmosphere where many of the girls went barefoot.

'I think we're a long way up here.'

'Right on top of the city, with a superb roof garden and swimming pool above. For the exclusive use of the players, of course.'

'Of course,' she repeated drily.

Carter smiled, casually lighting a cigarette and slipping the lighter back into his jeans pocket.

'This will be home for you over the season. During the summer months most of the players go abroad, to the Caribbean or the Far East, though it is possible to keep a room here if you prefer.'

'Will I have to share with anyone?'

He shrugged. 'Only if you want to. I've arranged a private room for you but that can be changed any time you like.'

Roz said nothing, staring out at the city sunset for another minute or so before turning away and prowling restlessly about the room. This place felt oddly claustrophobic, she thought. It might be quite difficult to settle down here, especially knowing how she was expected to perform at every tournament they played. The rewards might be overwhelming, she told herself grimly, but this particular tour could end up being less of a circuit and more of a treadmill for her. She was not entirely certain if she preferred the idea of going back to those backstreet pool halls to this glamorous but demanding lifestyle.

'So how often do we play?'

'Once every few weeks. It depends on demand.'

'And last night,' she muttered. 'Was that typical of what I should expect after every match?'

Carter nodded, drawing heavily on his cigarette as he watched her pace about the room, back in her comfortable hipster jeans and plain white T-shirt.

'Pretty much, if you carry on winning. Which I suspect you will. Though some of our regulars have rather more . . . exotic tastes, shall we say? You might find some of the demands they make difficult or you might enjoy them. It's all down to what sort of person you are inside, where your natural limits are.'

She stopped pacing and looked at him straight, hands on hips. 'Last night was hard for me, bloody hard. So tell me truthfully, Carter. Do you think I'm up to this?'

'Yes.'

'You sound so sure.'

Carter smiled, relaxing back onto one of the black leather sofas as he finished his cigarette.

'I was sure the first minute I saw you in that pool hall. There's just something about you, Roz.' He shook his head impatiently. 'I can't put my finger on it but it's exactly what a player needs to succeed. This is a difficult place to be if you're weak . . .'

'I thought last night was all about weakness,' she interrupted him, eyes blazing. 'About vulnerability, powerlessness.'

'No, it's about strength,' he contradicted her quickly. 'The strength to let go of your control and see how far it will take you.'

'To hell, I should imagine.'

She had expected that sharp-tongued remark to make him angry. But the tour manager merely laughed, leaning across to the ashtray and stubbing out his cigarette with strong careful fingers.

'That sense of humour's important too. Don't lose sight of it.' He looked at her, meeting her eyes. 'Whatever happens at a tournament, Roz, you can't take it seriously afterwards or it will destroy you. Some of the girls over the past few years have been damn good players, but they burnt out too quickly. They forgot to shrug it off once they got back here and it ate them up inside.'

Her face thoughtful, Roz indicated the expensive furniture and deliberately muted decor around them.

'So this is a safe house?'

'More or less.'

She frowned. 'What does that mean?'

'There aren't many rules up here, but it's still possible to step out of line and risk punishment.'

'What sort of punishment?'

He smiled, his eyes lingering on her body under the tight jeans. 'Use your imagination,' he murmured drily. 'Our clients aren't the only ones who like to watch a pretty girl taking the cane.'

The door to the room opened at that point and a man she had never seen before came in, briefly scanning the room until he saw her. In a dark expensive-looking suit and crisp white shirt, he was much taller than Carter and somewhere in his mid-sixties. The grey hair had been cut sparsely above a striking face, fleshless and hard-boned, his eyes a startling blue which seemed to pierce her to the bone as the man strode purposefully towards her.

'McNaughton,' he said, clasping her in a firm handshake. 'You must be our new star player. Welcome to the tour, Roz.'

'Thank you,' she said uncertainly.

Ignoring Carter, who had stood up at his entrance, the older man looked her up and down in the hipster jeans and white T-shirt. The eyes reminded her of an eagle's, fast and frighteningly observant. Then his mouth twisted into what appeared to be a smile.

'Very clean, very innocent,' he said succinctly. 'I just hope you're a little dirtier underneath.'

'I'm sorry?'

The man called McNaughton took a few steps back, gesturing to her clothes. 'Come along, I know you're young but there's no need to act the child. I don't have time for it today. Just take your clothes off and let me see your body.'

Flushed and embarrassed, she glanced sideways at Carter for some reassurance and was surprised to see a tense look on his face.

'Roz, this is the boss,' he murmured, his tone light but laced with careful respect. 'Mr McNaughton owns this building, and he runs the show up here. So do what he says.'

Realising that her options were extremely limited if she wished to remain on the tour, Roz took her T-shirt in both hands and pulled it firmly over her head. She had not bothered wearing a bra that morning and her breasts sprang out free and proud, nipples already semi-erect. Then her hands dropped to her button-up hipsters. Calmly undoing the buttons one by one, she wriggled the tight jeans down to her ankles and stepped out of them. She was already barefoot and it took only a few more seconds to remove her black lace thong.

She stood there, absolutely naked, waiting for his next instruction. McNaughton's expression had not changed as he watched, but Roz could see the tell-tale bulge in the front of his suit trousers and realised that he wanted her. Was this part of an initiation ceremony, she wondered, guessing that she would soon be required to relieve the boss in whichever way he chose. Funnily enough though, the idea of having sex with McNaughton did not appal her. In spite of his age, he was still an attractive man and she suspected that his sexual prowess might not be far behind that of men half his age.

McNaughton examined her carefully and then glanced at Carter for the first time since entering the room.

'Where did you find her?'

'Hustling in some backstreet club, sir.'

The older man made an amused noise under his breath, turning back to look at Roz with speculative eyes.

'Ever been fucked up the arse?'

The sudden crudity of that question made her blush scarlet. She shook her head, hearing herself stammer like a schoolgirl.

'No, sir.'

'Excellent. We'd better hurry up and grease your arsehole then, so I can stick my cock up it.'

Carter hesitated, seeing her face pale at his words, then signalled her towards him as he bent to open a drawer in the dark oak chest against the far wall. Handing her a pot of what she guessed to be clear lubricant, he flashed her a brief smile and squeezed her fingers reassuringly.

'Do whatever he says and don't make him angry,' he whispered in her ear. 'Everything will be OK.'

Turning reluctantly back to the older man, she saw McNaughton had already unzipped his trousers and was massaging his large penis to erection. She was taken aback by its impressive length and the fat bulbous head, purpling darkly as it stiffened. That could do her some damage if she resisted, she realised, wincing internally. No wonder Carter had warned her not to make the boss angry. He probably did not want to see her torn by rough handling.

Silently handing McNaughton the little pot of lubricant, she dared not meet his eyes in case he saw how scared she was and thought her spineless. He gestured her to kneel over the sofa and she hurried to obey him, leaning her cheek against the smooth black leather with her legs spread wide and her bottom vulnerably high in the air. This was not what she had expected from her first day, she thought, swallowing hard as she considered what he intended to do. It would hurt, she was sure of that. It always hurt the first time. But it was clear that obeying him without question was the only course of action open to her. Even having anal sex for the first time with this rather well-endowed man would be better than going back to the streets.

Tense and hot-cheeked, Roz felt a long finger rubbing grease in and around the puckered entrance to her rectum. It tried to slide in there and had to push hard at the opening, eventually forcing its way inside and spreading the grease along that narrow muscular passage.

'Nice and tight,' McNaughton murmured in satisfaction, his voice close behind her. 'I'm going to enjoy this.'

'Should I leave, sir?' It was Carter's voice and he sounded oddly uncomfortable.

'Stay where you are,' the older man replied sharply. 'Sit down and smoke a cigarette. You might learn something. This won't take long and we've got business to discuss afterwards.'

Her heart racing, Roz felt McNaughton drag her hips determinedly backwards. Then the swollen head of his penis lodged itself in the slippery crevice between her buttocks and she imagined its purplish slit oozing fluid, already eager to enter that tightly closed hole. Some rebellious part of her wanted to push him away and refuse to go through with it, but with her logical mind she knew this stranger was about to take her in the bottom and she was helpless to prevent him.

Closing her eyes, Roz buried her face deeper in the sofa to smother any cries at the moment of penetration. The last thing she wanted was to embarrass herself with a display of cowardice.

The puckered skin stung and burnt as he pushed hard at her anal orifice and gradually forced the first inch or so inside. His grunt seemed to indicate that he was finding it pleasurably hard to enter her. Realising that she had been holding her breath for some time, she tried to let it go in short controlled bursts, her chest hurting. But the pain was too much to bear and she soon began to gasp, her dignity dropping away as he rammed his hips impatiently against her buttocks. There was a moment of obstruction and then his penis just seemed to slip past it, her sharp muffled protest ignored. Once properly inside, McNaughton did not even allow her to get used to the sensation but pushed further and further in until she thought the agony would never cease, inexorably stretching the walls of her rectum.

She smelt smoke and realised that Carter had lit another cigarette as ordered. She wondered what on earth he must be thinking, watching as McNaughton buggered her ruthlessly across the leather sofa. From his vantage point behind them both, he must have been able to see her buttocks held apart by insistent fingers and the boss's penis shoving up inside her bottom hole, stretching the taut skin around the entrance with every thrust. It must have appeared quite disgusting to an observer, she thought, becoming a little red-faced as her bottom began to make odd farting noises. The pain had lessened now, for which she was naturally grateful, but there was still something inherently humiliating about this position, kneeling face-down with her bottom in the air while a complete stranger sodomised her.

McNaughton's pace had quickened now, pushing in and out of her bottom in long steady strokes, the rhythm just forceful enough to make her wince. She suspected he must be nearing his climax though. His girth seemed to have increased substantially since he had entered her and he had begun grunting with every inward thrust. Fighting the urgent desire to slip a couple of fingers between her legs, Roz tried not to think about what the man was doing. But it was hopeless. She was becoming flushed and breathless. Her hips were lifting slightly to meet his thrusts. She was sexually excited and she could not hide it any longer.

What made her arousal worse was the knowledge that she had only just met this man. Yet here she was, bending obediently to take his penis in her virgin bottom. If anyone had been going to break her in anally, she would have preferred Carter to do it. Firm as he had been when she sucked him off in the men's toilets, Roz suspected there was a soft side to the tour manager which might have spared her such embarrassment on her first time.

His hands suddenly tightened on her body and he slammed his penis right up to the hilt inside her bottom, hips jerking two or three times, his balls pressing hard against her empty vagina as he groaned loudly. Seconds later, as McNaughton shifted position, she felt a warmish pool of spunk escape her stretched anus and trickle down the narrow cleft towards her sex. He had shot his full load in her rectum and now that creamy white ooze must be soaking right through the walls of her bowel.

The filthiness of what he had done up there was too much for her. Finding the slippery nub of her clitoris, she rubbed at it fiercely until she arched into her own high-pitched orgasm. Then she slid another finger into the loose cavity of her bottom and screamed, her muscles twitching uncontrollably as she came again and again.

Not caring what the two men might think of her wanton behaviour, Roz writhed against the black leather sofa in an ecstasy she had not felt for a long time. The musky mingled smell of her juices and his sperm was still on her fingers when she slid them into her mouth afterwards and licked herself clean.

'You were right,' the boss was murmuring to Carter, accepting a cigarette and watching her recover from those violent orgasms. 'She is a dirty little whore. Absolutely perfect for the tour.'

'They adored her last night, sir.'

'So I believe.'

Carter glanced in her direction as she straightened, sweaty and dishevelled, to reach for a box of tissues on the coffee table. But he said nothing, quickly looking away as though it might be dangerous to be seen showing her any sympathy.

McNaughton was zipping his trousers up, a slight edge to his voice as he continued. 'Though it's a pity I didn't have a chance to enjoy her privately before the tour started.'

'She only arrived a few minutes before the match, I'm afraid.'

The boss nodded curtly. 'Next time, Carter.'

'Yes, sir.'

There was a peremptory knock at the door and McNaughton frowned. 'Come in,' he called.

It was Paula. The dark-haired girl stood in the doorway, taking in the scene with angry narrowed eyes. From the ugly look on her face, she had not missed a single detail, from McNaughton's relaxed features down to the way Roz drew her sperm-slick thighs closer together and tried to stand up without trembling.

Paula's hands settled on her hips in the see-through black lace dress. There was not a single shred of underwear in evidence beneath that dress, Roz thought in disgust, and the girl's shaven pussy was clearly visible. It was their free time now, as Carter had emphasised to her, saying there was no need for the girls to wear anything revealing unless they wanted to. Clearly Paula was the sort of girl who needed to show everything at all times.

'Yes?' the boss said sharply. 'What do you want?'

Paula pouted and smoothed her dress down against her body, presumably to ensure the two men could see her dusky-pink nipples outlined beneath the skimpy material.

'I had to come, sir.' In a pair of slender black stiletto heels, she swayed across to McNaughton, throwing Roz a contemptuous glance as she passed. Throwing herself extravagantly to her knees, she looked up at the older man from under lowered lashes.

'This new girl's no good, sir. I watched her last night and she's going to put the punters off.'

'Why's that?'

Paula shrugged. 'She can play pool all right. But she's not a genuine submissive. Not like the rest of us.'

McNaughton laughed drily, taking a last drag on his cigarette and throwing her the still-smouldering butt. Paula gasped at the unexpected heat between her palms but seemed to recover her composure remarkably quickly, crawling to stub it out in the nearest ashtray. She hid her blackened hands behind her back as if she were ashamed of them and stayed where she was, kneeling submissively beside the coffee table.

'I just enjoyed the new girl myself and you're wrong. She's raw and unpolished, that's perfectly true. But she's got all the right instincts and Carter is an excellent trainer. He trained you too, I believe.'

'Yes, sir,' Paula nodded sulkily.

After continuing to regard her steadily for a moment, McNaughton turned back towards Carter with a frown on his face. 'Is there some problem between these two girls?'

'Paula was upset when she failed to win last night. It's been nearly a year since she lost a final like that.'

'I see.'

Carter hesitated before speaking again, his tone carefully neutral. 'Should I punish her for you, sir?'

'I think that might be appropriate. The cane, Carter.'

'Yes, sir.'

McNaughton settled back onto the black leather sofa and waited in thoughtful silence until the cane had been produced. The fleshless face beneath his greying hair held a smile of cruel amusement.

'But whatever punishment you give Paula, make sure you give twice that amount to the new champion,' he insisted. 'Then we shall see whether this little slut has the makings of a true submissive.'

Carter nodded without speaking, but his eyes flicked sideways to Roz and she thought she detected irritation in them.

Both girls were ordered to huddle side by side in front of the sofa, dropping to hands and knees when instructed and obediently displaying their naked bottoms to McNaughton. Neither girl looked at the other but Roz could sense Paula's hostility and resentment coming at her in waves. She was not particularly bothered though. It was not the first time she had made an enemy playing pool. There were few people who enjoyed being beaten, after all, and it did make Paula's attitude easier to handle, knowing up front what her grievance was.

Carter stood beside them, flexing the thin white cane in his hands. Roz could not help remembering the pain of her last caning and hoped he would not be too brutal. To her relief though, he did not extend the waiting period but struck swiftly, bringing the cane down across Paula's buttocks with obvious expertise. Paula's entire body jerked and she cried out, her shoulders already beginning to shake as though in anticipation of strokes to come.

Then the cane came down twice in quick succession across her own raised buttocks and Roz had to stifle an instinctive scream, fingers digging into the deep-pile carpet like claws. That sudden flash of pain had seemed like fire and now her skin was throbbing terribly where the cane had struck, not yet recovered from the beating she had endured the previous night on the pool table.

After each stroke he gave Paula, the merciless Carter dealt a double amount to her without any attempt at gentleness. His boss watched in approving silence, occasionally making a satisfied noise under his breath when one of the girls could not help but cry out at the agony being inflicted on their tender bottoms. Roz closed her eyes and tried not to imagine what her own bottom must look like now, a criss-cross of cruel red lines tortured with stroke after stroke of that thin cane. It angered her to know that, if Paula had simply kept her mouth shut, neither of them would be undergoing this punishment now. But she supposed that this sort of barbaric treatment was a normal part of the tour regime. She could either live with it or leave. Those were her only two options.

But whatever she chose to do in the end, she dared not show any more weakness than Paula during this test. Otherwise she might lose her place on the tour. So she listened hard to the moans of the girl at her shoulder, feeling the way her body twitched in reaction to the cane, and tried not to surpass those signs of distress. After all, she had a reputation to protect now and there was no way Roz wanted the other girls to think she was a coward.

'That's enough!'

Both girls knelt shuddering with tearful relief as Carter stepped away, lowering the cane to his side.

McNaughton sounded pleased, standing up and coming forward to examine their quivering red-striped bottoms. 'She's impressive, this new girl. That was a good job you did in finding her, Carter.'

'She'll certainly draw the punters.'

'Absolutely.'

Carter hesitated. 'It's getting late. Should I send the girls back to their quarters, sir?'

But the boss did not seem to be listening. Instead, he put the tip of one polished leather shoe under Paula's chin and drew her head upwards, staring down into the girl's face with a cruel smile. 'Have you learnt your lesson, Paula?' he demanded. 'This new girl is far more submissive than you. She barely made a noise during that punishment while you squeaked like a novice.'

'I'm sorry, sir.'

'So you admit she is your superior?'

Paula's body seemed tense and she did not answer at first, her breath catching in her throat.

'I thought you wanted to hear me cry out, sir. It was a mistake, that's all.' Her voice trembled pitifully. 'I could have kept silent too if I'd realised that was what you wanted, sir.'

McNaughton's face hardened. 'It is not your place to judge what your masters require. You are merely to obey.'

'Yes, sir.'

'However,' he continued, glancing at Roz, 'it is true that you have taken the cane rather better in the past. So I will give you the benefit of the doubt on this occasion.'

'Thank you, sir.'

McNaughton paused. 'Which means we have still not established which of you is the more submissive.'

'There's always the Table Rack,' Paula said hurriedly, then softened her voice in a sickeningly obsequious manner. 'That's what you used on me when I first arrived, sir, and you said I was the best ever.'

'The Table Rack? We haven't used that punishment in a while.' Much to Roz's horror, the boss nodded and glanced across their kneeling bodies towards Carter. What on earth was the Table Rack and how much would it hurt, she wondered? It sounded even worse than the trials she had endured at the tournament last night. But whatever this new torture might entail, she was clearly about to experience it. Her hatred for Paula grew steadily as he continued speaking. 'Sort that out straight away, Carter. I think the best idea would be to leave her on the Rack all night. That way we can finish our business tonight and assess the girl's performance in the morning.'

'Yes, sir,' Carter murmured, his face expressionless as he yanked Roz to her feet and dragged her towards the door.

Six

Spread-eagled face down across the pool table like a helpless sacrifice to some ancient god, Roz tried unsuccessfully to move her arms and legs but she was too tightly secured to move more than an inch or so in any direction. Her groan of defeat appeared to satisfy Carter, who stepped back from the table and nodded.

'That should keep you out of mischief tonight. I'll be back in the morning to see how you've coped.'

She tried to lift her head to glare at the man, but a thick strip of metal positioned immediately behind her neck had been bolted to each side of the table, rendering movement almost impossible. A heavy-linked chain ran from each cuffed ankle and wrist to a metal hoop attached to each corner pocket, from where the chains rose to a fitting on the light shade above. Whenever she pulled angrily at her bonds, the light shade swung back and forth, making a loud rattling noise and sending eerie jerking shadows across the practice room.

'You can't leave me here like this,' she spat at him. 'It's barbaric. What if I need the loo during the night?'

His smile sent a cold shudder down her back. One of his large hands slipped between her thighs and stroked the damp crease running along her thong, making her body tense with frustrated desire. Roz swallowed hard, closing her eyes momentarily. She was longing for one of those thick fingers to slip beneath the leather strip and massage her clitoris until she exploded into an orgasm, but she had far too much pride to beg a man for sexual favours.

'That's simple, Roz. As I see it, you have two choices here. Either hold it in . . . or let it out.'

'So you don't care if I piss on the baize?'

'Go ahead. It's only the practice table and a few urine stains won't make any difference.' Carter bent down to her face, his eyes lingering on her parted lips as if he wanted to slip something between them. 'Besides, we can easily replace the cloth if you dirty yourself as well.'

'Filthy bastard!'

But that insult merely earned her another punishment. With an open palm, Carter slapped her bare buttocks several times in quick succession, her cries of pained humiliation apparently amusing him. Roz struggled in her chains again, pressed face down on the pool table, but she knew her position to be hopeless. She would not be going anywhere until he or McNaughton chose to release her in the morning. Though no doubt even that release would come at a price.

Her heart sank as she considered the long hours of torment which lay ahead for her, secured to this table all night like some criminal in the stocks. She had been stripped down to nothing but her leather thong for this punishment and the room was not entirely warm. Her skin was goose-pimpling with cold, her nipples almost painfully stiff as they rubbed against the smooth green baize of the pool table. To her inner fury, though, Roz guessed it was not only the cold which was making her nipples erect. The treatment she had received over the past 24 hours had left her constantly aroused and frustrated, although she had tried to hide that reaction. His slaps had not helped. Now she was horrified to feel herself oozing fluid between her open thighs, her wide-stretched pussy aching with desire. It was so embarrassing. And in this position she would not even be able to reach down and masturbate herself to a much-needed climax.

'I thought you were my friend.' Her tone was accusatory. 'But you're enjoying this, aren't you?'

Carter hesitated, then straightened up without taking advantage of her vulnerable position.

'Strangely enough, I am. But I'm still your friend. This isn't how I wanted you to spend your first night here, Roz. But now that you're stretched out like this and chained to the pool table . . . well, let's just say it's an arresting sight.'

Her sex throbbed in response to the note in his voice. But she struggled to sound angry.

'Why don't you just fuck me and get it over with, Carter? I know you're dying to.'

He laughed briefly. 'Because I can't.'

'What?'

'I'm not allowed to interact sexually with the pool players. Not once they've joined the tour. That sort of pleasure is strictly reserved for McNaughton and his clients during the touring season.' Carter shrugged, stepping away as if that restriction did not bother him at all. But she thought she could detect irritation in his voice as he checked her bonds for the last time. 'You girls are supposed to rest in between tournaments anyway. Otherwise you might not be charged up enough before going a match. And then the clients wouldn't get their money's worth. See what I mean?'

Her voice was dry. 'So you can look, but not touch?'

'That's the theory, yes.'

'But in practice?'

There was a moment's hesitation as he stood beside her, one hand reaching out to absent-mindedly stroke the pert curve of her bottom. This man must be so frustrated, she thought, her pussy hot and moist. Only a eunuch could look after eight scantily clad girls day after day, punishing and touching them as intimately as Carter did, and not feel the urge to bury himself inside one of them occasionally. Her heart was beating hard as she imagined the tour manager suddenly breaking the rules and climbing onto the table behind her, his thick penis ready to push deep into her sex.

Then Carter laughed, turning away. 'You won't get me into trouble that easily. Other girls have tried before and failed.'

'Man of stone, huh?'

'I'm just doing my job, sweetheart. Which doesn't include what you've got on your mind.'

'So you're a psychic now.'

'No, but I can see the damp patch on the baize between your legs.' Carter left the practice room without rising to her bait, his laughter mocking as she found herself abandoned on the pool table, staring into darkness beyond the swinging light shade. 'Goodnight, Roz. Sweet dreams.'

The practice room fell silent as his footsteps receded and she realised that she was alone. Struggling against the chains attached to her ankles and wrists only made her feel frustrated, so she stopped and listened instead, hoping to hear one of the other girls passing in the corridor so that she could call out for help. But the corridor stood silent and empty.

Nobody went past at all, not even one of the dark-suited minders whom she had seen patrolling these rooms during the evening. In fact, there was no sign of anyone still awake on the entire floor. Roz found that difficult to accept, so she tried shouting for a while. But all she got in return was a dry throat and an odd sensation of loneliness.

It took nearly an hour to get used to the fact that no one was coming back to release her. That was the point when her body stopped aching and started really hurting. The chains dragged inexorably at her ankles and wrists, forcing them into an unnaturally high position while her trunk was kept low by the iron band securing her neck to the table. Although she tried to remain stoical about her plight, a few exhausted moans escaped her lips from time to time. But at least there was no one around to witness her degradation, she kept telling herself.

In spite of such incredible discomfort though, Roz realised she was finding this imprisonment arousing. How stupid to get sexually excited by something so frustrating, she thought, feeling more than a little irritated by her own weakness. But there was no point trying to pretend that the Rack was having no effect on her body. Her sex lips were gaping wide and moist with juice. Much to her humiliation, she could even feel them tingling at the possibility that Carter might come back during the night and touch her again.

Suddenly, a muffled noise near the doorway made her lift her hot cheek from the baize. She could not turn her head properly to see who had come into the room, but Roz sensed she was no longer alone and felt her heart begin to thud with anticipation.

'Who's there?' she whispered.

There were hurried footsteps behind her, then the dark-haired girl she had beaten at the tournament appeared. She put one slim finger to her lip as if to caution silence, then glanced back over her shoulder for a few moments, clearly worried that she might have been seen entering the practice room. But nobody else appeared in the doorway and eventually she turned back, leaning over the table to meet Roz's eyes. Her voice was attractively quiet and melodious.

'Do you remember me?' The girl seemed almost too well-spoken for a pool player. 'My name's Lauren. You beat me the other night.'

'I remember.'

The dark-haired girl smiled at her sympathetically. 'Are you OK? It can be pretty rough, stretched out like this for hours.'

'Sounds like you've done it yourself.'

Lauren nodded. 'It used to be one of McNaughton's favourites. Though now he seems to prefer the Frame.'

'The Frame?'

'Don't worry, you'll find out about that soon enough.'

Roz groaned and closed her eyes in pain, aching and trembling from her unnatural position. 'I hope not.'

'I bet you wish you'd never agreed to join the tour.'

'Damn right.'

The dark-haired girl stroked her cheek reassuringly. 'Everyone feels like that the first week. But it's funny. You get used to it after a while. It even gets sort of exciting. The punishments, I mean.'

Her sex still hot and moist, Roz could not help laughing a little in wry agreement. 'I can understand that.'

Lauren hesitated, watching her for a moment. Then she bent down to her face again, those dark eyes wide with sympathy.

'You're turned on right now, aren't you?' she whispered, her breathing quickening as their eyes met. 'My goodness, you look tense. Are you feeling really frustrated?'

'Yes.'

Lauren moved around her body, a gentle hand creeping along her inner thigh and sliding up towards her slick wetness.

'Would you like me to help you come?'

'I'm . . . not sure.'

'Is this your first time with a girl?'

'Not entirely.'

Her laugh was low and wicked. 'Carter would be absolutely livid if he could see what I'm about to do. It's forbidden to help a girl who's being punished. Especially like this.'

'Like this?' Roz echoed, her mouth dry as the other girl stroked the damp outline of her sex lips under the leather thong. 'What do you mean?'

By way of reply, Lauren lowered her head between the wide-spread thighs and licked at those pouting outer lips.

Roz allowed a moan to escape her lips, pressing her face against the baize cloth. Her nerve-endings were leaping with electric shocks as that clever little tongue brushed like a feather over her outer lips, then pushed aside the thong to slip into her hot sex itself. Her fingers soon followed it, stroking and then holding apart the swollen lips so the dark-haired girl could reach her tongue even further inside. The sensitive inner flesh flooded with juice at her touch, a warm rush of fluid between her thighs that could not signal anything but excited arousal.

'No,' she groaned, her voice shaking, but it was too late to hide how she was feeling. The fierce reaction of her body had already betrayed her desire for release.

Lauren slid two fingers experimentally into her sex and held them there while she continued to lick. Then she began to ease her long fingers back and forth, in and out of the sticky hole, still flicking her tongue across the fleshy nub of her clitoris until it stood up like a tiny penis. Secured to the table and unable to stop her, Roz could do nothing but gasp and writhe in her bonds, waiting for that inevitable moment when the dammed-up pleasure inside would burst its banks and sweep through her body. She had been aching to be touched down there for hours and now at last it was happening, even if this was not how she had imagined it. For it was not Carter but a young dark-haired girl between her thighs, bringing her to orgasm with these delicate flicks of her tongue.

She thought her head was going to explode with excitement. Her legs began to shake so violently that the chains attached to her ankles rattled against the light shade and shadows swung across the room. She felt her face go hot with shame and excitement, then her muscles seemed to clench internally and she knew it would not take much longer for her to orgasm.

'Do you want to come in my mouth?' Lauren asked her in muffled tones, her face still buried in the throbbing mound of Roz's sex.

'Hurt me first.'

The girl raised her head slightly to stare at her. 'What?'

'Hurt me. Bite me, slap me.'

Lauren's mouth slowly returned to her sex as if she could not quite believe what she had heard. But Roz did not have long to wait. Sharp little teeth soon caught up her clitoris in their grip and gave it a couple of hard nips, not quite breaking the flesh.

She cried out in pain and clamped her eyes shut. Her raised buttocks and thighs shook under a sudden rain of slaps. Lauren was not taking it easy on her either; the skin burnt and stung almost as badly as if she had taken a whip there. While she was still recovering from that onslaught, the tongue that had tormented her clitoris now forced its way into the aching hole of her sex, jabbing in and out until she thought she would go mad. Then one long finger slipped between her buttocks and found her anus, pushing deep inside its stiff ring of muscles at the same time as that clever tongue was working in her sex.

It was this last intense stimulation she needed to reach orgasm and Roz climaxed at last, screaming in pleasure and rubbing herself against the unyielding surface of the pool table without giving a damn that her nipples would suffer afterwards. The sensation was too much though and she blacked out for a minute or so. When she came back to full consciousness, the other girl was standing beside her head, stroking her flushed cheek with an amazed expression on her face.

'You dirty crazy little bitch,' Lauren said with an odd laugh.

'Probably,' Roz agreed breathlessly.

Unfortunately, the rest of the night did not pass quite so excitingly for Roz. Chained to the table with her legs spread wide, she soon realised she needed the toilet but would be unable to go unless she wet herself over the baize. Roz held on valiantly for some hours, dozing fitfully between bursts of needing to wee, but it was not long before she became genuinely desperate. Indeed, by the time McNaughton returned in the morning, accompanied by Carter and Paula, she was in gut-wrenching agonies at having to hold back such a fierce desire to urinate.

'Did you have a peaceful night?' McNaughton asked in a smooth voice, unceremoniously reaching between her legs and fingering her sex lips through the leather thong.

They must still have been damp from her orgasm because the boss smiled, unfastening the thong at each side so that it fell away and left her pussy open to his inspection. She blushed, wondering how far this latest humiliation would go as the musky scent of her arousal filled the air. McNaughton's breathing seemed to quicken, his fingers exploring her dampness more thoroughly. Then he began tugging at the taut exposed nub of her clitoris until Roz gave a little gasp of anticipation, fearing that at any moment she might let go of her control and spray his fingers with hot wee.

'Come here and feel this, Carter. I think the slut enjoyed her night on the Rack. She's absolutely soaking up there.'

McNaughton's hand was replaced by Carter's, those thick fingers rubbing slowly across the oily slickness of her sex as though he now wanted to enjoy what he had refused last night. Yet when he spoke, his voice sounded as flat and emotionless as ever.

'Yes, there's no doubt about it.' His hand dropped away, leaving her empty and aching. 'She's easily as submissive as Paula. Even more so, perhaps.'

'Perhaps . . .'

'Should I release her, sir?'

'Not yet.'

McNaughton seemed oddly hesitant as he felt between her thighs again. Then his hand slipped up over the slight swell of her belly in an experimental fashion, only pausing when she tensed every muscle in a desperate attempt not to open her bladder over the table.

'I think this slut needs a piss.'

Carter came round to her head, forcing her neck back until she had to meet his eyes.

'Do you?'

'Yes,' she whispered, hot with embarrassment.

Paula was beside the table in a second, yanking so dreadfully at her hair that Roz yelped in pain, wishing her hands were free so she could slap the nasty bitch in the face.

'You should call him sir,' the other girl spat, still wrenching at her hair with long spiteful fingers. 'You're on the tour now. That means you have to show respect or be punished.'

Carter sounded angry. 'I'm perfectly capable of disciplining these girls on my own, Paula. This has nothing to do with you.'

The other girl hesitated for a moment, fingers still wound viciously around Roz's hair, as though waiting for McNaughton to intervene. But when the boss said nothing in her defence, Paula stepped back sulkily and fell to her knees a few yards away from the table. Her glossy hair fell forward over her face in a shining curtain as the other girl bowed her head, yet Roz guessed there was nothing genuinely submissive about that gesture. She could sense the resentment emanating from her in waves and knew that Paula was only hiding her face in case the anger showed. No doubt further argument might have resulted in a beating, whether she was the boss's favourite or not.

'So you need to wee?' Carter continued, lifting her chin with his finger so he could study her expression.

'Yes, sir.'

He glanced across speculatively at McNaughton, who must have made some signal that Roz could not see because Carter nodded in silent agreement, reaching down beneath the pool table to produce a small silver bowl. Then he placed it carefully beneath her wide-spread legs on the baize and moved back to her head, staring into her eyes.

'Can you guess what happens next?'

Her mouth was dry, her heart thudding. 'Erm . . . I hope not.'

'Come on, don't bother trying to refuse this time. Trust me, it's not worth risking a punishment over something this trivial. Now be a good girl and do what you're told. I want you to let go of your muscles and urinate into the bowl for me.' He stroked her hair as though she were some sort of domesticated animal he was training. 'Nice and slowly please, so you don't spill any on the cloth.'

'I can't,' she stammered.

Carter smiled at her fearful expression. 'Of course you can.'

'Not here. Not in front of . . .'

His voice became stern and he stepped back, his eyes growing cold as they narrowed on her face. 'Look, you agreed to undertake this basic training. It was part of the original deal and you can't wriggle out of it now. Or would you prefer to leave the tour and go back to hustling in those backstreet clubs where I found you?'

'No.'

'Then shut up and piss into the bowl.'

Roz closed her eyes, swallowing hard as she saw there could be no escape from this situation. Though it was almost impossible to imagine herself carrying out his order and relaxing her muscles enough to urinate over the pool table. She had never done anything like this before in her life. Yet the thought of what he was asking her to do both repulsed and excited her. She wished fervently that Paula was not present, her own face flushed as she tried not to consider how she must look to the other girl, poised naked above the little silver bowl with her legs spread high and wide by the chains. Her sense of resentment grew alongside her excitement. This whole scenario was designed to humiliate and debase her, that was obvious. They all knew that wetting herself like some silly little schoolgirl without any self-control would be the final blow to her dignity and that was why Carter was insisting she obeyed.

Yet even though she kept fighting the urge to urinate, clenching those internal muscles, Roz knew it was only a matter of time before she could not contain the flow any longer and would be forced to let go. And as if the tour manager understood exactly what was going through her mind, Carter put his hand between her legs, teasing and tickling the sensitive skin around her wee hole.

'Stop struggling and relax your muscles. Just let it go.'

'You don't understand . . .'

'I understand perfectly, Roz. That's why I'm asking you to do what you're told. This test is all about agreeing to relinquish control over your own life. Learning to obey without question is an essential part of being a player, a genuine member of this tour. If you can't yield up your control to the clients and let them dictate what you wear, how you behave, what sexual acts you perform, then how on earth can you ever be part of the team here?'

'But it's obscene!'

'Yes.' McNaughton stepped forward, his face taut with excitement as he watched her struggling not to wet herself. 'And that's what makes it wonderful. Now obey the order and let me see you piss.'

Groaning in defeat, Roz lowered her eyes to the cloth so that they could not see the desperation in them. Then she concentrated on relaxing her muscles until she felt a warm trickle of wee begin to ooze out from between her stretched pussy lips. But it was hard, she found, to simply let go and urinate in front of these people. Much harder than she had realised when he first gave her the order. She wanted to wee, to please him and the boss, but for some reason her body would not obey. It was too used to urinating in private. For a few terrible minutes, she thought the act would prove impossible.

Carter sensed her inner struggle and put his hand back between her thighs, tugging at the damp fleshy hood which covered her clitoris and making her head spin in uncontrollable ecstasy. Within seconds, she felt the trickle of wee turn into a steady flow.

She raised her hips, arching towards his hand as he removed it to leave her sex empty and bereft, and the flow became a sudden gush which flecked her thighs with hot tiny splashes. Roz heard the hissing and tinkling of her own urine filling the silver bowl beneath her body and groaned aloud in excited humiliation. It was happening at last and there was no longer anything she could do to prevent it. Her pelvic muscles had relaxed completely. She was wetting herself while they watched and her head felt so excited she thought it might explode.

McNaughton's voice was suddenly close by. 'That's excellent,' he was murmuring in her ear, his voice unsteady. 'Now keep pissing for as long as you can. I want you to fill the bowl right up.'

The boss leant forward over her tortured body. His fingers felt for the damp flesh between her thighs as that hot gush gradually slowed to a trickle again, cleverly manipulating her body until Roz found herself gasping and trying to writhe away from his touch. But the chains prevented any movement except a slight twitch and jerk of her limbs as she felt an orgasm begin to build inside. She fought the sensation for as long as possible, but the growing heat in her body made it inevitable that she would come in the end.

How sluttish she must seem to these onlookers, wetting herself over a pool table without the smallest shred of dignity, legs spread wide by these chains, burning pussy exposed for them all to see, the tinkling sound as her urine struck the sides of that little silver bowl and filled it to the brim. Paula was probably still on her knees beside the pool table, she thought, closing her eyes in desperation. That jealous bitch must be able to see right up into her piss-soaked vagina, trembling now with desire under McNaughton's skilful fingers. How the other girl must be laughing at the sight of such a filthy shameless whore, chained with her legs apart for any man to penetrate and abuse.

That last mental image sent Roz spinning out of control. The deep grunts issuing from her throat sounded more like an animal in labour than a woman coming. Yet come she soon did, groaning and squealing with long-deferred pleasure as McNaughton's fingers shoved up inside her and brought her to orgasm. She had pissed herself in front of them like a shameless slut and now she was coming, over and over, lost to the fingers working so urgently between her legs.

Her body arched impossibly beneath the restraining chains, head straining upwards like a hunting dog's at its master's whistle, and she met Carter's eyes. The tour manager was watching her struggle to resist the force of that orgasm, his expression unreadable. But the bulge in his groin told her everything she needed to know.

Their eyes locked and Roz felt a final explosive shock that seemed to impact in her sex, radiating in waves along her spine to the white blast-zone of her brain. Even knowing that Paula was still watching did nothing to prevent those spasms rocking her body. She gasped out loud and allowed herself one long cry of pleasure as the orgasm peaked and began to fall away, her bladder relaxing so completely that the last few drops of her urine trickled down McNaughton's intrusive fingers and along his wrist.

Finally withdrawing from her pussy, the boss lifted his hand to his lips and licked speculatively at the sticky fingers.

'Perfect,' he muttered. 'Utterly perfect.'

Carter released her gaze with obvious difficulty and turned away from the pool table in silence, returning after a few minutes with a thin white cane. This he handed to McNaughton without any comment, his face shuttered. Then he took a couple of steps back into the shadows of the practice room, leaning against the wall and lighting a cigarette as he watched the proceedings.

McNaughton flexed the cane experimentally in front of her face, his smile unnerving.

'Does it ever scare you, Roz?'

Too breathless and confused to answer him at first, Roz stared up at the silver-haired man as her body slowly recovered from that mind-blowing orgasm.

'Does it ever scare you?' he repeated. 'Listening to the footsteps behind you and waiting for the pain to start?'

At last she realised what he meant, belatedly focusing on the cane in his hands and hoping there might be some way to avoid that particular punishment. But she knew that any such hope was forlorn. They had already pointed out to her that she was supposed to relinquish control over her life while she was on the tour. Being caned and humiliated by these men was part of that loss of control. It would give McNaughton pleasure to cane her, and that was precisely why she was here this morning, chained to the pool table: to give him and his clients pleasure. Not to mention herself, she thought drily, her sex still aching from the multiple orgasms which had wracked it so violently only a few minutes before.

But taking the cane was such a mixture of pleasure and pain for her, it was hard to know where one finished and the other started. Still marked with raised weals, her bare buttocks twitched in reaction to the sight of that long cruel stick, the memory of her last caning prominent in her mind as she replied with complete honesty.

'Yes, sir.'

'The helplessness a girl feels before the cane descends for that first stroke, the sheer vulnerability of her nudity,' he continued, walking around her as he flexed the cane in his hands. 'It must be hell for you, knowing there's nothing you can do to escape. That you can only wait until the punishment is over and hope you don't disgrace yourself by screaming or fainting.'

'Y . . . Yes, sir.'

At her stammered reply, McNaughton nodded with approval and moved to take up his position somewhere behind her, disconcertingly out of sight. Yet she could still hear the preparatory passes of the cane through the air, that terrifying whispered swoosh past her ear as he tested its weight and speed in his hand. He was right. It was utter hell, simply waiting there for the first stroke and hoping the pain would not be so overwhelming this time that she embarrassed herself in front of Carter and the other girl. Roz wanted to be stronger than she had been during her last caning, to take this punishment with complete resilience. But she knew that once the caning had begun, her resolution to endure each agonising stroke in silence might quickly be defeated by a very natural desire to scream and beg McNaughton to stop.

The first stroke came down without warning and she bit her lip so hard there was blood in her mouth, head jerking up as she stared across at Carter. But his face seemed dark and impassive, leaning against the wall in the shadows while he smoked his cigarette. If the tour manager cared what happened to her, he gave no sign of it.

'Good girl,' McNaughton said softly, and brought the cane down again on her raised buttocks.

That time she could not stop herself yelping a little, though she caught her breath before making any greater noise. The third and fourth strokes were equally hard to bear without screaming, yet somehow she managed it. By the sixth time that thin white cane had cut across her already marked and sore buttocks, her lips had been chewed almost to shreds as she fought not to embarrass herself by shrieking aloud. Yet it seemed strange to her that these men wanted her to relinquish control over her own life to them, whilst rigidly continuing to control her reactions during a punishment like this – though this was not the time to point out that inconsistency to either of them, her entire body struggling to cope with the white-hot pain shooting across her buttocks.

'Seven,' he muttered, raising the cane even higher above her body. His breathing had quickened and it was obvious that the sight of her caned bottom had excited McNaughton beyond the point of arousal. Putting his full strength behind the cane, he brought it down with such explosive force that she thought her heart was going to stop. Then the pain abruptly kicked in and Roz broke down, sobbing helplessly like a child into the green baize of the pool table.

'Please stop,' she begged him, ashamed by her own weakness but unable to stay strong any longer. 'I can't take any more.'

Paula, still watching the proceedings on her knees beside the pool table, burst into peals of vicious laughter.

'Listen to that,' she purred triumphantly. 'The girl's far too weak to be top dog on this tour. Let me finish the beating for you, sir. I'll soon have the bitch squealing for mercy.'

'Shut up,' McNaughton said, sounding a little out of breath now, and Roz heard him unzip his trousers.

Less than a minute later, McNaughton had climbed up onto the pool table behind her and positioned his erection between her sex lips, shoving it inside with a deep-seated grunt of satisfaction. He did not hesitate but began to thrust in and out immediately, grasping her hips as she bucked violently against the chains. The gold-fringed light shade above their heads swung back and forth in a rhythmic motion, sending flashes of light across Carter's face as he watched from the shadows. Roz gasped and soon moaned with an answering excitement, McNaughton's thrusts taking her rapidly towards orgasm.

Not for the first time she found herself wishing it could be Carter inside her, still remembering the feel and taste of that thick-veined shaft in her mouth as Roz knelt to suck him off in that filthy pool hall. It might be against the rules for him to have sex with any of the players during the season, but she was sure he must want to bend those rules on occasion.

Perspiration sprang out all over her body, her pussy on fire as she imagined how it would feel to have Carter fucking her from behind instead of McNaughton. The dark eyes were hooded now, still watching from the shadows as their boss ploughed her tight channel with ever-increasing force. Anyone might be forgiven, she thought, for assuming that Carter did not find her sexually attractive. Her woman's intuition, however, told her the tour manager was far from indifferent to her looks. There was a visible tension in the way Carter held himself, bending now to stub out his cigarette without once taking his eyes off her sweat-slick body.

McNaughton leant forward, driving himself against her bruised buttocks as he laboured over her like a stallion mounting a mare. The skin there was stinging horribly from the cane, exacerbated now by the rough material of his suit trousers. Her breath hissed out in protest and her fingers clenched into automatic fists against the baize. Yet Roz found even that pain oddly exciting, a dangerous and unpredictable pleasure, gyrating her hips to allow him greater access in spite of the restrictive chains attached to both ankles. She was so close to orgasm now, she could practically taste it in her mouth.

She raised her head slightly and fixed her gaze on Carter. They stared at each other again like two silent combatants, ignoring the man grunting and pushing himself into her from behind. He was no longer important. Her heart immediately began to thud in that familiar off-rhythm, all her muscles tightening as if for some supreme effort, and Roz knew she was on the verge of coming. Yet what was it about Carter watching her with McNaughton which so intensified her excitement? Sometimes it was almost as though she belonged to Carter and had done ever since the first moment she had accepted his penis in her mouth. Feeling his eyes linger over her flushed cheeks, her body wracked with pleasure as she was fucked so forcefully by their mutual boss, was like some spine-tingling voyeurism between lovers, a sexual collaboration between possessor and possessed which deliberately excluded McNaughton.

Just as she reached her own orgasm, crying out in abandon as that wild heat burst through her body, she heard the man inside her give a final deep grunt and ram himself home. McNaughton must be coming too. She was almost surprised to feel the warmth of his sperm spreading inside her and then dribbling out as he rapidly withdrew, wiping himself against her stinging skin. She had forgotten he was there. His hands seemed rough on her hips now that he had finished, pushing her away as he jumped down from the pool table. She struggled to readjust her balance within that network of chains and the fringed light shade shimmied like a wild thing above her head, a strobe light illuminating Carter's face as he stared harshly into her eyes and then plunging him back into shadow again.

Paula was bleating at McNaughton in a childishly high-pitched voice, struggling to her feet without permission.

'I've been the best ever since the tour started,' she was saying, even daring to tug at his sleeve as McNaughton tried to leave the practice room. 'It was only one match, sir. Let me play her again. I can prove to you . . .'

'That's enough!'

McNaughton's hand swept down and suddenly Paula was on her back on the floor, gasping and covering her face.

'I've tried to be understanding,' he said angrily. 'To remember how well you've served me over the past few years, Paula. But no amount of seniority can excuse your behaviour tonight. Carter?'

Carter moved forward out of the shadows, his face instantly alert. 'Yes, sir?'

'I want this irritating little slut hobbled and muzzled for at least the next twenty-four hours,' McNaughton said, ignoring the girl's horrified gasp as she backed away, shaking her head. He zipped up his trousers with a vehement gesture and headed towards the door. 'Perhaps that will teach her to respect her masters in future.'

'Yes, sir.'

'And release the other girl. She's very promising. I must make sure you're rewarded for finding her.'

Carter glanced back at Roz for a moment, his face unreadable once again as he took in the sweat-covered body chained above the pool table with her legs wide open.

'Yes, sir,' he murmured.

Seven

Carter selected an almond croissant from the breakfast buffet, poured himself a cup of scalding black coffee, and made his way carefully up the narrow flight of stairs to the roof garden.

It was a cool bright morning outside and the city below hummed with the distant sound of traffic. The garden itself was exquisite. Originally designed to impress wealthy foreign clients, its main use now was to provide fresh air and exercise for the players so they did not have to leave the McNaughton building between tournaments. In front of a gunnera plant whose vast green leaves dominated the garden in summer was a collection of ornate cushioned wooden benches surrounded by old-fashioned shrub roses, the flagstones around them strewn now with fallen petals. Although it was still early, several of the girls were already out of bed and outside in the garden that morning.

Lauren was sitting cross-legged on one of the cushion-covered benches, holding one of her bare feet and painting the toenails pink with a look of complete absorption. Beside her sat Roz, sipping at a hot drink as she stared out across the rooftops of the city.

Carter smiled at the sight of the two girls sitting together. He liked Lauren. She was the best behaved and most soft-spoken of all the players on the tour, yet there were hidden depths to the girl. Noticeably subdued and ladylike in front of McNaughton, he knew she possessed a wild streak beneath that calm exterior. Pleasingly curved and dark-haired, it was usually Lauren who satisfied the greatest number of clients at tournaments, totally uninhibited when it came to indulging her insatiable sexual appetite with members of the audience, male or female, young or old. Carter knew little of her background, of course, though it was clear to everyone that she had received a good education. One of their older girls at twenty-one, Lauren could always be relied upon to look after the new players. So he was pleased to see her already hanging out with Roz. Having someone more experienced around for support and advice could only help the younger girl settle more easily into her new life on the tour.

'Good morning, girls,' Carter said, seating himself on the bench opposite with his black coffee and croissant in hand. The soft almond-filled pastry smelt delicious and he licked his fingers appreciatively, smiling across at the two girls. 'You look far more relaxed today, Roz. I take it you slept well last night?'

'I slept like a log. The beds here are incredibly comfortable,' she replied, turning her head shyly towards him.

'They're not bad. The performances can be pretty demanding so McNaughton tries to make sure the players are comfortable between matches. There's a sauna and private gym on this floor too, to keep you all in top matchplay condition.'

'A sauna?' She looked startled, putting down her cup. 'Just for us? I've never had a sauna before.'

'That's not a problem. If you need any help, I'm sure Lauren will be happy to show you how it works,' he murmured, glancing briefly at the other girl for confirmation. 'It is quite important to make proper use of the facilities though. They were specially installed for the players and McNaughton likes everyone to look their best for the clients.'

But at his words the new girl sighed, turning to stare across the city again with a distracted expression. Carter drank his coffee and watched her with a sense of unease. There was a restlessness in her face which made him wonder how long Roz would last on the tour. It was no place for the half-hearted, he thought wryly. This lifestyle could become difficult to endure if a player did not make a proper commitment to the tour from the beginning. McNaughton liked to call that process an act of submission, enforcing his belief with the cane or the tawse. Which sometimes worked, and sometimes did not.

Personally, Carter preferred to let the girls choose this lifestyle freely, without the need for coercion or the threat of punishment if they questioned the system. The pleasure always went both ways after a genuine choice had been made, something he found deeply satisfying. Under those circumstances, it was never about money or a player's status on the tour. If they chose submission freely, none of the girls would ever feel as though they were being used. On the contrary, everybody would be getting what they wanted and life could only be more exciting.

But he was not the boss. All he could do was supervise the girls during their basic training as he had been instructed to do by McNaughton and hope they would eventually come to enjoy themselves of their own free will. But could an independent-minded girl like Roz, used to calling the shots and choosing her own sexual activities, ever see the tour in such a submissive light?

He finished his coffee and placed the empty cup on the flagstones, his voice becoming businesslike.

'Our next tournament is in less than a week,' he said, scrutinising Roz's face and figure with a critical eye. 'Your game may be OK but your body needs to be better prepared before you can perform again. We have a superb masseur here on twenty-four hour call. His name is Tyler and I'd like you to see him later today. First though, you'll have to be thoroughly cleansed and depilated, head to foot.'

'What?'

Carter smiled at the girl's horrified expression, standing up as he checked his watch. He ought to get back to work now. It might have been pleasant, sitting out here in the garden with them as he finished his breakfast, but there were several important duties to attend to before lunch and he was losing time. Besides, if he was not wary about the way he handled her initial training, he might end up forming a special attachment to Roz. Which was probably the most dangerous thing he could ever do in this job, given McNaughton's strict rules about sexual interaction between players and management. There were plenty of spies about who would happily inform on him, Carter thought with sudden bitterness. Paula, with her obsessive jealousy of this new player, was the likeliest candidate at the moment. And if the strength of his attraction for Roz was ever revealed to the boss, he could face immediate dismissal for it. But if he played this particular game with a little more caution and tried not to show the girl any favouritism, he might be able to enjoy her at some point in the future without being disciplined for it.

His voice hardened deliberately. 'A full body wax has been booked for you at eleven o'clock this morning. Lauren will show you where the salon is.

And don't make that face, sweetheart. It doesn't suit you. Pain is something you had better learn to enjoy here . . . or lose your place on the tour.'

On the far east side of the penthouse floor of the McNaughton Building, the marble-tiled communal baths were lit by a series of muted spotlights concealed in the walls and ceilings. Three tiled steps down along the full length of the baths brought the girls into pleasantly warm water at knee height, then a gentle slope led them in deeper until they were almost submerged. During the daytime, sunlight filtered down through a frosted-glass roof positioned centrally above the water, rippling over the bare shoulders and breasts of the bathers.

There was a hushed atmosphere as Roz stepped into the shallows and glanced around at the other bathers. There were three naked girls whispering together at the deep end who had watched her emerge from the changing rooms and were now quite clearly criticising her naked body. Unbothered by their catty looks, she shrugged and continued to look around the baths. A well-tanned blonde was lying passively on her stomach beside the water while a younger girl knelt astride her body, stroking some sort of oil into her thighs and buttocks. Only one other girl in the room seemed to be actively washing herself, standing like a nymph in the centre of the bath as she soaped her slim body, and that was Lauren.

The dark-haired girl raised a hand in welcome when she saw her, a look of relief on her face. 'There you are at last! You took ages getting undressed. Come on in. You'd better hurry up and wash yourself, we can't be late for the salon.'

'Why? Do they chop your head off if you're late?'

Lauren shot her a quick sideways glance and put a finger on her lips, cautioning silence. There was a

111

warning look in those dark slanted eyes as she waded towards her. 'Don't even joke about it. If you can't follow the rules here, they'll always find some way to punish you.'

'I handled the Rack without any trouble, didn't I?'

'But that was only for starters.'

Roz frowned, staring at the other girl across the rippling water. 'You mean there's more to come?'

'More and worse.'

Lauren stepped closer, hurriedly checking that none of the other girls were listening before continuing in a low voice. Her breasts brushed lightly against Roz's shoulder as she turned, pretending to splash water across her glistening thighs to wash away the soap suds.

'Look, we're all here of our own accord. That's part of the original agreement. Because we want to play pool. But it's not easy being one of the players outside tournament time. There's no chance just to relax and be yourself. There's always something extra they expect you to do, some duty you have to perform. And you either obey them or you get punished. It's as simple as that.'

'So I might get caned again?'

Lauren shrugged mysteriously. 'That, and other things.'

'Oh come on . . .'

'You don't have to believe me. You'll find out soon enough when you break the rules. Now take this bar of soap, give yourself a proper wash and for God's sake stop talking so loudly. One of those other girls might hear what you're saying and then we'll both be in trouble.'

'OK, no need to get so excited.' Roz took the slippery bar of soap and slid it across her shoulders and breasts, enjoying the warm fragrant scent of ylang-ylang as she worked it to a lather. 'I was just curious what you meant. This is all new to me, remember.'

Pushing the soap down to the rounded curve of her belly, she closed her eyes to shut out Lauren's frown and tried to concentrate on the relaxing warmth of the water against her thighs and buttocks. She let her hand slip lower, right below the surface of the water, massaging the soap into the fine curly hair between her thighs until the bath was white with thousands of tiny bubbles.

Her hand worked at the same gentle rhythm she had seen Lauren using on her own body, round and round, and over and back again, pressing firmly against the mound of her pussy. It was strangely arousing, knowing that the other girls were still watching as she cleaned herself. It must look to them as though she were masturbating, one hand lost beneath the surface as she worked. But she did not stop, even when her cheeks became flushed. The embarrassment was worth it for these gorgeous sensations growing inside her body. The skin of her inner thighs was soon smooth and creamy from her cleansing routine, that luxurious scented lather washed away by the constant lapping of water against her thighs and buttocks.

This was so much better than a shower, Roz thought with a deep appreciative sigh, feeling her muscles begin to relax after the tension of the last few days. The soap almost slipped away from her but she caught it again with a deft flick of the wrist, parting her legs slightly to allow herself better access. It felt incredibly good to be surrounded by all this soporific warmth, the moist air of the baths leaving her drowsy, a sheen of perspiration across her cheeks and forehead. Once her pussy felt cleaner than it had ever been before, she moved the slippery bar of soap round to her bottom, pushing between the firm white cheeks and rubbing at the tight little hole there.

Lauren had dipped herself under the water at her side, rising again with her breasts dripping and her dark hair sleeked back. She looked like a shiny seal as she moved through the bath, sliding lithely behind Roz and removing the bar of soap from her hands.

'Here,' the older girl murmured in her ear. 'I'll do that for you. Bend over a little more, I can't reach properly.'

Taken aback by that unexpected offer, Roz immediately did as she was told, bending forward with her hands resting on her thighs for balance. It was merely a question of ensuring she was clean up there before the waxing procedure, she told herself. There was nothing more interesting to be read into the situation. Indeed, she expected Lauren to be rough with her, matter-of-fact even, just in case the other players suspected there was some sort of relationship between them. But the hands parting her bottom cheeks were gentle, almost reverent, exposing the tender skin without any hint of practicality. Perhaps Lauren did not care what the other players thought. Roz's mouth went dry as she felt the soap pushed inch by inch into that wet-skinned crevice, only to be pressed up against her bottom hole with tantalising brevity. She thought her low moan was a clear enough signal for Lauren to stop, but the older girl merely leant a little closer.

'Stop squirming, for God's sake. You need to be thoroughly cleaned before going to the salon,' Lauren explained, her voice a little breathless as she prised those buttocks apart again. 'Try to relax your muscles. This won't take long.'

One slim finger began to penetrate the tight ring of her bottom hole and Roz groaned this time, unable

to control her reactions any longer. This was surely
not a normal part of the washing routine, she
thought, her cheeks burning. No one else in the bath
seemed to be soaping their friends' backsides in quite
such an intimate fashion. But it felt good, she could
not deny it. As the intrusive finger pressed deeper
inside, her spine arching with desire under a series of
electric shocks running through that sensitive inner
flesh, Roz suddenly became aware of the other girls
staring at them across the steamy room. Their eyes
had narrowed maliciously on her small high breasts
and the flush on her cheeks. There was no hiding her
arousal now.

The sound of a loud cough made them both turn,
their faces hot with embarrassment as they realised
that Carter had entered the baths and was standing
on the tiled floor above, arms folded across his chest
as he watched what they were doing.

'That's enough for now, Lauren,' he said sharply.
'I believe Tyler is waiting for our new arrival.'

'Yes, sir.'

Lauren dropped the soap and nudged Roz back
towards the side, a panicked look in her eyes. The
two girls stepped hurriedly out of the bath, seizing
several of the thick fluffy towels that had been laid
out for their use and rubbing themselves dry under
his silent scrutiny. Slipping back into her clothes, Roz
felt that hot familiar ache between her legs and
wished the other girl had been able to finish before
Carter had appeared to spoil their fun. Now she
would have to go to the salon in this state of
unsatisfied arousal, every movement hell as her thighs
pressed tightly together beneath the little black skirt
she had decided to wear that morning. She had not
even bothered to find herself any underwear. Without
even the tiniest of thongs to contain her juices, it

would be obvious to anyone who felt between her thighs that she was excited and ready for sex.

When they were both dressed, Carter escorted them back along the hushed corridors of the penthouse, eventually leaving her and Lauren outside the glass-fronted door to the salon. Roz had expected some sort of verbal explosion once they were out of earshot of the other girls in the bath and had prepared herself to be chastised. But the tour manager did not seem particularly angry with them, as she had at first feared. There might even have been a glint of amusement in his hooded eyes as he instructed Lauren to stay with Roz until her appointment with the masseur after lunch.

'After that, McNaughton wants to see you in his private rooms,' he told the older girl, his tone clipped. 'Unfinished business,' he said. 'You'd better not keep him waiting. Is that understood?'

Lauren nodded, avoiding his eyes. 'Yes, sir.'

Once Carter had disappeared back towards his own office, Roz glanced across at Lauren without bothering to hide her curiosity. She did not want to appear too inquisitive when they had barely known each other more than 24 hours, but she was dying to know what that conversation had meant. It seemed strange to her that a sweet-tempered girl like Lauren should have any sort of personal dealings with McNaughton, a man whose sadistic and domineering nature had been only too obvious the other night.

'OK, so what on earth was all that about?' she asked, her eyes fixed avidly on the other girl's face. 'Is there something going on between you and McNaughton?'

'Don't be ridiculous. But he is the boss, remember? I can hardly refuse if he asks me to visit him.'

'Does that mean what I think it means?'

'Probably, yes.'

'Jesus Christ.' Roz stopped and stared at her in disbelief. 'I don't know how you can do that, Lauren. Not after the way he treated me the other night. Can't you just say no to him? I thought this tour was about free will?'

Lauren bit her lip as if not sure how to answer that, pushing open the door and motioning Roz into the quiet entrance hall of the salon. Her voice was wary as she glanced back over her shoulder. 'Look, you don't understand. McNaughton's not so bad when you get to know him. It all depends what you're looking for in a man.'

'You've got to be kidding!'

'It's nothing to get upset about, Roz. I give him what he wants and he gives me ... what I want.'

'Which is?'

Her face slightly flushed, Lauren pulled back a curtain in the salon and gestured Roz to lie down on the clean-sheeted bed.

'Let's talk about that another time, OK? You just take your clothes off and get comfortable. I'll tell Tyler you're here.'

Roz slipped reluctantly out of her tight black skirt and top, folding them onto a nearby chair and stretching out on the neat white bed. Her head was full of lurid images which she failed to suppress: Lauren in bed with McNaughton, his hands grasping her full breasts and slipping intimately between her thighs. Roz exhaled sharply, staring up at the ceiling in confused anguish. She found it hard to endure the thought of that beautiful pale skin marked by his cane as the girl jerked and moaned under every stroke. No doubt Lauren had her reasons though. It was even possible that she genuinely enjoyed the pain and brutality of a session with McNaughton. Roz

117

herself had felt excited at times by his domineering cruelty, though she suspected that having Carter's eyes on her body the whole time had tipped the balance between pain and arousal. The cane itself had been nothing but an instrument of torture for her. It was what happened inside her head between each stroke which brought the real excitement.

It felt odd to be lying there in the nude, hidden by nothing more substantial than a curtain as she waited for her massage. The whitewashed room was very clean and tidy, smelling of the bottled lotions which lined the shelves around her. A pile of clean white towels lay on the table beside her, folded and ready for use. Green plastic gowns hung in a row behind the door.

She was reminded of routine check-ups with the doctor, drawing up her knees and letting her legs flop gently apart while some cold metal object was inserted inside her vagina. Those latex-gloved hands moving mysteriously between her legs, his clinical air of disinterest as he bent forward for a closer look. Her breathing increased as she remembered lying there on her back, staring down at his bald patch in anticipation. In her imagination, the doctor would always fumble with his flies at that point, hoisting her ankles over his shoulders without asking for permission and shoving his cock deep inside her until the examination table shook beneath his thrusts. The nurse standing behind him like a professional observer, watching with barely concealed jealousy, the tip of her tongue protruding from between pointed white teeth as she played with herself beneath her uniform.

But of course the doctor had never done anything that out of the ordinary during those internal examinations. He had simply withdrawn the cold metal object and left her frustrated, her legs splayed wide apart, waiting in embarrassed silence as the nurse passed her a paper towel to wipe between her thighs.

Suddenly the curtain was pulled back with a sharp rattle and a young man stood there, smiling across at her in a friendly way. His white uniform was immaculately clean and pressed, hair caught back in a neat dark ponytail. Roz could not help staring, her mouth dry. He was wearing shorts and the tanned muscular legs beneath them were still damp as though he had just stepped out of the shower. So this was Tyler, their masseur. After the thick-set minders she had seen about the penthouse in the past few days, she had simply not expected someone so good-looking to walk into the cubicle.

'You must be Roz,' he said cheerfully, closing the curtain behind him. He took down a bottle of oil from one of the shelves and shook it like a cocktail, examining her naked body with professional ease. 'My name's Tyler and I'm going to give you a full body massage. It may be a little uncomfortable in places, but that's normal. Just tell me if it actually hurts. Before we start, do you have any areas of injury I should know about?'

Silently, Roz lifted herself to let the masseur see her bottom, still aching and marked from the cane with long raised weals.

'OK, no problem.' Tyler opened the bottle and squeezed a little oil into his hand, heating it gently between his palms as he approached her. 'I can help you with that if it's causing discomfort. Now could you roll onto your tummy, please? I prefer to start with the spine and buttocks.'

The oil was scented and felt heavenly as Tyler began to knead and smooth the skin of her shoulders and upper back. He was so skilled at his job, in fact, that it was not long before she forgot

119

the embarrassment of her naked body and allowed herself to enjoy the massage. It was such a change not to feel under constant pressure to perform, she thought, sighing with pleasure. His hands slid repeatedly along her spine and over the curve of her buttocks until the muscles were completely relaxed and she felt as though she were melting against the white sheet. Her head turned to one side and she closed her eyes, not really sleeping, but drifting into a kind of dream state where her imagination could play. There was an ache between her legs and a dull heat beginning to stir in the pit of her stomach. She imagined his expert fingers parting her sex lips and stroking her clitoris, finding that moist cleft where she hoped he would sink himself before the massage ended.

'Turn over,' he murmured, helping her with careful hands as she forced herself to roll onto her back.

The cool air was a shock at first but she shut her eyes tight again and let him carry on. He stroked along her shoulders and across her breasts, caressing the taut nipples without emphasis, his fingers moving down along the flat plane of her stomach until she sighed aloud with the need for him to go further. Yet Tyler seemed oblivious to her arousal, continuing his massage in an easy silence. He massaged each leg in turn from thigh to the tips of her toes until they felt like rubber, only then moving back up to the prominent mound of her sex so that her legs parted and she arched her back towards him in yearning.

His fingers twisted in the light wispy curls of her pubic hair, tugging at them with a playful laugh.

'These hairs are charmingly old-fashioned but they need to come off, I'm afraid. Just stay in that position while I heat up some wax and we'll soon have you properly nude.'

'Will it hurt?'

'Only a little.' Tyler smiled, glancing down at her with an ironic expression. 'Is that going to be a problem? I thought you girls were here because you enjoyed pain.'

'I'm here to play pool.'

'And get fucked,' he added drily.

She shrugged, not meeting his eyes. 'So long as I keep winning, that's the only thing that matters to me.'

Tyler stepped away without any further comment and she heard him moving amongst his utensils for a while at the other side of the cubicle. But she guessed from his silence that the young masseur did not believe a word she had said. When he returned, he began smearing her legs with warm wax and pressing long strips of white cotton against them. Watching her expression, he ripped off the first wax-coated strip and gave a little smile as her body reacted to the pain. There even seemed to be a hint of amused cruelty in his face as he continued without even allowing her to catch her breath, ripping off the remaining cotton strips one by one. The strips under her arms hurt slightly more than her legs and she began to whimper, gritting her teeth in order not to humiliate herself by screaming. He was right, after all. As a player, she was supposed to be used to having pain inflicted on her.

Having her sex waxed, though, was a thousand times more painful than she had anticipated. Tyler held her down on the bed with one iron hand as she yelped and struggled to be free. The delicate skin along her bikini line and between her sex lips stung and burnt with terrible fire as he yanked the hairs clean off the skin. Yet even while she was writhing like an abject coward and begging him to stop, she

121

could already feel the tell-tale flare of heat along her body and knew that she was becoming excited. There was something about her ignominious position, held down forcibly while this man stripped her pussy of hair, that made her wish he was inside her.

But she was not the only one to become sexually excited during the waxing. When it was over and her stinging body had been denuded of hairs, Tyler moved to the head of the bed, hurriedly undoing the zip on his shorts and freeing his penis. To judge by the rigid swollen length, it was clear her cries and struggles had aroused him too.

'Shut up and suck me,' he muttered and pushed her head towards him. It was not entirely what she had hoped for after that intense experience but she did not bother to argue with him, sucking his penis deep into her mouth and sliding her lips back and forth over the thick blue-veined shaft.

As her mouth moved obediently on his penis, Roz allowed her fingers to slip between her thighs so she could masturbate. Without even the slightest hint of hair left on her ravaged skin, her clitoris and sex lips were amazingly sensitive to the touch. She let her fingers circle and press against them, moving inside to find juice dripping down the crack of her backside and her inner flesh already poised for orgasm. She pushed first two and then three fingers into her sex right up to the knuckle, far too well lubricated to need any preparation for their entry. Within a few moments, she felt her body heat begin to build to a crescendo, her breathing quicken and knew she would soon come.

She let his shaft slip from between her lips and took it in her free hand instead, milking it into her mouth while the other hand worked frantically at her clitoris and soaking labia, pressing round and round in an ever-increasing rhythm until her back arched in climax and she bucked her hips in the air, imagining his penis inside her beginning to twitch and pump. Gasping and moaning, Roz closed her eyes and let the orgasm pulse over her at last in an intensely pleasurable wave.

His penis still hovering against her wet parted lips, Tyler grunted and drew her head closer. He obviously could not even wait for her to finish before he enjoyed his own turn.

She let her mouth open wider as he pushed deeper inside, her lips stretched around his thick shaft. He began to piston urgently in and out of her mouth and it did not take long before she felt the first hot bolts of his sperm shoot against the back of her throat.

His hand clutched her head as Tyler continued to pump for another few seconds, hips working energetically against her face until he had emptied his balls. The thick salty fluid filled her mouth almost immediately and began to ooze messily down her chin. In no position to argue, she swallowed it down and heard the man above her groan in satisfied approval.

'I can see why you were so popular at the tournament,' Tyler said hoarsely as his penis slipped wetly from between her lips.

The sound of footsteps outside made them pull quickly apart, Tyler zipping up his shorts and tidying his white uniform while Roz hurriedly wiped her mouth with a corner of the sheet and rolled onto her back again, a little too shaky to try sitting up.

They were just in time. Seconds later, the curtain was pulled back and Carter stood looking down at her, his face expressionless as ever. She could smell faint smoke on the air as he came towards her and guessed that he had only just put out a cigarette.

'Finished?' he asked Tyler without glancing at the young man, a suggestion of irony behind the question.

'Yeah, she can go now.'

Carter took her by the arm and helped her down off the high bed, his eyes moving slowly over her denuded body. From his usual shuttered expression it was hard to decipher whether the tour manager had any idea what the two of them had been doing seconds before he came in. Though if he had guessed, there was certainly no hint of anger in his demeanour as he pulled her closer. One finger brushed the smooth skin just above her pussy where the curly pubic hair had been growing. The area was still slightly reddened and tingling from the wax. It felt tight and sensitive under his touch.

'Tyler seems to have done a thorough job on you,' he commented. 'Not a single hair in sight.'

His voice seemed too smooth, deliberately devoid of expression. It was almost as though he were hiding something. She considered for a moment whether he could be jealous of Tyler, then dismissed the idea as unthinkable. There was no reason for him to be jealous, not over the newest arrival on the tour. And even if Carter did have his suspicions, he had no proof that anything had been going on between her and Tyler. He was probably this distant with all the girls, she thought, not just her. The blank expression and cold air of professionalism were simply part of his working personality.

'Did it hurt?'

'Yes,' she replied tartly.

'Excellent.'

Her intake of breath made him glance sideways at her. She shook her head in amazement. 'You're quite a bastard, aren't you?'

'That depends on my mood.'

Her flashed smile was tight, deliberately saccharine. 'And is this a good or a bad mood, Carter?'

'Shut up and get dressed,' he said flatly. 'I've got a meeting later this afternoon and you're holding me up.'

Roz shrugged and collected her little black skirt and top, wriggling into them as Tyler muttered some half-hearted excuse and disappeared into another cubicle. She had the distinct impression the younger man was not meant to have availed himself of her mouth like that. But she decided not to mention what had happened between them and concentrated on getting dressed instead. Carter had already told her that sex between the tour staff and the players was forbidden. There might come a time in the future when she needed someone like Tyler to break that rule and satisfy her need for penetration. Getting him into trouble now over some minor indiscretion would not help that happen, especially when they had both enjoyed themselves equally in the end.

'So where now?' she asked idly as Carter led her out of the beauty salon, surprised by how her thighs seemed to press more sexually against each other now that she had been completely denuded of hair. Roz could even feel juice trickling out of her sensitised lips and moistening the tops of her thighs as she walked. She was amazed that one simple procedure could have made such a difference to the way she felt inside. Being waxed down there had so highly eroticised her body that every movement she made now, however tiny, seemed to bring her one step closer to orgasm.

'I've got a little training session lined up for you downstairs,' he said coolly. 'It's routine for new players. Just to make sure you know your way around the latest equipment.'

'Sounds like fun.'

Those unreadable eyes flickered towards her face,

then slid down along the narrow shadow of her cleavage.

'For you or for me?' Carter murmured, and pressed the button for the lift before she could reply.

Eight

Carter selected the specially modified swan-neck from the rack and strolled back to where Roz was waiting for him, bent forward over the baize with that ridiculously tiny black skirt hitched up to display her buttocks. She must have become accustomed to adopting such humiliating positions, he mused to himself, deliberately taking his time as he studied her rear view.

It was an inspiring sight, each firm white globe still marked with faint bruised lines from earlier punishments. No wonder Tyler had been tempted to amuse himself with her body, he thought, in spite of the possible consequences if they had been discovered. She was standing on tiptoe now, the calf muscles in each smooth-skinned leg straining to hold the required position.

Carter's penis twitched appreciatively in his trousers as he ordered the girl to bend even lower and she obeyed in embarrassed silence, the brownish puckered skin around her anus fanning into a wide-stretched star as her breasts sank closer to the cloth and her buttocks moved naturally apart. It would be pleasant to take advantage of her as Tyler had presumably done, judging by the way those two had sprung apart when he entered the cubicle. She was undoubtedly a temptation, this one. He could not help imagining how it would feel to nudge between those pale rounded cheeks and sink himself into the darkness beyond.

It was unusual to find himself so intensely aroused by one of the players. He found all the girls attractive, of course, and had often gone back to his rooms at the end of the day feeling frustrated and in need of relief. Constantly surrounded by these players, witnessing their lewd and sexually provocative behaviour at every tournament, it was difficult at times to follow McNaughton's orders and rein in his instinctive desire to fuck them. Yet as soon as he had met Roz at the pool hall, he had felt a difference in his physical reaction to her body. The sensation was too visceral to be simple lust. It was more compelling and far less easily controlled, especially in a situation like this, where he was alone with the girl and could so easily bend the rules without fear of discovery.

But it would be stupid to risk McNaughton's anger – and possibly dismissal from his position as tour manager – by allowing his control to slip for even a minute.

'What's that in your hand?' she was asking, her voice a shaky whisper as she tried to see what he was holding.

'It's a specially modified rest that we call a swan-neck,' Carter told her calmly, holding the curved metal tip close to her face so that she could examine it in greater detail. 'It's used in snooker rather than pool, to bridge over an awkwardly placed ball. But we always keep one on hand at tournaments in case a client wishes to use it.'

'For what?'

'In most cases, to check for the presence of natural lubricants. If it goes in with reasonable ease, the player is excited enough to be entered. It's quite a simple device. This side is intended for the anus.' He pointed to one of two elegant prongs at the end of the swan-neck, its narrow blunt tip rounded to ease entry. Then his fingers lingered over the neighbouring prong, its thicker metal cold to the touch. 'This for the vagina.'

'They both go in at the same time?'

'Of course.'

'And if there aren't any "natural lubricants" inside?'

He shrugged. 'Then it hurts.'

'Jesus.'

His voice hardened at her tone. 'Stop talking now and face front. You're here to learn how to take these implements, not discuss our reasons for using them.'

He steadied the modified swan-neck between her spread buttocks, one prong poised against the brown star of her anus, the thicker one already nudging her sex lips apart, feeling his own arousal increase as he anticipated sliding both prongs inside at the same time. He wished it were possible to see her face at the same time, for although this rear view was tantalising enough, it would be perfect if he could also gauge her reaction to each encroaching inch of the swan-neck through the changing emotions on her face. He had watched other girls take this particular implement for the first time and could remember how their expressions always changed from apprehension to startled arousal as the cold prongs entered both their orifices at the same time.

'Keep perfectly still and try not to tense your muscles. It can hurt if you resist penetration.'

Proceeding at an unhurried pace, Carter gradually increased the pressure until her sharp intake of breath told him the more rounded prong was beginning to enter her anus. Then he turned his wrist deftly to the left, ensuring that the thicker prong would soon push its way between her sex lips so she could be entered in both holes simultaneously. The ornate wooden handle of the swan-neck stretched almost the length of the pool table itself; it took experience to be able to line both prongs up to the right orifice at that distance. His arousal grew though as he heard her breathing quicken and knew that the slimmer prong must be entering her anal cavity.

'How does it feel?'

'C . . . cold.'

'But does it hurt?'

'Yes,' she hissed through clenched teeth.

He smiled at her tone and continued to press the swan-neck into her body. The other prong had already slipped between her vaginal lips and was beginning to push against her sex. She groaned a little, twisting her hips as though she wanted to escape from its cold metal intrusion.

'I told you to keep still,' he muttered.

Exasperated by her lack of obedience, Carter lifted the cane by his side and dealt her a cracking blow across her buttocks. The thin whippy stick came down on her skin a little harder than he had originally intended, less of a warning and more of a severe punishment. From her agonised yelp of pain though, the cane had presumably made the right impression on her. But he was mistaken. In her distress, Roz seemed to forget the cardinal rule: never answer a master back. She sounded upset now rather than angry, perhaps even on the verge of tears, which was not surprising after a blow like that.

'I was trying my hardest,' she said faintly. 'But how am I supposed to keep still with that thing inside me?'

So the cane had to fall again, this time criss-crossing the ugly red mark left by his previous blow.

She swore once, loudly, then lapsed into a recalcitrant silence. It was like trying to teach some sulky schoolgirl to behave, he thought grimly, wrestling with a sudden desire to finish this part of the exercise and give her a full caning. That might be the only way he could get the message through to her. But there was only a limited amount of time available for training each new player and he needed her to understand the correct use of each implement before the next exhibition match.

'When are you going to learn obedience?' he demanded, still enjoying the way her body had writhed helplessly beneath that second blow. 'You know the rules by now. Perhaps you should try following them if you want to avoid any further punishments like that. You will remain completely still during this training session and not open your mouth until instructed to do so. Have I made myself clear?'

'Yes, sir.'

'Everyone knows that because I'm in charge of training the players, I'm inclined to be a little more lenient than your other masters. But there are limits to my patience –'

'I'm sorry, sir.'

In response to her interruption, however apologetic and soft-voiced it might have been, Carter brought the cane down again across the exposed tops of her thighs, satisfied by her tormented gasp and the cruel red mark which sprang up there immediately. It was odd how he wanted to hurt her, even enjoyed hurting her when it meant she might learn some self-discipline, and yet so often felt the need to protect her when another man was administering the punishment. He had recruited most of the other players, yet for some reason he only felt possessive about Roz, as if she were his private property. Which was a dangerous and uncomfortable way to start behaving towards a player, he reminded himself. Never get attached, never get involved. That was an absolute basic rule on the tour. But perhaps it was simply because he suspected she would turn out to be their best player ever. She had already attracted McNaughton's special attention, after all, and would probably continue to outshine the other girls until the last match of the season.

'Did I say you could speak?'

'No, sir.'

'Then learn to obey and shut up.'

He allowed her to experience the sensation of metal inside both orifices for a few more minutes, revelling in her taut silence and the way her body quivered whenever he twisted the implement from one side to the other, then slowly withdrew the swan-neck to examine it. He had not thought she was finding the exercise particularly arousing. But to his surprise, both metal prongs showed signs of moisture. It was not entirely unusual for the vaginal prong to be damp on withdrawal, of course, but it was obvious from the warm slick metal of the other prong that her rectum was also well-lubricated. Clearly she had been aroused by having them both inside her at the same time.

Contemplating the raw and unadulterated sexuality that must lie behind those cool blue eyes, he felt a familiar stirring in his groin and wished again that he was allowed to enjoy the players himself. Just the mental vision of gripping her hips and sliding into that damp tight passage had him hard within seconds. It was frustrating to realise that he could insert any damn thing he wanted into this girl's anus, except his penis. But those were the rules and he had to abide by them.

'Well, you didn't do too badly in the end,' he murmured, carefully laying aside the swan-neck. 'Following the withdrawal of the swan-neck, a client would enter you either vaginally or anally. Sometimes two clients might enter you simultaneously and you would be expected to climax with them both. Even if they come at separate times. Do you think you could manage that?'

'Yes, sir.'

'Has anyone ever used a tawse on you?' he asked, forcing himself to turn away from the inviting sight of her buttocks before the temptation to fuck her there became too intense.

He put back the cane and selected one of the tawses instead, a particularly sturdy piece of equipment whose flat tongue of leather – split at the end into three short strands – would soon have her gasping for breath. When Roz admitted that she had never even seen a tawse, he showed it to her briefly, tested the flexible leather against his palm a few times, and took up a comfortable position behind her.

'It can be quite a painful but exhilarating experience, your first taste of a tawse. That's why it's so important for you to be fully prepared before it's used on you in public.' He raised the tawse above her pale, vulnerable buttocks. 'Make no mistake. This will hurt. But as with most punishments on the tour, there are techniques you can learn which should control your reaction to the pain.'

Her stifled scream as the first blow struck home left him in no doubt that she had grasped the efficiency of a tawse as a dispenser of punishment. Carter stood there a second, watching a deep blush come up on her cheeks, with a little bruising where the split ends had landed, then raised the tawse again. The thick slap of its impact was always such a deliciously satisfying sound, he thought to himself, bringing it home against her buttocks with something akin to reverence. The second blow overlaid the first ever so slightly, deepening the colour in her cheeks and making her whole body jerk in reaction. This time she made less noise but he could tell by the way her hands clenched into tight fists that the impact had been just as powerful.

He felt a sudden surge of pride in her ability to accept such pain without struggling. Few players on the tour had ever been this stoical when receiving the tawse for the first time.

'Describe the pain.'

There was a moment's hesitation as she collected herself enough to answer him, dragged herself back from the muteness of suffering.

'It's a complete shock when it first hits, like getting slapped in the face by a wave of icy water. It leaves you breathless.'

'And then?'

Her voice wavered and nearly broke, but she caught it in time. 'Then it's a slow burn, followed by agony.'

'What sort of agony? Don't be so imprecise, describe to me exactly what you're feeling.'

'Searing bloody agony that seems to last forever. You want to put your hands there, rub it to make the pain go away. But you know you can't, so you just hang on and try to move through it to the other side where you can . . .'

'Yes?' he prompted her.

'Breathe again.'

'Very good.' Carter nodded, satisfied by her reply. 'Next time you hear the tawse coming, focus on something in the near distance. Pick a spot in the room and really concentrate on it. Describe it to yourself in minute detail if that helps. Location, dimension, colour, even its texture. Don't take your eyes off it until the pain is controllable.'

He was impressed by her instinct, the way Roz had seemed able to manage the pain without needing to be given a technique. But he said nothing. It was better not to give individual players a sense of their importance. That was something which should only happen on the table. Away from it, they had to remember their place on the pool tour and behave accordingly. Lifting the tawse above her marked buttocks, Carter stood in silence for a few seconds, considering where to place the next blow. That was part of the training too, of course. It was important to make the girls wait for their punishment occasionally, not be given it so regularly that they imagined there could be an escape through learning the particular rhythm of the tawse or cane. That might lead them into a dangerous complacency.

He picked a sweet spot and brought the tawse across to it without hurrying, enjoying that slight whoosh as it travelled through the air and aware that it must make her anticipation of pain even worse. Though the sound was much louder with the paddle, one of his favourite implements for punishment. Some of the players actively cringed on hearing the whoosh of the paddle, even when it was being administered to somebody else. This girl was a much faster learner than the other players though, and she did not cringe. Her body jerked but she made no sound and her fists remained unclenched this time. It was also pleasing to note that her head was a little higher than before, eyes presumably fixed straight ahead as she had been instructed.

He eyed the glowing buttocks below him, tantalisingly warmed by the split leather ends of the tawse, and thought of how it would feel to part those cheeks with his fingers and push himself into the tight puckered opening which he could just see from here, winking at him above the gaping invitation of her shaven mound. Not for full penetration – which was strictly forbidden to him – but simply to lodge his swollen cockhead there for a few moments, to demonstrate how she might be expected to take a client in her anus after the tawse had been administered. The thought made his mouth dry with desire and he had to adjust the bulge in his trousers, reminding himself not to risk any loss of control like that. It would be too dangerously easy to push further inside once he was positioned there, inch by seductive inch, deeper and deeper, until he was moving back and forth between those painfully flushed buttocks in a rhythm which could only be called fucking.

Clenching his teeth in an effort to regain control, Carter forced himself to drop the tawse back on the pile, ordering her in a brusque voice to turn around and sit on the pool table. Roz must have sensed his tension because she moved quickly to obey, submissively facing him on the baize with legs wide apart as she had been taught to do when sitting in a master's presence. But her feet needed to touch each corner pocket, spreading the hairless lips of her sex wide apart in preparation for her next training exercise. So he arranged her with rough hands, trying not to dwell too much on the taut jut of her nipples or the delicious bruising he had inflicted on the tops of her thighs.

'This is quite a popular game with our regulars. The girl sits on the pool table like this, opening herself wide to each side, and the client uses the butt of a cue to impale her.' He took up a suitably thick-ended pool cue and positioned it against the lips of her cunt. 'It's quite a sizeable implement to take, and any carvings or special ornamentation on the butt end could damage you internally if you're not relaxed. Take a few deep breaths and try to push out as the cue goes in.'

But the cue butt went inside her easily enough, those shaven outer lips parting to reveal a pinkish interior slick with arousal. Roz had fixed her eyes on his face when the butt entered and now she gave a soft gasp as it began to stretch the walls of her vagina. Not a gasp of pain this time though, but one of increasing excitement. Her hips moved slightly on the baize table top, wriggling further down as if eager to accommodate more of the thick wooden pool cue. That was not part of the exercise, he thought, pausing to consider it. But for once, Carter chose not to punish the player for moving without permission. It was a gesture which only served to increase his desire to fuck her until she begged to be allowed to come and he knew their clients would love her for it too. That innate willingness to be penetrated, the sheer sexuality of her body as it opened itself up to take even more of the cue butt, these were things that could not be taught to a new player. A player would either possess them naturally or not at all, and Roz possessed them in spadefuls.

There was little he could teach a player like this in the ways of pleasing men, he thought wryly, watching her squirm with unconcealed pleasure as the ornate cue butt pressed deeper inside her body. The little noises she was making under her breath could not be faked. Roz was so highly aroused now, her juices were beginning to trickle out and leave a damp stain on the baize cloth beneath. He could only hope to discipline that hungry sexuality and point it in the right direction.

'Arch your back a little more,' he murmured, not wanting to spoil the mood. He followed her movements through half-closed eyes. 'That's good. Try to take it like a cat on heat.'

'Mmm.'

He withdrew the butt end until it was resting against the outside lips of her vagina, not quite removed but not inside either. The ornately carved inlay along the tapering butt end was running with her juices. The thin whitish fluid streaked the darker carvings, gleaming superbly further up where the polished wood began. His gaze met hers properly for the first time, their eyes locking together as she waited for him to push the cue back inside. She looked completely submissive, knees pulled up slightly and her legs wide apart. The lust began to beat like a pulse in his groin. He wanted to unzip his trousers and drag her towards the edge of the pool table, pushing her thighs even further apart as he fed his cock straight into that moist opening.

'Carter,' she whispered, still looking at him, her eyes drowsy with desire.

'Don't speak,' he said hoarsely. 'The training isn't finished yet. If you speak, I'll have to punish you again.'

Her hips moved in response, drawing his attention back to her juice-slick cunt where the cue butt still rested against her outer lips. She smelt of female arousal, hot and musky. An urgent desire for sex was pouring from her body and he could barely control his own need to climb inside her, ride this girl until he had emptied his balls into that soaking cunt. Her voice had become almost inaudible, a mere thread of sound in the quiet practice room.

'You want to punish me again? Hurt me again?'

'Yes,' he breathed.

Her gaze invited him without further words, making it clear that was what Roz wanted too. In a sort of erotic daze, Carter found himself reaching back for the cane and raising it above her pale splayed legs as if in response to a request. Without ever once taking his eyes from her face, he brought it down with a sharp crack across one of her thighs and almost felt the impact with her. An ugly thin red line appeared as if by magic where the cane had landed, instantly drawing itself along the white skin. The blue eyes closed on a high-pitched cry of pain and then opened again, misty with tears but somehow grateful. Carter struck the other thigh without waiting for her to recover, hungry to hear that terrible cry again, watch her face wince as he administered this reward for good behaviour, gave her what she wanted.

His penis was stiff and aching, pressing against the folds of his trousers as he rammed the cue butt back into her sex and worked it in and out at a hard pace, continuing to criss-cross her thighs with a series of blows as he thrust. The pattern of vicious red lines left by the cane grew more complex with every blow, her body twisting on the pool table with agonised desire. There was genuine anger behind his arm, only too aware that he was one step away from fucking this girl and possibly losing his job. Carter could feel sweat dripping from his forehead and wiped it away with a jerk of his wrist, bringing the cane down once more into the soft yielding flesh of her inner thigh.

Roz grunted like some kind of wild animal under that final blow of the cane and arched into orgasm, suddenly expelling the cue butt as her internal muscles contracted on the thick wood and it slid away. He shoved it back in without hesitation, watching her with undisguised amazement as her cries intensified and a dark red flush sprang out across her breasts and upper body.

He had never seen a player take so much pleasure from such a brutal training session. It was as if the pain and humiliation had brought her to orgasm on their own. His head felt ready to explode. He would go insane, he thought desperately, if he could not find a way to satisfy his need for sex as soon as possible.

The door behind them creaked and he spun, instantly tensed in case it was McNaughton.

But to his relief it was only Misha standing in the doorway, one of their domestic staff, a pretty young brunette he had noticed a few times before in the corridors around the penthouse.

Misha's command of the English language was not very good but he had always been aware that she was curious about the players on the tour, how the girls were punished and trained outside tournaments. There was a wedding ring on her finger, a thick gold band which had prevented him from propositioning her before. But on this occasion, he could not afford to waste time on such niceties.

'Misha?'

He signalled to the young woman to come nearer, turning his back on Roz and casting aside the cane. It clattered on the floor and he saw the cleaner's eyes move to it warily, then she was standing next to him in her white apron and short black skirt, waiting silently for him to speak. He examined her figure with a speculative eye: large firm breasts, a trim waist, and hips a man could easily hold onto if he wanted to fuck her from behind. But would she be interested in him? It was well known that some of the minders had sex with the cleaning staff from time to time, as he himself had done on numerous occasions, but there was no pressure on the women to comply. They were not bound by the same contract as the players.

He pointed without ceremony to the bulge in his trousers, still a little breathless from his exertions. 'I have a problem, Misha. Do you want to help me with it?'

'Sir?'

'I need to fuck.'

Misha clearly understood that word. She looked scared, backing away from him a little, but her lips had parted slightly and she was licking them as if her mouth were suddenly dry. She lowered her eyes and twisted the ring on her wedding finger, shaking her head in an apologetic fashion. 'My husband . . .'

'You don't like me?'

The brunette hesitated, gazing past him to where Roz still waited silent and wide-legged on the pool table, her thighs a mess of cruel red lines and bruises.

'I won't do that to you,' he promised quickly. 'That's not what I want. I just need to come. Do you understand?'

He was already reaching for the hem of her skirt, his need far too urgent for polite negotiations, but she shook him away.

'Not in there,' she whispered in a thick Eastern European accent, her face flushed. She glanced guiltily back over her shoulder as though afraid they might be seen by one of her superiors, then dropped to her knees in front of him. 'Only in my mouth, sir.'

'There's no need. I'd pull out in time.'

'Only in my mouth,' Misha repeated stubbornly and he suspected it was a phrase she had learnt through long experience.

Realising that any further argument would be pointless and might even prove counter-productive, he hurriedly unzipped his trousers and pushed his swollen penis into her waiting mouth. It was such a relief to be enclosed in a warm channel of flesh at last, her lips sliding obediently over his shaft as it went in, that he gave a strangled groan of triumph. Grasping her dark glossy head with both hands, he thrust himself in and out of that slender throat without even giving her a chance to get used to the intrusion. She knelt there submissively in her short black skirt and white apron, head tilted right back so he could use her mouth as ruthlessly as he pleased.

He wondered fleetingly what Roz must think, watching him take his relief in another woman's mouth. Her need to be fucked had seemed almost as compulsive as his need to fuck her. Had she understood why he could not satisfy both their appetites?

The memory of her cane-marked thighs and that glistening hole still plugged by the butt end of a pool cue was exactly the trigger he had been trying to avoid. But there was no chance of holding back an orgasm now. The spunk had begun to rise in a great inexorable wave and he was forced to release it.

His hands tightened like a vice on Misha's head. He groaned and pulsed a thick stream of come into her throat, imagining it was Roz he was fucking instead, her naked body with its criss-cross of red lines writhing against his as he shot his load deep into her belly. Carter closed his eyes and let the orgasm take him over in a wave of liquid heat. Spasm after spasm of raw pleasure jolted through his frame. He dragged the young brunette up against his groin, ignoring her muffled protest as he emptied himself into the warm recesses of her throat.

But when Carter swung back to her afterwards, keen as a boy to see the reaction on her face, Roz had vanished and the stained pool table – still damp with her juices – stood empty.

Nine

It was late afternoon and the city was hazy with sunshine. Roz turned away from the window, chalking her pool cue thoughtfully as she considered her next shot. It did not really matter whether or not she potted the ball since she was playing alone. There was no opponent to beat on this occasion, except herself. But even during a practice session she liked to play each shot as perfectly as possible, taking pride in that satisfying thud as the ball hit the back of the pocket and dropped.

She took her time sizing up a difficult pot to the far right-hand corner pocket, then sank gracefully into position with her legs apart and her head well down as usual. The other girls might think it was enough to practise once or twice a week, but Roz preferred to spend several hours a day at the table in between matches. That was the only way to stay on top of her game, to ensure that she kept improving.

Suddenly the door to the practice room burst open and she glanced up to see Cherie standing in the doorway. The other player had a wicked smile on her face.

'Lauren's about to seduce the pizza delivery guy. Do you want to come and watch?'

'What?'

'There's CCTV in the lounge and that's where they are now, Lauren and this bloke.' Cherie made an impatient face when she did not react. 'Hurry up if you're coming. We've all piled into the monitor room to watch and I don't want to miss the fun.'

'But I'm practising.'

'Oh, sod that and put the cue down. It won't kill you to join the party for once.'

Roz allowed herself to be dragged away from the table by the exuberant Cherie, reluctant to leave her precious cue unattended for any length of time but aware that she did not have much choice in the matter. The girl's excitement was too infectious.

When they reached the small monitor room, she found nearly all the other players packed into every corner, crammed together on chairs or crowding up against the walls. On every monitor screen, larger than life, she could see Lauren from several different angles, lying on a sofa in the lounge with a stout man in black biker leathers. The couple were already kissing and he had his hand up her short PVC skirt. From the satisfied noises she was making, Lauren seemed to be enjoying the attention.

'We're recording it for a laugh,' Cherie whispered in her ear as they squeezed past the girls in the doorway and found a tiny space in the far corner. 'It'll make a great Christmas present for Lauren. She'll go crazy when she finds out we're all watching.'

'Won't we get into trouble?'

'The security guy's gone out for a cigarette and Sally's on lookout in case he comes back early.'

Roz stared at the row of screens, her heart beating hard. She could imagine the punishment they would all be facing if anyone ever found out about this. It was completely forbidden for them to have sex with non-clients and Lauren knew it. Not that she seemed to care at the moment. The delivery man had unzipped his leather jeans now and Lauren was already down between his legs, head moving in a steady rhythm as she sucked. Even the grainy black and white picture could not disguise the dreamy look of pleasure on her face.

Cherie pinched her arm. 'It's OK. Don't look so worried.'

'But what about Carter?'

'He's gone back to his room for a sleep. He always does at this time of day. So there's no one about to catch us.'

Somebody changed the camera angle on one of the monitors, managing to zoom in on the couple so they could see everything in incredible detail. The tall blonde whose name she could never remember was passing round some of the pizzas the delivery man had brought on his bike, laughing and making crude gestures with the baked red chillies on top. But Roz refused the slice which was offered to her, not feeling very hungry any more. Instead, she turned back to watch Lauren's fingers moving down the swollen shaft to the root end buried in curly pubic hair, squeezing and pressing it with obvious expertise, her cheeks blown out by the size of the organ. To her, there was something shocking but fascinating about being able to see and hear their sex-play like this, as if they were watching a porno film being made in the next room.

Roz felt a familiar dampness begin to stain her panties and squirmed with discomfort, a slight heat in her cheeks as she glanced sideways at Cherie. But the other girl was clearly feeling the same way, lips parted moistly and her breathing becoming shallow as she too followed the action on the screen.

The delivery man, balding and with a slight paunch, had started wriggling out of his leathers now.

A raucous cry went up amongst the girls as his white torso and pendulous stomach were revealed, followed by thick hairy thighs with that bulbous-headed erection jutting between them. Still watching them both, eyes fixed on the screen, Roz felt a jolt of sexual arousal and swallowed hard. Lauren had bent forwards over the sofa, down on her knees now as she yanked up the short skirt to reveal a shaven pussy beneath smooth pale buttocks. She spread her legs to allow him access and the tiny puckered hole of her anus came into sharp focus. Behind her, the delivery man knelt down on the carpet and ran both hands over her buttocks in a careful exploratory fashion. They could not see his face properly from that angle, but the rigid length of his penis was already pressing between her thighs with obvious urgency. One finger slipped without warning into the shadowed cavity of her anus, no doubt pushing inside as the man leant forward over her body. Lauren tensed and cried out, the word too muffled to be heard on camera, though it could have been 'yes'. But the man withdrew without paying any attention, sniffing at his finger and clearly undecided, his penis still nudging the slick gaping mouth of her vagina.

Roz felt Cherie move even closer, their bodies pressed together like train commuters in the confined space. Seconds later, a cautious hand had slipped beneath her skirt and was brushing the tops of her thighs. Roz found her breath caught in her throat as the hand traced the pouting hairless outline of her sex lips before crawling slowly around to the firm swell of her bottom, locating the crease which hid her anus. She knew she ought to move away, tell the other girl to stop, but in truth she was dying to be touched there too. She glanced around the room but nobody seemed to have noticed what they were doing. The others were too intent on the row of screens.

The delivery man was parting Lauren's sex with clumsy fingers, the bulbous tip of his penis beginning to push inside as he decided on a straight fuck. She laid her flushed face against the sofa, a soft groan audible to everyone in the room as he entered her. Lauren might have preferred the other hole but she was clearly happy to take whatever he chose to give her. The man withdrew right to the edge of her outer lips, gazing down at her shaven mound in obvious admiration. He must be unable to believe his luck today, Roz thought, her mouth dry as she watched him push back into that well-oiled slot with a grunt, gradually building up to a steady rhythm punctuated by the sound of moans and sighs.

Lauren spread her legs even wider as he fucked, eventually raising her bottom in the air to encourage a faster pace. Although he was already sweating profusely, the delivery man obliged, gripping her hips with both hands and pumping in and out like a dog mounting a bitch. They could see every detail on the monitor in close-up, even his large hairy ball-sac swinging and banging against her thighs with each thrust.

It was still and quiet now in the monitor room. Neither of them looked away from the screen as Cherie pushed up between her buttocks and rubbed gently against the tight opening, not moving inside but teasing her, making her shift from one foot to the other in silent frustration. Lauren's moans and the man's loud grunts as he ploughed her body were making the juice pour from her pussy now. It was all Roz could do not to finger herself openly, although she noticed that some of the other girls were doing just that, hands working silently beneath their own skirts as the couple on screen continued to fuck. Tormented by the sight, she shifted her feet further apart and leant forward slightly to allow Cherie better access.

Her gesture seemed to work; the finger moving cautiously between her buttocks hesitated over the tiny aperture once more, then pressed inwards with just enough force to make the star yield and open. She bit down hard on her lip, stifling an instinctive groan. Her nerve-endings came vibrantly alive as the girl's finger explored inside the rim, finding the strange slimy channel where she had already taken several men over the past few weeks and enjoyed it. Roz felt herself beginning to sweat with desire, even moving her hips backwards in an attempt to be entered more fully. She knew though that however much she wriggled about, one slim finger would not be enough to satisfy her.

Cherie must have read her mind, speaking low in her ear. 'You want to go somewhere quieter? How about the laundry?'

'But this is wrong,' she whispered back tensely. 'You're Paula's girlfriend. She'd kill us if she found out.'

'Better make sure we're not spotted then.'

'I'm not sure . . .'

'Look, do you want to fuck or not?'

Roz glanced at the other girl uncertainly. They might be taking a risk by sneaking away together, but at least she would get some relief at last for her aching pussy. It was not easy, doing all this training every day and rarely being satisfied enough to relax. McNaughton seemed to want the players in a permanent state of arousal.

She drew a deep breath. 'OK.'

They slid unobtrusively from the monitor room, leaving just as the delivery man dragged his penis free of Lauren's pussy and lodged it between her buttocks.

He's planning to take her up the arse now, Roz realised with a stab of jealousy, but was too desperate for sex to stay and watch any longer.

She followed Cherie along the corridor towards the laundry room, passing several minders and domestic staff on the way, her nerves jangling in case somebody asked where they were going. She was not particularly scared of Paula; the girl was nothing but a loud-mouthed bully. But she knew there would be serious trouble if any of them started a fight amongst the tour, and Paula was bound to lay in with her fists when she discovered what was going on. Which she probably would, given that everyone here always seemed to know what everyone else was doing. Her sex was absolutely soaking though, and if she was honest with herself, she was still smarting a little from Carter's rejection the other day. It would feel pretty good to break the rules for once, as though she were putting two fingers up at him and his precious tour.

It was dark and cramped in the laundry room. One of the tumble-driers had been left on, the large drum spinning rhythmically in the background as they stumbled past shelves of clean, neatly pressed laundry towards the washing area. They spoke in muted whispers, pointing further into the room where they would be safer from prying eyes, giggling slightly and climbing over piles of dirty clothes which had been abandoned on the floor there until the next day.

Cherie wasted no time on preliminaries, pushing Roz face down over one of the washing-machines and dragging her skirt up to her waist. Roz cried out in surprise, even though it was what she had wanted. She was used to women being gentler than men, to being kissed and caressed with eyes shut and fingers trembling over her skin. But a few leisurely hours spent in her neighbour's apartment had not prepared her for such a ruthless assault. Her panties were yanked down across her thighs and a hot tongue stabbed into Roz's anus, then licked so torturously around the rim that she was ready to scream with frustration.

'Please . . .'

'What do you want?' Cherie whispered hoarsely.

'I need something . . . inside me.'

'This?'

The girl's probing finger entered her anus again, setting alarm bells ringing all over her body and triggering yet more clammy heat between her thighs. Roz arched her back, finally allowing herself to moan aloud at the intrusion, but knew it was still not enough.

Her eyes closed convulsively. 'More.'

Two more fingers joined it inside her anus, forcing their way past the tightly puckered sphincter until Roz gasped and bent even further forwards to help their progress. They felt intolerably large and unwieldy, all knuckles and unexpected fingernails, not like the real thing at all. Not like Carter's would have been – smooth and thick, driving straight up inside.

For a moment she remembered the delivery man's penis – swollen-headed and still gleaming from Lauren's slick pussy – pushing between her friend's buttocks and tried to imagine how it must have felt to take that hard length into her rectum. Cherie's three fingers worked deeper, in past the knuckle. There was genuine discomfort now. The washing-machine felt so cool under her hot face.

'That better?'

'Only a little bit.' Roz could hardly believe what she was saying. 'I still need more.'

'Wait a minute.'

The fingers withdrew rather too abruptly from her anus and she hissed at the pain, but continued to lean over the washing-machine in a state of frustrated anticipation. She could hear Cherie moving slowly about the laundry room in the half-darkness. What on earth was she looking for?

She came back after a few minutes, laughing to herself, and Roz almost jumped in shock when something thick and rubbery nudged between her waiting buttocks.

'What the hell is that?'

'A double dildo.'

'What?'

'Shhh. It belongs to Paula. She keeps it hidden here. I just strap it round my hips, one end goes in my pussy and the other . . .'

There was a tense moment of fumbling and Roz cried out as the dildo was pushed up inside her anus without warning.

'It hurts!'

Cherie sounded amused. 'Of course it hurts. It's bloody enormous.'

'Take it out.'

'No way, sweetheart.' The girl stroked a hand down her straining bottom, beginning to ease the double dildo back and forth between their bodies like a sadistic see-saw. 'You said you needed something bigger. So you're going to get it.'

Roz whimpered, gritting her teeth and hanging on to the cold sides of the washing-machine for support. Each time Cherie rocked her hips forward, the dildo stretched the tight walls of her rectum as it pushed deeper inside. But when she rocked backwards, it was dragged out even more painfully until the sphincter had almost closed against the huge rubber tip and had to stretch wide again as it was pushed back in. After a few more thrusts though, the pain did begin to fade and was replaced by a growing sensation of

151

heat. It was not long before Roz was moaning again, a wild flush on her cheeks as she actually tilted her hips back to receive the dildo more fully.

Cherie reached forward to fondle her breasts through the silky black top, rubbing and squeezing, bringing her nipples quickly erect. She too was becoming aroused, uttering little high-pitched cries each time the double-ended dildo slid back up her pussy.

With her eyes tightly closed, Roz could almost imagine she was being anally fucked by a man. Except that she could feel a soft body leaning into her from behind. Warm breasts on her back. The musky scent of a woman's pussy running with juice. That thought brought her close to orgasm and she groaned, pressing against the hard contours of the washing-machine, barely able to breathe anymore. Her hand slipped down between her thighs and Roz began to manipulate her clitoris, panting like a dog in the sun. But there was such a terrible sensation of fullness in her rectum, she was afraid that if she came with the dildo in place she would embarrass herself by making a mess.

'Please, I can't . . . '

Cherie seemed to understand her feelings. 'Just let it go, darling,' she muttered in a strange voice, lost in a sort of trance as she too approached her climax. 'I know it makes you want to shit. But it's OK. Stop holding back and come.'

The sheer crudity of the words brought a heated flush to her body and Roz trembled into orgasm, crying aloud with pleasure. She was being fucked in the arse by another girl, taking a fat rubber penis up the hole which should only ever be used for the toilet, pussy juice running freely down her spread legs, skirt pushed up round her waist, bent over the washing-machine like some cheap filthy whore. Spasms rocked her until she was sobbing into the cool plastic facia of the machine, buttons and dials grinding painfully against her skin, her rectum convulsing as the dildo squeezed itself into the last available inch.

'Dirty, dirty, dirty girl!'

Roz groaned with horror at Cherie's mockery, knowing that it must have happened, that she must have messed herself as the dildo was being withdrawn.

'I'm sorry,' she babbled. 'I'm so sorry . . .'

'You deserve a good slap.'

'I didn't mean to do it. I'll clean it up.'

'Yes, you bloody will.' Cherie spun her around and pushed her violently to her knees on the cold floor of the laundry room. Pulling the dildo clear from her own sex, she shoved the dirtied end towards her mouth with a threatening tone in her voice. 'Look what you've done to Paula's favourite dildo. Suck it clean. And I don't want to see any filth left on it when you've finished.'

'Please . . .'

'Suck it clean, you dirty slut.'

Whatever she had expected to happen when they came into the laundry room, it had not been anything like this. The mingled smells of latex and her own foul slime were enough to make Roz retch. But she decided to obey, tentatively placing her lips over the bulbous-headed dildo and starting to suck even though her throat burnt with the taste of it. When she came to the end which had been inside Cherie's pussy, to her relief she found the latex streaked with a familiar creamy white fluid, its bitterness quite exciting to lick away. She worked both ends again with her mouth and tongue until the dildo was clean and she was able to look up at Cherie for permission to stop.

'Is it clean now?'

'I think so.'

'Good.' Cherie snatched away the double dildo and handed her the starched edge of a white sheet instead. 'Now rub that inside your mouth. Make sure it's clean in there too. Finished?'

'Yes.'

The other girl hiked up her skirt and stepped forward over her kneeling body. The pungent aroma of her pussy filled the air. Roz stared up between her spread thighs, admiring the shaven mound with its glistening hairless slit right on her eye-level.

'You've had your fun. Now I want mine.' Cherie straddled her face and leant forward over the washing-machine. 'Stick your tongue in me and don't stop licking until I've come in your mouth.'

Obediently, Roz strained upwards on her knees and let her mouth cover the bare pussy, sucking both shaven lips inside and working them with her tongue. From the deep groan Cherie immediately gave, she guessed it must be having the desired effect. Using her fingers with care, she pulled the lips further apart and stuck her tongue right up inside. The hidden channel was moist and bitter and delicious. Moving slightly higher within the protuberant folds, she located that peaked hood of flesh over Cherie's clitoris and flicked it back and forth with her tongue, teasing the other girl until she heard her cry aloud. Then she clamped her mouth over it and sucked hard, hard, hard.

Both lost in Cherie's sudden and violent orgasm, neither one of the girls noticed the door to the laundry room opening. Then they heard a familiar voice above the sound of the tumble-drier. 'Get your tongue out of there. That's my girlfriend's cunt!'

Light was streaming in through the open door. Paula stood in the doorway, rage in her eyes as she

154

stared across at them both. They sprang apart, Cherie hurriedly dropping her skirt and trying in vain to recover her composure, but it was too late. It was only too obvious what they had been doing together.

'Just who the hell do you think you are, new girl?' Paula started to cross the laundry room towards them, an ugly snarl in her voice which meant a fight was imminent. 'You turn up like you own the place, cheat your way into winning matches that don't belong to you, bat your eyelids at McNaughton and Carter . . . and now here you are again, sticking your tongue up my girlfriend.'

'It was my fault,' Cherie stammered.

'Shut it, slag.'

Roz stood up warily, adjusting her clothes without once taking her eyes off the bigger girl. 'There's no need to get so uptight. We were just having fun, that's all.'

'She's my property. And you put your tongue in her.'

'I'm not looking for a fight.'

'But you're going to get one, you bitch.'

Paula lunged at her furiously, her unco-ordinated blow half punch, half slap. The washing-machine was right behind Roz and she could not step out of the way in time. They tangled together, hands up at each other's faces like claws and feet kicking out. It was an ugly little struggle. Roz felt something catch her painfully in the eye. She lashed out blindly in return and heard Paula swear. Then somehow they were both down on the floor, rolling together like wild cats and knocking over baskets of clothes while Cherie shrieked at them from the sidelines to get up.

Then the shrieking stopped abruptly.

It took Roz a few seconds to register that someone else had entered the room. By then it was too late to disentangle herself. A strong hand had plucked her away from Paula and she was sprawling on her back several feet away, staring up at the angry figure of Carter.

'Is this some kind of bloody joke?' It was the first time Roz had ever heard the tour manager shout. 'I try to grab some sleep for half an hour and when I come back, all hell seems to have broken loose in the monitor room and you three are in here brawling.'

Carter stood there completely naked in front of them, his penis swinging flaccid between those muscular thighs and his arms folded across a hairy chest. Under different circumstances it might have been funny. But there was no humour in his face as he stared at each of the girls in turn, his eyes narrowed in fury.

'Now, who's going to tell me what's going on here?' He looked hard at Cherie. 'Well?'

Trembling, she could not meet his gaze. 'Nothing, sir.'

'What were these two fighting about?'

'I don't know, sir.'

Carter stood there in silence for a moment, looking at them all, then his voice became menacingly low and silky.

'Either someone tells me the truth right now or all three of you get the whip until I hear it.'

Roz clambered to her feet, sore and trembling. 'Please don't punish Cherie. It's not her fault, it's mine. We came in here together because . . .' Then her voice faltered and suddenly she could not look him in the eye, her cheeks flushed with embarrassment.

But Carter seemed to understand without needing to hear the rest. His eyes moved slowly over her body, presumably noting the messed-up hair and tell-tale stains on her skirt. She suddenly felt very cheap and wondered what he thought of her behaviour, knowing it must be obvious what she and Cherie had been doing alone in here. But was that really a punishable offence? She was not sure whether or not it was allowed for players to have sex with each other during the season, though everyone knew that fighting was strictly forbidden.

'And Paula found you?'

She nodded reluctantly. 'I didn't mean to start fighting with her. It just happened.'

'Don't blame it on me, you lying bitch,' Paula spat. 'She started it. Just ask Cherie if you don't believe me.'

But Cherie shook her head, still scared of her girlfriend but clearly determined not to give in this time. 'Paula's the one who's lying. She came in here and started shouting at us –'

'I can see what happened,' Carter said flatly. His expression unreadable as ever, he took a clean white sheet from one of the drying shelves and wrapped it sarong-style about his waist. 'You can go back to your room, I'll deal with you later. But Roz and Paula will both be punished for this little fiasco.'

'Please –' Cherie began.

'You know the rules. Fighting is not allowed at any time and they have to be punished.'

Paula was straightening her clothes, a sulky look on her face. She shrugged as Carter pointed them silently towards the door. 'I don't care about being punished. But she'll be crying like a little baby within five minutes. I can take anything you want to give me.'

'Even the Frame?' he said sharply.

Suddenly afraid, as though that was the last thing she had expected to hear, Paula's face turned pale and she stopped dead in the doorway. Her eyes had widened and Roz was surprised to hear a note of pleading in her voice. Whatever the Frame was, she thought, it must be a fairly formidable piece of equipment.

'But we were only fighting –'

'I'm sick of your attitude, Paula. It's about time you had a real test of obedience. You can both be strapped into the Frame together, and then we'll see which of you can take the most punishment.'

Roz stared at Paula across the narrow divide of the Frame, trying not to let the other girl see how much she was suffering as the painful metal clamp bit into her soft breasts. It had taken nearly fifteen minutes for them to be strapped into the unusual device, a wooden frame which locked them together at the wrist and ankle so they would be forced to face each other during their beating. The Frame had been dragged into one of the communal rooms by two minders and set up in the middle of the floor according to Carter's instructions.

Both girls had been ordered to strip completely naked, their humiliation complete when the tour manager positioned them in the Frame himself, ignoring Paula's protest as he placed thick restraining straps around her wrists and ankles. Roz tried to signal to him apologetically when he bent to fasten hers, eager for him to know how sorry she was, but he avoided her eyes. Not for the first time, she wished there was some way to tell what he was thinking, uneasily aware that the punishment in store for them both tonight would be more severe than any she had suffered so far.

Back in a plain white T-shirt and jeans, his face freshly splashed with cold water, Carter seemed less angry than he had been earlier. He strolled around the Frame for the last time, no doubt checking that both girls were properly secured and would not be capable of any movement during their punishment. Roz thought the tour manager sounded much cooler and more distant now, back in professional mode.

'It was clearly stated when you arrived here that there would be no fighting amongst the players. That rule was broken tonight. You will both be beaten in turn until I am satisfied that you have learnt your lesson.'

'Will it be the cane, sir?' Roz dared to ask in a small voice, unable to forget the agonies inflicted by that dreadful instrument.

'Perhaps.' Carter stopped at her side, those strange unreadable eyes lingering over her face. 'Does the cane frighten you, Roz? Maybe you would prefer me to choose another punishment?'

She sensed this might be some kind of test. 'N . . . No, sir.'

'Good,' he said bluntly. 'Because it will be the cane.'

'Yes, sir.'

The air felt cool and almost refreshing on her exposed buttocks. Yet Roz could not relax, only too aware that her vulnerable skin would soon be stinging and burning under the cane. She waited in a tense silence for that first blow, steeling herself not to cry out. But her mind was whirling with doubts. How many strokes was he planning to inflict on her? The leather restraints had been fastened so tightly at her wrists and ankles, they were biting into her flesh – a clear indication of his displeasure. Perhaps this was yet another of his experiments, she thought grimly, designed to see which of the two girls was the stronger. Which made it even more important not to cry out under the cane. It would be too humiliating to seem weaker than Paula. Meeting the other girl's eyes with what she hoped was a defiant stare, she raised her chin, mouth set firm, determined not to break first.

She watched Carter move round to the other side, standing beside her rival as he checked the other girl's restraints. 'Comfortable, Paula?' he asked mockingly, tightening the metal clamp over her breasts.

'Yes, sir. Thank you, sir.'

His glance was ironic. 'So submissive all of a sudden. But how long will that last once you've been released?'

The other girl did not reply, cheeks slightly flushed as she hung her head and waited for the beating to begin.

'As you can see,' the tour manager carried on, shaking the wooden Frame with one hand as he passed to test its sturdiness, 'This rather unusual device is used to punish two girls at once. The idea is that you face each other while you take your punishment, able to watch every expression of pain or fear produced by the cane. I can stop the punishment at any time you request, of course. But whoever breaks first and begs me to stop is the loser.'

He moved to stand behind Paula, flexing the cane experimentally between long fingers.

'You may cry out at each stroke or take the cane in silence. That is entirely up to you. The only rule is that you must not shut your eyes at any point during the punishment. Is that understood?' Both girls nodded and he gave an odd little smile, stepping back to take up his position about a cane's length from the other girl's exposed bottom. 'Good. Then it begins.'

Roz heard a cruel whooshing sound as the cane travelled rapidly through the air, then she watched Paula's expression change from mute defiance to shocked pain. Those narrow blue eyes stretched wide and her mouth gaped suddenly open, dragging air into her lungs as if she had been drenched by a bucket of icy water. The other girl's cheeks turned pale, then flushed with a surprised pink, and there was even a slight suggestion of trembling from the naked body imprisoned opposite hers. He was making damn sure it hurt, that much was obvious from Paula's reaction. But to her disappointment the other girl did not cry out, somehow managing to control herself so that Roz realised she had been silently challenged to respond in the same way. If she was unable to hold herself together at the first stroke of the cane, crying out in pain like a little girl, Paula would appear to be the stronger of the two.

Now it was her turn. She tensed herself for the inevitable shock of that first stroke, hearing Carter shift behind her as he took up his new position and tested the cane against the air.

The cane was like a strip of white heat across her bare buttocks, making her jerk involuntarily against her fastenings so that the whole wooden Frame shuddered and her breasts shook painfully under the metal clamps. Yet she clamped her mouth shut on the cry which had welled up inside her as the cane struck, allowing herself nothing but a terrible gasping grimace which she knew Paula would enjoy witnessing. This was no time to display weakness, not when they had been secured mere inches from each other's faces and could see every change of expression betrayed by the eyes and skin.

With slow deliberation, she lowered her eyes to Paula's mouth. The pale lips had been bitten but were not yet bleeding. The other girl was frightened and Roz wanted her to know she could not hide it.

But what could Carter be thinking, she wondered in a moment of dizzy ecstasy, still standing behind her in the aftermath? The man was so dangerously silent, she wished she could read his mind. Perhaps he was simply admiring his handiwork before moving round to administer the next stroke to Paula. She could hear his breath in the stillness, seeming faster now after the exertion of the two strokes. Or was that a sudden excitement she was hearing? Roz could not help imagining how the mark must have sprung up on her white skin in glorious scarlet, one more thin raised weal to add to the others she had suffered since joining the tour. It must be an arousing sight.

'Two strokes each this time,' he muttered, taking up his position again behind Paula. She had expected to see something in his face, some clue to let her know what he was thinking, but his eyes were hidden in shadow, the mouth a thin determined line as he raised the cane and brought it down on Paula's vulnerable skin.

'Then three strokes each, then four . . . and so on, increasing every time, until one of you begs me to stop.'

However much Paula might have wanted him to stop though, the end of their joint punishment was not imminent. A cry of pain was wrenched from her lips at the second stroke of the cane and her hands clenched briefly into fists against the wooden Frame but the girl showed no other signs of weakening. She was clearly tougher than that. With an aggressive air of defiance, she locked eyes with Roz as they both waited for Carter to change ends, as if to indicate that she was still in the game and would not be beaten that easily.

Licking her lips as she waited for her turn again, Roz was not sure which ordeal was worse: her trembling anticipation of the cane or the cane itself. It was certainly not an easy punishment to take, facing her rival in such close proximity without betraying the pain she felt. Carter was behind her again. She sensed his slight hesitation before he raised the cane and wished she could close her eyes, blot out the spiteful look on Paula's face that made her want to claw the other girl's cheek until it bled. But closing her eyes was against the rules and she would not be the first to break them. That would look like cowardice. So she waited for her next two strokes in what must have seemed an obedient silence, eyes fixed straight ahead and her face composed, while her heart hammered through her body like a man taking an axe to a tree.

She took the next few bouts of strokes in mute submission, her body forcing itself against the Frame each time as if the wood could soak up the impact and save her from the pain. The other girl was much less successful at controlling herself, her cries strangled but audible as the cane bit repeatedly into her soft flesh. Roz felt an odd pride at her ability to remain silent, merely allowing a little gasp to escape from time to time and knowing that Carter was impressed by the look in his face whenever he moved past her.

She kept her eyes straight ahead, teeth clenched hard and with a clammy sweat beginning to run down her naked spine and the backs of her thighs. Yet in spite of her awareness of Paula's gaze, she could not help feeling that strange tingle of arousal between her legs and at the erect tip of each breast. Guessing how Carter must admire the cruel raised stripes he had created on her flesh, and excited by her own new-found burst of submissiveness, she was soon moist and eager for the punishment to go further. But what would be the reward if she won this test of endurance?

Roz imagined the tour manager releasing her from the Frame after the punishment and pushing her unceremoniously to the floor on her hands and knees, his hands parting her tortured buttocks and examining the marks he had left there. She would still be trembling with the pain of her punishment, her body damp and bruised under his probing fingers, but she would not protest as he forced himself between her sore buttocks and took his pleasure. Just imagining the painful moment of his entry was enough to make the juices flow more freely between her legs, embarrassing her as they trickled openly along the inner thighs and down towards her feet.

'Whore,' Paula hissed into her face, obviously not having missed the flush of arousal on her face. 'Filthy little slut.'

By way of reply, Roz merely smiled and continued to grind her hips against the wood of the Frame as though it were Carter's body pressing into hers, gasping with shocked pleasure as his final stroke caught her across the tops of her thighs.

Carter moved round to stand behind Paula. He had sweat stains on his T-shirt and there seemed to be a wild look in his eyes. 'Five strokes each this time.'

Paula moaned. 'Please . . .'

'What is it?' The tour manager stepped forward again and raised her chin with his finger, staring down into her pale face. 'You want me to stop? Is that what you're saying?'

'I . . .'

'Are you conceding the game, Paula?'

'No!'

He stepped back and raised the cane, his voice abrupt. 'Very well then. No more interruptions.' The uncompromising cane flashed down and Paula's naked body leapt in response against the Frame, her sudden cry piercing. But he did not even hesitate, his strokes falling almost one on top of the other. 'One . . . two . . . three . . . four . . .'

'Stop!'

The other girl was sobbing openly now, her body writhing and her face dripping with sweat.

'You admit that you've had enough?'

Her groan of defeat was followed by a brief, almost imperceptible nod. So she had won at last, Roz thought with a sudden fierce burst of triumph, watching Paula as she reluctantly conceded the game. It had been a hard-won surrender though. The other girl had bitten down into her lip so hard that she had tiny beads of blood along the skin, and her buttocks probably looked like a war zone after taking so many strokes of the cane. But it was clear Roz was not the only one to have found the intensity of their punishment exciting. Paula seemed limp now and almost drowsy as Carter bent to release the restraints, a warm flush of exertion in her face. There was not even more than a sharp ecstatic gasp of pain when he removed both nipple clamps and rubbed gently at her breasts to bring the circulation back.

Yet Paula's tearful blue eyes flashed across at her with as much defiance as ever, as though to say she had only won the battle, not the war. 'Next time, bitch,' she mouthed silently as he helped her step down out of the Frame. 'Next time . . .'

Ten

'Don't just stand there looking like an inexperienced virgin. Turn round, bend over and display yourself. Like this.'

Lauren seemed in an impatient mood this morning, positioning Roz face down over the table and spreading her thighs unceremoniously apart. In one smooth movement born of long expertise, she dragged the tiny thong from her friend's hips and abandoned its wisp of thin black lace on the floor, ignoring Roz's instinctive protest. Then Lauren pushed the PVC skirt to her waist and reached between her thighs, tugging at her exposed outer labia to make them stand out more prominently. The other girl's hands were swift and rough on her body, even though they hesitated slightly over the soft hairless sex as if curious to explore further.

'The audience wants to see your body, Roz. Not only see it, but feel it and use it.' She urged her to lean forward over the table, pushing down on her spine so that the buttocks raised naturally and invitingly. 'Nothing must be hidden. You can't give these punters a half-hearted striptease and expect them to go home satisfied. The tour doesn't work like that.'

'But it's so . . . humiliating.'

Lauren sighed, hands dropping to her sides. 'I can see why Carter wanted me to give you some performance tips.'

'I don't need to be taught how to perform.'

'Darling, you play a sweet game of pool. I'm not denying that. You're a star player, you leave the rest of us standing. But as far as the tour goes, you lack the all-round game. This isn't just about results on the table, remember. '

Roz straightened up angrily, reaching for her cue. 'I thought we came in here to practise?'

'We are practising,' Lauren pointed out gently.

'I meant to play a game.'

'Where's the difference?'

Roz slammed one of the pool balls down towards the far pocket in a burst of temper, then bit down hard on her lip. It was not fair to take her frustration out on Lauren. The older girl was only trying to help her fit more smoothly into the tour regime. She ought to be listening instead of complaining and acting like a spoilt schoolgirl. Ever since she'd joined the team, Roz seemed to have done nothing but get herself into trouble with Carter or McNaughton; she badly needed this sort of advice to get her back into favour, even if it hurt to admit it.

'OK,' she muttered, turning to face the brunette. 'So you think I'm not playing the game properly?'

Lauren hesitated. 'It's not a question of that. There isn't a right or wrong way to play this game.'

'Then why are we here?'

'So you can learn how to develop . . . desire.' The other girl stroked her face with one hand, tracing the outline of her jaw up to her cheekbone. To Roz's surprise, there seemed to be a look of sympathy in her eyes. 'Can I ask you a personal question, Roz?'

'Shoot.'

'I see you looking at Carter sometimes. You want him, don't you?'

Roz flushed and pulled away. 'So what?'

167

'What you feel for Carter, you need to feel for the others too. OK, maybe not quite the same desire. But something similar. It's a desire to fuck and to be fucked. But you have to allow yourself to feel it, Roz, to actually want them inside you or standing behind you with a cane in their hands. You can't force yourself to want that. You have to genuinely need it, to think about it every day until it becomes a way of life. Then you can consider yourself a submissive.'

Roz stood beside the pool table, turning the cue ball over and over in her hand like a lucky charm. She was listening but only through the sound of blood in her ears, feeling an excitement that she hated to acknowledge but knew she could not escape from. It was inside her, that desire Lauren was talking about, even if she kept pushing it away and refusing to look at it head-on. Because she suspected that once she let her desire make any important decisions, like the ones that involved her enjoying what happened at the end of each tournament and even looking forward to that ritual pain and humiliation, she might never regain her self-control. It would be with her for life.

'So Carter's not happy with me?'

'I didn't say that.'

Roz felt inexplicably angry. 'What more does he need to please him? He can't accuse me of not trying my best, for God's sake. I took more punishment than Paula the other day.'

'This isn't about Paula. This is about the game.'

'I can play the bloody game in my sleep. It's what happens after we've finished playing that I find difficult.'

Lauren smiled, leaning forward over the baize under the dazzle of the overhead light. Her neat full breasts rose from the tight leather dress, white and unblemished except for a few fading marks from the cane. She was wearing little make-up that morning,

168

just pale lipstick and a faint smudge of gold shadow across each eyelid. She looked beautiful and elegant and somehow untouched by her hungry sexuality, even though Roz had seen her in the midst of the action after every tournament: down on her knees by the pool table or lost somewhere in the audience, taking a penis like an iron bar deep in her throat or milking two men at once with those long expert fingers. Yet those sticky heated moments on the tour seemed to wash over and past her, leaving the brunette as languid and composed as ever.

'Climb up on the table then and let me show you how it's done,' she said persuasively. 'There are a few tricks you should learn.'

'Tricks?'

'The sort of thing that amuses the punters.'

Roz allowed the other girl to position her on the table, watching in confusion as her legs were spread and her sex checked for lubrication. Then her eyes widened in horror as Lauren reached for the white cue ball, polished it with a cloth, then tested its size against her gaping sex.

'Where's that cue ball going?'

Lauren smiled. 'Where do you think?'

'You've got to be kidding!'

Roz tried to scrabble backwards, but her thighs were caught and held apart in a surprisingly strong grip while the other girl came closer and started to push the cue ball into her sex. There is no way this ball is going to fit inside me, Roz thought wildly, struggling to escape. Her outer lips burnt and stung against the cool rounded surface, slowly peeling back and opening under the pressure. Yet the cue ball still felt impossibly large, forcing itself into that narrow entrance with what felt like the diameter of a watermelon.

'Breathe out and relax your muscles,' Lauren said impatiently. 'It's easier to take than you think.'

'Look, there's nothing easy about having a cue ball stuffed up inside your . . . ouch!'

'Just a little further. One more push.'

'I can't.'

Moments later though, it was over and the cue ball had wedged itself painfully in the entrance to her sex, stretching the delicate tissues until Roz felt they must be thin as paper. The sensation of internal pressure was almost intolerable, a feeling of fullness in her rectum that made her squirm with discomfort. She put an experimental hand down to the hairless mound, tracing the smooth cold outline of the ball with her fingers as it protruded from between the protesting outer lips of her sex. Still perched there on the table with her legs apart, knees bent and her belly aching, she stared at Lauren in a bemused silence. It was as though an alien head had appeared between her legs, a cue ball emerging from her womb, ready to be born.

'Amazing, isn't it?' Lauren gave her an odd smile, wiping her hands on the cloth. 'Now use your muscles to squeeze it out towards the corner pocket. The idea is to pot the ball from that position.' The other girl laughed at her stunned expression. 'Go on. The punters love it.'

It was a horrific mental image. But what goes in must come out, Roz reminded herself grimly. She clasped both hands on her thighs for support and pushed down hard, grunting with the effort. For a few alarming seconds it seemed to both of them as though the ball was not going to budge. It was wedged in there so tightly. Then suddenly the cue ball exploded from her vagina like a cork released from a bottle of champagne. Now sleek and shining, the ball rolled across the table and rattled against the corner pocket, not quite dropping but leaving behind a thin viscous trail of fluid on the cloth.

'Je . . . sus!'

Lauren clapped gleefully, her breasts bouncing. 'Fantastic!'

'It . . . didn't go down.'

'That doesn't matter, it was close enough. Give it a little practice, you'll be able to pot a ball into any pocket on the table.'

'You mean I have to do that again?'

' 'Fraid so.'

Breathless and exhausted by her efforts, Roz collapsed back on the pool table with her legs wide apart, staring up at the ceiling light in a daze. Fluid was now trickling embarrassingly down the inside of her thighs and she could feel how erect her nipples had become. She ought to be ashamed of herself for reacting to that exercise in such a lewd manner. Her sex was sore from stretching to hold the full rigid diameter of a cue ball and then ejecting it with enough force to shoot it straight across the table towards the corner pocket, yet somehow she had found the experience exciting. What she craved right now was a long cool tongue between her legs, preferably a woman's, to soothe the stretched and fevered flesh. But was that the wrong or the right response to pain? Her mind was spinning and she could no longer hold onto reality, a sense of perspective to save her from this internal confusion. Perhaps what she actually needed was to repeat the experience, to allow Lauren to push that slimy cue ball back inside and then squeeze it out again with all her might, concentrating on the aching centre of her body where the ball strained at her labia. Now that the cue ball had been ejected, it felt curiously empty in there.

'Ready for a second attempt?'

'Oh Christ.'

Roz heaved herself back into a sitting position, this time holding out a hand to take the ball from Lauren. When the brunette tried to pull away, she shook her head and insisted, feeling the heat burn in her face as she listened to her own words.

'It's OK. I can put it in myself.'

Lauren gave her a wry smile. 'Not in your arse, you can't.'

'What?'

The other girl slapped her playfully on the thigh. 'Turn over and kneel up on the table. Legs wide apart.'

This time the pain was more excruciating than she could have imagined. It hurt far more than any penis she had ever taken in her anus, even the thickest and most rigid. She had intended to be brave when she first knelt and offered up her exposed buttocks to the other girl, accepting this final humiliation with silence and composure. But as the tightly puckered hole began to burn and stretch under the penetration, Roz found herself squirming like a little girl, though that merely served to intensify the pain she was feeling.

When she tried to remain still, the pressure against her rectum became even more intolerable, and when she squirmed again, the cue ball seemed to enter her more fully. Her cheeks flushed and she began to moan, shaking her head from side to side in muted denial of what was happening between her legs. Her anal passage felt like the barrel of a cannon, loaded and ready to fire.

'That was well done,' Lauren murmured approvingly. 'The cue ball's right inside you now.'

'I don't ... think I can ...'

'You need to move slightly to your right,' Lauren continued in a calm voice, ignoring her muffled words and stroking the inside of her thigh with a soothing finger. 'To line up with the corner pocket so you don't miss the shot.'

Roz could not speak but grunted, her face hot, shuffling her knees a little as she tried to obey. What must she look like from behind? Her anus felt so huge and swollen, like that of a baboon on heat.

'Touch your forehead to the baize. Now look back through your legs . . . you see where the pocket is?'

She was in a direct line with the pocket now. Closing her eyes, Roz grimaced and squeezed hard with her anal muscles until she felt a terrible oozing pop and knew that the cue ball had been ejected. Almost in the same instant, she heard the ball hit the table with a loud thud and roll away in the direction of the pocket. The immediate sense of relief was enormous, her anus contracting gratefully after being stretched to the absolute limit. Her eyes flew open just in time to see the cue ball drop into the pocket, its smooth white surface slimy with mucus, and felt a strange triumphant whoop rising in the back of her throat. She had done it. It had hurt intensely and been one of the most humiliating experiences of her life, but she had done it perfectly.

'Superb,' Lauren breathed, her fingers moving across the tortured flesh of her anal hole.

'I did it.'

'It was incredible. You must have muscles of steel up there. I've never seen it done so well first time.'

Roz made a face, unable to get up and embrace her friend, her flushed face still hidden against the pool table.

'It hurts.'

'Let me help you.'

The other girl leant forward between her raised buttocks. Suddenly there was something warm and wet lapping against that stretched hole out of which the cue ball had just been catapulted. The sensation was almost too intense for pleasure, jolting those burnt nerve-endings and making her quiver uncontrollably. Roz gasped and closed her eyes even more tightly, pressing her face harder into the table. However much she might have wished this would happen, it was no longer merely in her imagination. Lauren was softly licking her anus, each delicious stroke of her tongue taking away the pain inflicted by the cue ball's entry and making it seem like a distant memory.

'Is that what you need?'

Roz nodded, once again unable to reply. That terrible aching sensation was still in every muscle between her legs, vagina and anus alike, both holes burning and over-stretched, yet now there was an illicit pleasure mingled in with it. Her fingers dragged and scraped at the baize cloth covering the pool table as if she could pull it straight off in her frustration. This close, she could smell chalk and see tiny bits of the cloth caught under her fingernails.

In a moment of sheer physical longing, she wished Carter could be here in the practice room with them, to witness the wantonness of her behaviour, to see her writhe with this deep-seated desire to be forced down and mounted. He needed to take her as much as she wanted him inside her, she was almost certain of that now. Her breath faltered as she imagined it in her mind's eye: his erect penis pressing deep inside the stretched channel of her rectum, ploughing her body on this stained pool table like a whore he had hired for the night. The thought was almost too much for her, taking her straight to the verge of orgasm. Her belly clenched with anticipation and she heard herself groan loudly. She wanted the other girl to push her

174

tongue deeper inside, perhaps right past the battered rim of her anus into the darker passageway beyond, but she did not know how to say it.

'What else?'

Roz gave a low moan and shook her head. Her buttocks rose even higher though, straining towards that invisible mouth.

'You have to tell me. Ask me properly.'

'Please . . .'

Lauren laughed, teasing the rim of her anus with one damp finger. 'That's not enough. You know what I want to hear.'

For a time there was silence between them, the other girl's fingers still playing with the sore and trembling flesh around her anus, her head occasionally dipping to lick around the rim. But she did not go any further than that. She would not let her come. It was almost as though she were deliberately withholding pleasure. But why? Roz could not understand such cruelty, though she suspected that this might be some kind of test. Yet another test, when she had passed all the others as well as any other girl on the tour. It was not fair. Her cheeks burnt and she shook with the need to come, pressing her thighs back against Lauren in the hope that such a mute entreaty would not go unnoticed.

'Darling, I can read you like a book. You want me here . . . and maybe there too afterwards.' Lauren let her fingers move down, idly tracing the bruised outline of her sex. She laughed mockingly when Roz jerked and moaned in reaction, withdrawing her hand. 'But you'll never succeed on this tour if you can't learn to beg.'

'Please . . .'

'Use the right words. Tell me what you want.'

'Lick me.'

175

'That didn't sound very submissive.'

Roz's voice trembled. 'Lick me, please. Tongue me.'

'Where?'

'In my . . . bottom.'

'Do what you're told and use the right words,' Lauren told her insistently. She circled the puckered gaping skin of her anus again, this time pressing much harder against the flesh so that a fingertip slipped inside and made Roz groan aloud. 'I don't care if it sounds dirty. You have to be taught how things are done here.'

'In my arse,' Roz whispered, hot-faced.

'Properly.'

She writhed in shame. 'Please, I want you to lick my arse. I want you to fuck my arse with your tongue.'

By way of reward, Lauren bent without any sign of hesitation and pushed her tongue deep inside the tortured anal opening. Every nerve-ending in that muscular channel came jolting to life in one incredible flash of voltage, so bright and electric it was as though a string of Christmas lights had been pulled taut around the walls of her rectal passage and switched on. Roz gave a piercing cry and slumped forward onto her chest, squashing her breasts against the unforgiving surface of the pool table. Completely by instinct, her hands found their way between her thighs and rubbed feverishly at her clitoris. The erect flesh there quivered and moved under her fingers like a creature with a mind of its own, too slippery to stay still. The gaping outer lips of her sex stung pleasurably with every accidental brush of her fingers.

Once again she allowed herself to imagine Carter kneeling behind her, holding her by the hips and sinking himself deep into her abused bottom hole.

Her nipples scraped painfully against the rough baize, making her squirm with abandon and heightening her excitement as Roz imagined receiving spurt after spurt of his thick hot come inside her bowels. Now the tongue in her anus had started moving in and out with a violent stabbing motion. That new sensation proved more than she could bear. Her groan as she finally reached orgasm was a mixture of joy and shame-faced despair, eyes clamped shut and her mouth wide as she felt her body go into spasm.

The other girl moaned as she realised what was happening. Hurriedly she removed her tongue from Roz's anus and climbed up onto the pool table beside her. In one brutal move, she dragged away the hand which Roz had pressed so urgently into her sex and placed it between her own slim thighs.

'Rub me too,' she ordered her with a sharp gasp, not bothering to hide how excited she was. 'Hard.'

That tense slippery flesh responded eagerly to her touch and Lauren was soon groaning and writhing around like a wild animal, lost in her own powerful orgasm. The brunette drew her legs up towards her chest, head thrown back, her beautiful loose hair tumbling in disarray as she let the climax take hold of her body. Their sweat-drenched bodies slid against each other on the pool table, eventually lying entwined in each other's arms, hip to hip and with their breasts pressed together as they kissed. The silence between them afterwards was heavy and beautiful. It was as though neither of them wanted to spoil the moment by rolling apart. Even when both their orgasms had faded there was still a heated flush on Lauren's face, her eyes dark and drowsy with satisfaction.

The fingers that had worked inside Lauren's sex slipped out easily enough, sticky with juice and smelling of arousal. Roz raised her fingers to her lips, cleaning carefully under her rings, along the knuckle joints and between each finger. It gave her an incredible sense of achievement to know that she had given Lauren such pleasure, using nothing but her hand.

'Enjoying the taste of my pussy?' Lauren smiled up at her, lazy and contented in the crook of her arm.

'Delicious.'

'Your arse was delicious too. If I hadn't needed to come myself, I could have kept my tongue stuck up there all day.'

Roz paused, still licking her fingers. The deliberate crudity had made her heart quicken but she was too tired now to follow it up.

'I've never had a woman do that to me before.'

'So was it good?'

Roz grinned. 'What do you think?'

'To be honest, I think you were imagining something rather different while I was sticking my tongue up inside your arse.' Carefully, Lauren sat up on the pool table and looked across at her with unexpected seriousness. 'Or should I say someone different?'

Roz caught her breath sharply. 'Drop it, Lauren.'

'You can't keep thinking about him like this, Roz. It's too fucking dangerous. If McNaughton ever found out . . .'

'There's nothing to find out, OK? End of lecture.'

Lauren was still watching intently as she swung her legs over the side of the pool table and slid to the floor.

'You're not falling in love with him, are you?'

'Don't be ridiculous.'

'Oh my God.' Lauren shook her head in dismay, seeing the wild tell-tale flush on Roz's cheeks. 'Don't fall for a man like Carter, please. Not Carter.'

Roz stood still a moment, staring down at the floor and steadying herself against the side of the table. Was that what was going on? Was she really falling for a man who had ordered her to be beaten and punished on a daily basis ever since she had arrived here, a man who had watched her have sex with stranger after stranger, encouraging her to be abused by each of them and taken ruthlessly in her mouth, her vagina and anus according to their desire?

'No.' Her voice trembled. 'Not Carter.'

Carter had unzipped his jeans in front of the row of monitors, certain that he would not be disturbed by the security guard for at least another half an hour, masturbating himself with long easy strokes as he watched the two girls touching each other on the practice table. It had been the usual thing at first. More exciting to watch because they were unaware of his scrutiny, but nothing out of the ordinary. Then he had listened to Roz speaking to Lauren about him afterwards, his penis still swollen and tense with the need for release, and watched her face change as she spoke his name. Falling for him? His hand had stilled on his penis, his eyes narrowing on the screen. That was an impossible dream and one he was not even sure that he wanted.

But it had not been his imagination. Roz did want him as much as he wanted her. Though neither of them were likely to get a chance to consummate that desire. Not during the season, anyway. For as Lauren had quite rightly said, the whole thing was too dangerous. He could lose his job as tour manager and Roz could not only lose her place here, she would also be risking an unimaginable punishment at the hands of McNaughton for disobeying one of the cardinal rules of the tour. Yet the idea that she actually wanted him inside her, even after everything he had done to her and would probably do to her in the future, was enough to make his heart thud in his chest with excitement.

Carter turned his back on the monitor as the two girls finally left the practice room, giving the shaft in his hand a hard squeeze. It responded instantly, rearing up again with its fat bulbous-tipped head. He was too aroused to zip himself up again and simply walk away. But none of the players were available to him during the season and most of the domestic staff would have gone home by now. So it would have to be a hand job.

Hurriedly, he flicked through all the channels on the closed circuit system, but was unable to find anything happening on the penthouse floor which would bring him to orgasm quickly enough. The security guard would be back from his evening break soon and it would be too embarrassing to be caught in here with an only-too-obvious erection. So he stopped recording in the practice room and rewound the tape to the point where Lauren had first bent her head and started licking the other girl's anus. From that particular camera angle, it was possible to see the look on Roz's face as well as the inviting twin mounds of her buttocks. Her thighs were so widely spread that he caught an occasional glimpse of her sex, its hairless slit still gaping and almost purplish-looking from the cue ball which had been inserted earlier.

He wondered how much that had hurt the girl, taking the cue ball up there. Enough to make her hiss and writhe. But not as much as it must have hurt when Lauren forced it into her anus, he thought, wishing he could have ordered her to suck his penis

180

at the same time. Ever since he had first seen her in that pool hall, he had known that Roz would make a spectacular addition to the tour. She was easily the most desirable of all the players, her body so naturally attuned to sex and sexuality that she could be relied upon to respond to any treatment, however harsh or bizarre.

His mouth was dry as he followed their antics on the monitor and fingered himself. His erection was uncomfortably large and stiff now. Carter usually left it to the girls to teach each other trick shots. His role was to introduce new players to the rules, administer punishments and generally keep order. But he was beginning to regret not having watched this show in person.

He shuffled a little closer to the screen, his penis almost resting on it as he jerked the tense purplish head back and forth. He watched Roz sinking her fingers into Lauren's sex and imagined himself there in the room, standing behind them. His eyes fixed on the pale globes of her rear, the smooth cleft between them and the flashes he could see of that mysterious little hole that was her anus. Darker and slightly ragged-looking from having to accommodate the cue ball, that dimpled hole beckoned to him.

If the slut really wanted him, that was how she would have to take him. Right up her dirty little backdoor. He had seen Roz take men there often enough, he knew how much she loved it up the arse. So many men, so few protests. His penis rigid now with the need to impale her, he too wanted to clamp those squirming buttocks with both hands and drive himself deep into her rectum. Down on her belly, arse in the air, an attitude of total and utter submission. That was what she wanted, what she needed to complete her as a player.

His penis was touching the screen now, desperate to get as close as possible to the real thing. His hand flicked the swollen head up and down so fast it had become a blur against the grainy black and white image of their naked bodies. The girls were pressed up against each other like Siamese twins, breast and hip, fingers working steadily in each other's orifices. One blonde and one brunette, caught together like a couple of bitches on heat sniffing at each other's arses. Such hungry little sluts, he thought wildly.

He imagined both of them together, down on their knees in the practice room, their greedy upturned faces inviting him, taking his cock alternately in their mouths. Those slow powerful sucks from Roz that would leave him ready to explode in the darker cavity of her anus.

With that image in his mind, Carter grunted and erupted over the monitor in a burst of semen, a red haze in front of his eyes that seemed to take ages to clear.

It took some time to reconnect to his surroundings. Then, as his heart rate returned to normal, he realised with a sudden jolt of horror what he had done. Pushing his sticky penis back into his jeans with an unsteady hand, Carter zipped himself up before the security guard could return to find him in an embarrassing situation. He could scarcely believe he had behaved like that, especially in such a dangerously public place. Even an inexperienced teenager would have had more sense. The monitor in front of him was smeared with thick bolts of come, white streamers hanging from its neat trim and dripping to the carpet. Carter searched his pockets for a piece of tissue, anything he could use to clear up the mess, but there was nothing.

In the end, he stumbled away from the monitor room in a paroxysm of guilt and relief, taking with him the memory of her grimace as she climaxed and the newly planted suspicion that Roz had been thinking about him too when she came.

Eleven

Don't fall for a man like Carter. That was what Lauren had said to her in the practice room – an unambiguous warning from a girl who was experienced enough to know how this game operated between players and management – and her words continued to reverberate through Roz's head as they approached the end of the season. Yet somehow she managed to play better than ever at most of their tournaments and exhibition matches, beating the other girls without much difficulty and maintaining her superiority over Paula. However her feelings might have changed towards the enigmatic tour manager, she was not going to allow any kind of emotional weakness to affect her game. Much to her relief, Lauren seemed the only player who had noticed the way she looked at him. The other girls were unaware of the situation and she did not intend to let that change.

Their next major tournament was in north London. The venue was a converted warehouse on a disused industrial estate. The interior had been redecorated in fine style for the occasion, a false ceiling hiding the rusted old beams above the match table itself and red carpets laid down for the audience. Away from the main arena, the place was a maze of

corridors and outbuildings, so that the girls kept
getting lost on their way to and from matches.
Beyond the well-lit warehouse the rest of the industrial estate had a lean and sinister air. Grass straggled
untidily through cracks in the concrete and a few
abandoned cars lay burnt out on their sides around
the periphery.

As soon as they arrived, Carter performed a slow
cautious sweep of the place and advised them all to
stay close to the venue.

'We've only got security in the warehouse itself,' he
told the girls bluntly. 'So you need to be extra careful
tonight. Sometimes the punters get greedy for a little
one-on-one action. Stick together between matches
and watch each other's backs.'

The dressing room was a cramped draughty room
at the back of the warehouse, with only one toilet
cubicle between all of them. Paula grabbed the best
spot immediately, right in front of a row of three
full-length mirrors, and stripped down to a see-
through sequinned thong and bra in spite of the cool
weather. While she was applying her make-up, her
eyes kept wandering to Roz in the mirror as though
she were planning something unpleasant. Ever since
that night of punishment in the Frame, Paula had
been careful not to spend any time in her company
outside tournament time. It was obvious she had not
forgotten her embarrassing defeat.

Roz guessed that Paula might be planning to cause
trouble that night, making a mental note to stay away
from the other girl when they were not playing. Those
narrow blue eyes seemed as malicious as ever and she
was not in the mood for a fight.

In fact, it was only when she had beaten one of the
Scandinavian blondes – the one with the pierced
tongue and clitoris, whose name she could never

remember – that Paula even bothered to speak to her. They passed in the narrow corridor between the arena and their changing room, so uncomfortably close that their breasts almost touched as they swung to avoid each other. Roz had expected a cold look from those blue eyes, or possibly none at all; an icy glance straight ahead was her rival's usual way of dealing with such encounters. Much to her surprise though, Paula slowed down and put a hand on her arm to stop her.

'Someone was asking for you in the dressing room,' she said shortly, her eyes unpleasant as they moved over Roz's skin-tight skirt and top. 'Some dark-haired man.'

'Who?'

'Dunno.' Paula glared at her impatiently. 'He came into the dressing room about ten minutes ago, said he was looking for you. Then he went outside for a cigarette. That's all I know.'

'You didn't ask his name?'

'No.' Paula shrugged contemptuously and continued along the corridor towards the arena. 'I'm not your bloody social secretary. Go and ask him yourself. He's probably still outside.'

Left standing alone outside the door to the changing room, Roz frowned to herself. She was perplexed. Who on earth could the man be? Maybe her landlord had finally caught up with her, though that seemed unlikely. The more logical explanation was that it was simply one of the punters here tonight, some admirer of hers keen for a private exhibition. Some of the other girls occasionally agreed to that sort of thing, even though they knew it could be dangerous. She ought to tell Carter about this man at once. But the last thing she wanted was for the tour manager to think she was going soft, running to him at the first suspicion of trouble. No, it would be better to deal with the situation herself.

It was dark outside the back of the warehouse and she could not see anyone waiting for her there. The rough ground surrounding the warehouse was now filled with parked cars, a distant streetlight glinting off their steel panels. She could hear men's voices coming from the front entrance, out of sight here, and the sound of engines as yet more cars arrived and were directed into parking spaces. But there did not appear to be anyone on this side of the building. Roz began to suspect it had been another of Paula's dirty tricks, something designed to throw her off balance before her next match in the hope that it would affect her game. She was just about to go back inside when she caught the acrid scent of cigarette smoke on the air.

'Who's there?' she demanded uneasily, her nerves jumping as she stared over the gleaming car bonnets at nothing.

When there was no reply from the darkness, Roz turned to fumble at the back door only to find herself being grabbed from behind and dragged away between the rows of parked cars. One hand clamped down over her mouth before she could scream for help. It was a man at her back, silent and unseen, too strong for her to break free. She bit hard at his fingers, tasting smoke and engine oil in her mouth, but he seemed oblivious to the pain. Struggling against her captor as he pulled her several hundred yards clear of the warehouse, far out of sight of the minders on the front entrance, Roz lost one of her high heels and felt the rough ground scrape painfully along her bare foot.

'Stop fighting, you bitch. You're only making it worse for yourself,' the man growled in her ear.

Roz felt soft material being dragged down over her head, probably some kind of leather hood by the faint smell, then everything was plunged into darkness. Her heart was thudding in her chest and she knew that she was on the verge of panicking. Had Paula found someone to take her away from the tournament so Roz could not beat her again? The thought seemed almost inconceivable, a cruel and unjust act of revenge for simply being the better player, yet her female intuition told her that anything was possible where Paula and her pride were concerned. But where was he planning to take her? And what the hell would he do to her once they were alone together?

She ignored the man's warning, kicking out at his shins in a final attempt to escape, and was rewarded with a slap to the head so comprehensive it left her ears ringing. She stumbled, sagging in his arms for a few dizzy moments. Whoever this man was, he was not playing a practical joke on her. This was a serious abduction.

'If you don't struggle, you might get out of this OK.' His voice was harsher now, the London accent pronounced. They were standing beside a large metal object. She could feel it jamming into her side. He put his hands about her waist and lifted her into the air as easily as if she had been a doll. 'Now get up inside there. That's it, use your hands. Crawl forwards about five or six paces and kneel up with your hands behind your head.'

She had no idea which way she was facing any more, the leather hood effectively blotting everything out except for the occasional glimmer of light from below her neck. But she had been hoisted inside a large vehicle and pushed forward towards the back, that much was obvious. The floor beneath her hands and knees was cold metal, damp to the touch as if it had been hosed down recently. From the hollow-sounding echo as the man jumped in behind her and shut the sliding door, Roz guessed she must be inside a lorry or large van. The whole place stank of the same oil she had smelt on his fingers when he first grabbed her. And he had her trapped in here now. She was alone with him and there was no one who would be coming to save her. So what would be his next move?

Seconds later, her senses adjusting to their new surroundings, Roz caught the sound of fast shallow breathing somewhere above her head and was startled to realise they were not alone.

'You took your bloody time coming back. I thought you'd run out on me or something.' It was another man's voice, younger and rather less confident. 'Anyone see you grab her?'

'Don't be stupid.'

'So we can do whatever we want with her?'

'The bitch is all ours.'

The second man gave a nervous laugh. 'Look at those legs. I've always wanted a slave girl.'

'I'll settle for a fuck puppet.'

'So when do we start?'

'Soon as you like.'

He laughed again, coming closer. 'I like now.'

She had listened in silence, turning her head almost imperceptibly from side to side as each man spoke. So that was their plan. To keep her imprisoned here until they had taken their pleasure with her. But what then? Roz paled under the leather hood, afraid to contemplate what might lie in store for her tonight.

The man who had abducted her in the car park bent forward and clasped something cold around her raised wrists. Handcuffs, she realised with sudden apprehension, feeling the metal snag at her skin. Roz found herself being dragged back without warning to the side of the lorry and cried out in alarm. She was lifted off her knees, the remaining shoe falling away until she was stretched on tiptoe with both wrists attached to what sounded suspiciously like a chain. The heavy links clanked against the metal wall above her as it was drawn up and tightened, leaving her struggling for balance. The short sharp gasps which she could hear so loudly beneath the hood were her own. Her sense of direction was completely screwed up now. She had no idea where the two men were standing, in front of her or to the side. All she knew for certain was that the evening's entertainment was about to begin.

Then the younger one was suddenly right there, inches from her body. He put his hand under her skirt. Less clumsy than the other man, in spite of his lack of confidence, his fingers seemed more precise as he felt for her clitoris through the tiny black lace thong. Much to her horror and shame, she knew her sex was already moist and eager.

'Christ, she's soaking.'

'Ready for us, is she?'

'Smells like peaches. Horny little bitch. Peaches and fucking cream, dripping right off my finger.'

Her cheeks on fire under the leather hood, she heard a man's zip descend to her left and then the heavy rustle of what sounded like jeans being pulled down. It was about to begin.

'I don't care what we agreed. I can't wait any longer.'

Roz felt his hands parting her thighs where she hung, helpless to prevent what was about to happen, and waited for the inevitable moment of penetration without bothering to protest. They were too far gone now to listen to her pleas. Besides, this had not been some opportunistic abduction. The first man had been too cool about the whole thing from the start, the second man too eager to get inside her. They had been planning this evening for some time, she suspected. But had she been their target from the beginning or was she merely unfortunate enough to have caught their eye at some tournament?

'No, not yet.' The first man sounded firm enough, even though his own frustration was obvious. 'Let go of the girl and zip yourself up. We agreed to break her in first, remember?'

'I know, but . . .'

The other man's voice hardened. 'Don't argue with me. We owe it to Paula to do this right.'

Hearing that all-too-familiar name, Roz felt her body go numb with shock. So it had not been her imagination after all. These men were either friends of Paula's or working for her. The other girl must have arranged her kidnap to ensure that Roz would be out of the running for tonight's tournament. She could hardly believe that anyone could be so spiteful and vindictive. But there was no time to wonder about it any longer, for the two men had moved closer and begun to tear at her clothes. The skirt was pulled off without ceremony and her little sequinned top quickly joined it on the floor. Hands tugged at her black lace thong. It ripped under the pressure and someone dragged the last shred out from between her legs. She was naked.

'What's this bruising on her skin?'

The first man ran his hand down her belly. 'They beat them after every tournament. It's part of the game. I think that single raised line must be from a cane. And that's a tawse, most probably. See the shape of it?'

'She's a mess. It must hurt really badly.'

'Of course it hurts.'

The younger man sounded incredulous. 'Then why the hell do the girls let them do it?'

'Because they enjoy it.'

'Jesus.'

There was a short unnerving pause in the conversation, both men touching and prodding her body with experimental fingers. Roz winced a few times, catching her breath as they located cane marks across her belly and along her thighs which had still not healed. Bizarrely though, she did not waste any more energy on struggling or begging them to stop. She had expected to feel angered by their remarks, the casual way they discussed her as though she were some alien creature whose strange ways were a matter of curiosity to them. But all she could feel was an odd excitement beginning to creep under her skin as they touched her. What sort of torture had they planned for her tonight? She imagined the cane again, feeling her sensitive nipples react to the thought with a sudden rush of blood. Roz tried to guess from their hands and voices whether they were cruel men or merely there to carry out Paula's orders. Not for the first time, she wished that she could see their faces.

'Does Paula let them do this to her?'

'Yes.'

'She always was a bit crazy.'

'Perhaps.' The first man was squeezing her breasts now, flicking the nipples until they became erect, his touch clinical and a little painful. 'If she enjoys the pain though, why bother worrying about it? Paula's a big girl now. She can look after herself.'

'We're her brothers. It's our duty to protect her.'

The older man sounded impatient. 'Shut up. You're getting on my nerves. We're doing this for her, aren't we?'

So these two men were Paula's brothers. She sagged a little on the end of the chain, almost losing her precarious balance. Vanished was any hope of bribing them to let her go and forget what they had promised her rival. This was a question of blood, not money. Paula had asked them to punish her for being the better player and that was what her brothers intended to do. But exactly what form would this punishment take and how long would she be held here?

She yelped as the fingers pinching her nipples became cruel, and the younger one pressed his hand down over the leather hood to stifle her cries. The darkness intensified. She could hardly breathe, her chest heaving as she realised the hopelessness of her situation. It seemed unlikely that she would be missed by Carter and the others until her next match was called, which might not be for another half an hour at the least. And who would think to look in a parked van or lorry several hundred yards away from the warehouse? Nobody but Paula even knew that she had left the building. So there was no chance of a daring last-minute rescue by Carter, however much she had been hoping for that. Her heart began to thud in an irregular rhythm as she faced reality. It was up to her to get through this ordeal alone.

The older one moved away and Roz tensed, trying to guess what might be coming next, only to hear a metal buckle being unclasped and the familiar dragging sound of a belt as it was released from the man's jeans. It was snapped through the air a few times like a bull-whip, mere inches from her body. Then the younger man took a step backwards, releasing her mouth so abruptly that her head fell forward onto her chest, and she gasped for oxygen like a fish out of water. Her skin tingled with the sudden realisation that they were planning to beat her.

Roz could not bear to stay silent any longer. Her voice sounded strange and muffled beneath the thick leather hood.

'Did Paula tell you to do this? I haven't done anything wrong. I don't understand why she hates me so much.'

The first man came forward, pressing his body right up against her naked skin with one knee pushing her thighs apart. Roz could smell cigarette smoke again on his clothes, strong and acrid. There was no attempt at gentleness or seduction in the way he handled her body. She might as well have been a piece of raw meat hanging from a hook in a butcher's shop. His fingers grasped at her small breasts first, cupping and squeezing them until she cried out. Then he slid a hand between her thighs and levered them open, pushing up easily into her moist sex as if to prove a point; in spite of his cruelty, her body was on the verge of climax. Withdrawing his fingers, the older brother wiped them across her bare belly with a grunt of amused malice.

'You beat her, that's what you did,' he whispered, his voice close to her ear. 'You came out of nowhere and beat my little sister. You humiliated her in front of her boss. In front of the other players.'

'It's only a game . . .'

'A game she's supposed to win.'

'Well, I'm sorry to have spoilt her plans. But if Paula wants to start beating me, she'll have to become a better player.'

The older man jumped back with an angry exclamation. That had definitely been the wrong thing to say to her rival's brother. She could see nothing through the thick leather hood but guessed from his ragged breathing that he had drawn back the belt and was poised to hit her.

194

'Keep talking to us like that and you'll get this belt where it hurts. Is that what you really want?'

'I'm not afraid of you. Or your sister.'

'You will be soon.'

She laughed at them both from under the darkness of the leather hood. These men could do what they liked to her, she was not going to weaken and promise to let Paula win.

'I doubt that.'

'So you want me to give you a belting?'

'Fuck you.'

He sounded enraged. 'I told you, don't speak to me like that.'

'Fuck you,' she repeated with deliberate emphasis, those two words falling like bombs into the silence between them.

'Belly or tits?'

'Tits,' she spat back defiantly.

The words were barely out of her mouth when the belt was swung across her exposed breasts and she jerked in reaction, unable to prevent a high-pitched cry of pain. It was odd and disorientating, not being able to see the belt before it struck and so prepare herself for the blow. It was not the fiercest stroke she had ever taken across her breasts, but the leather hood over her eyes and the chain suspending her from the side of the lorry made her twist helplessly as if she had experienced such terrible punishment. These men know precisely what they are doing, she thought grimly, fighting to keep control of her response. But within seconds of the impact, she was embarrassed to feel heat spreading down her belly and between her legs, a familiar tingling sensation in her groin which told her she was becoming sexually excited.

'I warned you,' the older man said hoarsely. 'I didn't want to have to do that. You left me no choice.'

'Liar,' she gasped. 'You enjoyed it.'

He hesitated, then stepped closer. 'Only because you enjoyed it. You loved taking my belt, didn't you?'

'No.'

'So what's this?'

His fingers scrabbled between her legs once more, this time feeling for the sticky bud of her clitoris. It stood out from her lips like a beacon of excitement, taut and gloriously erect. Even though Roz was struggling hard to fight her growing arousal, she could not restrain a groan as the older man found and skilfully manipulated her clitoris. Her hips moved of their own accord, swaying towards Paula's brother in the hope that he might sense her desperation and slip his fingers back inside her. Her mind was reeling though. What the hell was she doing? No one could mistake the open invitation of her body as her breasts jutted eagerly forward and juice began to trickle out down the inside of her thighs. Yet the man was touching her there with calculated roughness, his fingers pinching and hurting the tender flesh of her sex. It was such a shameful response, she was suddenly glad the hood was there to cover her flushed cheeks and moist parted lips.

'I could have you right now,' he grunted in her ear. 'I could spread your legs and you'd be moaning like a whore.'

The second brother shifted position and pressed his body against her as well. He had said nothing for so long that Roz had almost forgotten he was there beside them. But she could feel a bulge pushing into her thigh now, hungry and cruel. So the younger one still wanted her. What was he, twenty? Maybe twenty-one? She tried to remember how old Paula was, their younger sister, but the memory kept slipping away into the breathless sweat-slick darkness behind her hood. Paula meant nothing to her, not here, so far away from the game and the lights of the pool table. All she could do was focus on these men and what they were planning to do to her.

The younger one had started touching her naked body now. His hands played clumsily with her breasts for a few moments, hurting her. Then she heard him drag his zipper down again and waited in silent anticipation, unable to stop herself picturing his rigid shaft as it was released from his jeans, the slit in that swollen purple head already oozing pre-come.

'Unchain her,' he was muttering to his older brother. 'I want her down on her knees so she can suck me.'

'That wasn't part of the plan.'

The younger man was masturbating himself as he stood there in front of her. She could feel the quick jerks of his hand and even the hard snout of his penis slapping rhythmically against her thigh.

'I told you,' he insisted, 'unhook the chain. You've had your fun with her. Now it's my turn.'

'We share or we don't touch her at all. That was the deal.'

'Forget the deal.'

Somebody gripped the back of the leather hood as if about to rip it off. It was the older brother, his tone suddenly threatening. 'You want to stick to the deal?' he demanded. 'Or do you want me to let her go?'

So she was going to take them both at once. That was what the two brothers had planned for her from the beginning. Her body grew hotter and wetter as she began to imagine what might lie ahead. It was actually a secret fantasy of hers, she realised with a stifled moan of horror, to have two men inside her at once. To take the younger brother in her throat and the older brother from behind, perhaps even in the tighter channel of her anus if he insisted. To be gripped and held by her hair at one end and her hips at the other. Would they remove her hood first though, or would it merely be pushed up to uncover her lips so she could suck the younger brother in this stifling darkness? Her body ached with the prospect of such enforced obedience. She would have to take them both at once, still hooded and on all fours, pinned down on this cold metal floor like a machine hammered by two pistons.

'Fair enough,' the younger one grunted. He ran a hand over her smooth buttocks and located the puckered opening to her anus. 'But which of us gets to use her arse first?'

'You said you wanted her to suck you.'

'I changed my mind.' One finger tried to intrude there, lodged deep between her buttocks. 'God, she's tight.'

'Don't worry about it. She'll be loose enough up there by the time I'm finished.'

Both men were touching her now. One of the brothers, Roz was no longer sure which one, pushed his fingers up into her sex again. The hot moist passage accepted them readily. She gasped and writhed as those unseen fingers stroked and manipulated her flesh. God, this was how she dreamt of taking Carter. In some secret place like this, hidden away from the rest of the tour, where they could act out their darkest fantasies without fear of discovery and reprisals.

For a moment, she dared to imagine that it was Carter's fingers inside her and felt the breathless climb towards orgasm begin. This was all wrong though. There was no future in her stupid attraction for the tour manager. It would only hurt her in the end. Don't fall for a man like Carter. But it could be so hot, the two of them caught in a camera flash in her mind, fucking like two dogs in a side street. The rough fingers working inside her began to press up against her clitoris, flicking repeatedly at the tiny nub until something seemed to break inside her.

She started to pant and urge them both on. More fingers. Harder. The other man was laughing at her helpless physical response, she could barely hear him through the strange buzzing in her ears. Blood pressure, she thought wildly. Then he pinched her nipples painfully between finger and thumb, calling her a bitch, a whore, a spunk-hungry little slut. It was the younger brother, she recognised the voice now.

'Eager little slut, aren't you?'

She moaned and shook her head as his mouth clamped down over her breast, licking and biting. The voice was muffled.

'You want this?'

'I hate you.'

Her body jerked at the end of their chain like a marionette, almost dancing for the brothers as they tormented her.

'You want this?' he repeated.

But what did it matter what these men thought of her? How they might jeer at her filthy behaviour? One of them was laughing out loud, she could hear him. Perspiration dripped down her face and emerged below the dark hood. Salt on her lips, she could even taste it now. Feel it trickle between the swaying valley of her breasts. Let them see it. She did not care any longer. Let them know who she was and what she wanted from them.

'Yes!' she hissed loudly.

Roz climaxed against the fingers in her sex – so hard, it almost hurt, the knuckles grinding against her flesh – again and again. Her body might belong to these men for the moment but her mind was somewhere else. With somebody else. She was even calling his name in a long incoherent cry. Carter. Carter. Carter.

She arched her hips with instinctive abandon and felt the cold chain drag at her arms and shoulders. The pain meant nothing to her though. The long series of orgasms had completely taken over. This was what she had been waiting for. They could do whatever they wanted to her now. It would make no difference. Pleasure was pouring through her pelvis like hot sunlight. Her mouth stretched wider under the leather hood, her head tipped back like a woman drinking, and she wallowed luxuriously in the tides of sensation.

'Now you can unchain the bitch,' the older brother said in a breathless voice, unzipping his jeans. 'And bend her right over. I'm going to do her arse first.'

Twelve

'What do you mean, she's gone?' Carter threw aside his newspaper and frowned up at Lauren. 'Gone where?'

'I don't know. That's exactly why I came to you.'

'When did you last see her?'

The brunette gave an elegant shrug, her bare shoulders set off to perfection by the thin white straps of her shift dress.

'Over an hour ago now. Roz went out to play her last match and never came back. The guy on the door says he saw her heading back towards the changing room after she won. But something must have happened on the way because there's no sign of her now.'

'She's not still in the arena, watching the other players?'

'No, I already checked.'

'Well, she can't have left here by the front entrance. One of the bouncers would have told me by now.'

'I'm scared. Where the hell is she?'

Carter stood up and glanced briefly at his watch. It was getting quite late and if she did not turn up to play her next match soon, it would be automatically forfeit and Roz would lose her chance of winning this tournament. He was feeling a little uneasy himself about her odd disappearance, to be honest, but he had no intention of allowing Lauren to see that. Although he might count the dark-haired girl amongst his allies on the tour, it would be stupid to reveal anything more than was necessary at the moment.

'Don't worry,' he said smoothly. 'I'll find her.'

It was quiet in the changing room area. Most of the other players had been knocked out of the tournament and the lights had been dimmed. Paula was still in there though, retouching her make-up in the far corner. She turned as he entered the changing room, a triumphant smile on her lips which she hurriedly hid when she saw his expression. His mouth hardened. Paula knew something about Roz's disappearance, he was sure of it now. She might even have engineered it herself. But the former top player was a cunning opponent and not easily broken. So how could he get the evil bitch to admit it and tell him where to find Roz without actually having to break her arm?

Carter stood there in silence for a moment, considering how he should proceed. One thing was obvious here; Paula could not have got Roz out of the way on her own, not without being noticed by one of the other players or the minders who had been constantly patrolling the warehouse area. No, she must have had an accomplice to help her with the vanishing act, or maybe more than one accomplice. But where had Roz been taken? It could not have been very far, surely. Using any sort of vehicle to spirit her away would have involved passing the checks on the front gate of the industrial estate. There was no other way out of the estate for a car or van; he had already established that fact with his security men on arrival. Not unless they had somehow managed to drag Roz away on foot. Which seemed highly unlikely to him.

'Have you seen Roz?'

Paula blinked before replying, the mascara brush wavering slightly in her hand. 'I'm not sure. Perhaps about an hour ago, out in the corridor. Is there a problem?'

'Only that she's gone missing.'

'Missing?'

Had he not known Paula better, her tone of surprised alarm would have been almost convincing. Carter folded his arms across his chest and surveyed her dispassionately. She was not an unattractive girl, but there was a suggestion of meanness in the narrow eyes and thin-lipped mouth which had never appealed to him. Though it would have given him immense pleasure just at the moment to bend Paula over one of these high-backed chairs in the dressing room and cane her bottom until it shone with red streaks.

'Nobody's seen her since she won her last match . . . and she's due back on the table within the next thirty minutes. You know our rules for match play as well as I do. If she doesn't make that official time limit, she'll be automatically kicked out of the tournament.'

'And no one can find her?'

'That's right.' He smiled at her coolly, taking his time. 'Unless you happen to know where she is.'

'Me?'

'Don't play the innocent, Paula. It doesn't suit you.'

He took a step closer, deliberately lowering his voice to make the accusation sound less dramatic. There was no point allowing her to see how much of this was pure guesswork.

'Let's face it, Roz is a great player. Far greater than you'll ever be. And you can't bear people seeing that, can you?'

203

Paula's face seemed flushed now. She threw down her mascara and faced him defiantly across the dressing room, hands on hips.

'I don't know what you're talking about.'

'You've been dying to get rid of Roz ever since she joined the tour. So what have you done with her? How did you get her out of this place without somebody seeing you?'

'You've got no evidence.'

'Don't worry, I'll find a way to prove it,' he continued relentlessly. 'And when I do, I'll see to it that you spend the rest of this season down on your hands and knees. Publicly taking it up the arse from one of the doormen or the pool cleaners . . .'

'You wouldn't dare,' she hissed.

'Watch me.'

Paula struggled in silence for a few moments, her sharp blue eyes fixed on his face. Then she turned back to the mirror, pouting sulkily like a child whose game has been spoilt. Her barely perceptible shrug confirmed his worst suspicions.

'OK, but don't expect me to apologise. She was asking for it. This is my third year on the tour and I deserve a bit more respect. Who the fuck does Roz think she is, cruising in here out of nowhere and getting the top spot without even having to work for it?'

Carter set his teeth, restraining a sudden urge to slap her until she begged him to stop. 'Where is she, Paula?'

'I don't know exactly. Probably still out there in the car park. It's a large unmarked blue van . . .'

The vicious little bitch was still talking but he did not wait to hear the rest; he was already hurrying outside into the cool of the evening. It took a few minutes for his eyes to adjust to the darkness, his heart thudding erratically in his chest as he walked down along the rows of parked cars. A large unmarked blue van. That should not be too difficult to spot amongst all these expensive cars, he thought grimly. But who else would be inside the van when he found it, apart from Roz? He was certain now that Paula must have had an accomplice or two. Otherwise she could not have kept her rival prisoner for the past hour whilst continuing to win matches in the arena. Had they hurt her?

Even though he had seen Roz take many strange and dreadful punishments, Carter still found his stomach clenching at the thought that she might have been tortured. Maybe he ought to be prepared for some kind of struggle when he eventually located the van and its occupants. Perhaps even a serious fight.

His feet grated on the weed-infested gravel as Carter put several hundred yards between himself and the last row of parked cars. Glancing back at the main entrance to the warehouse, now dark and quiet in the distance, he wondered for a moment whether he should call one of the bouncers over to help him in the search. Then his eyes fell on the large blue van parked beside a deserted warehouse to his left and Carter instantly abandoned the thought. This was one of his own girls – possibly the best player he had ever scouted for the tour – and it was up to him alone to get her back.

Standing by the closed back door of the van, he caught a strange low-pitched moaning from inside and identified Roz immediatcly. But was that distress or excitement he could hear in her voice? It was always hard to tell with Roz, he was forced to concede that, aware of a nagging sense of jealousy that another man might be enjoying her body where he was not allowed to do so. Then a deep male voice uttered some kind of command and there was a brief rattling noise in response, rather like metal clanging against metal. Chains, perhaps.

Another male voice spoke, echoing inside the van. This one sounded younger, less sure of himself. Then there was a soft heavy thud, as if a body had dropped to the floor, and Roz moaned again. His mouth tightened. What were those bastards doing to his girl?

But she was not his girl, he reminded himself sternly. Roz was anyone's girl during the season. She had given her body to the punters and her soul to the game. That was part of the rules by which they all lived, an absolute daily requirement of the tour. It was a situation he had always accepted in the past without any problem. So why should he be angry with these men for doing precisely what he wanted to do? Because she was being prevented from playing her match and winning the tournament tonight, yes. It was imperative that he should clear the way for her returning to the table. But if this stomach-wrenching desire to smash someone's face in was merely a consequence of possessiveness and sexual jealousy, then no. That was an unacceptable response to her abduction and he knew it. He was the tour manager, for God's sake. He had no business feeling like that about one of his own players. And she was a player, there had never been any doubt in his mind about that. Carter had known what she was from the first moment he had set eyes on her. The game meant everything to her. She was beautifully, entirely, supremely a player.

Gritting his teeth, he tried the handle to the back door of the van. It was not locked. He counted to three, then swung the door wide open and jumped inside the van as quickly as he could.

Roz was down on all fours at the back of the van, naked except for a black leather hood. Behind her, a well-built man in his early thirties was kneeling with his jeans unfastened and a thick purple-headed penis clasped in his fist. It was obvious that he had either just been inside her or was planning to enter her now.

The other man, several years younger and much slimmer, was staring across at him in dismay. He must have realised their little game had come to an end though, since he was struggling to yank up the faded blue jeans which had pooled around his skinny ankles.

'OK, that's enough. You've had your fun,' Carter said, steadying himself on the metal wall of the van. He rolled up his shirt sleeves to indicate that he would have no trouble decking either of them. 'Don't make me do something I'll regret. Just put your dicks away and let the girl go.'

'Who the fuck are you?'

'I'm her manager, mate,' he replied, fixing the older man with a cool eye. 'Which means it's my job to look after her and get rid of scum like you.'

'Jesus,' the younger man spluttered and backed away, hurriedly zipping up his jeans.

'That's unlucky. Because I haven't finished with her yet.' The well-built man shrugged and bent forward to rub his penis – still impressively erect, despite the situation – between her reddened buttocks. His laughter was deliberately coarse. 'Give me another five minutes and you can have the bitch back with my spunk up her arse.'

Carter lunged instinctively towards him, a red mist in front of his eyes, and slammed the older man to the floor. He winced as his shoulder met hard bone and then unforgiving metal. The van shook and swayed, both men winded by the impact as they rolled slowly apart. It had hurt like hell, but at least he seemed to have got his message across. The older man held up a hand, conceding defeat with a shake of his head.

He scrambled to his feet again and glanced across at Roz. To her credit, though, she had neither moved nor made a sound during the struggle. Most girls would have screamed or tried to run away. Roz was merely waiting in silence for the outcome, still down on all fours, the hood covering her face as though she were about to be executed. The pale marked skin along her spine shone with a delicious vulnerability. Her naked breasts hung down, unfettered, the dusky nipples taut and erect. Her thighs were slightly parted, her buttocks still raised in silent acquiescence, as though anticipating penetration. He thought she had never looked so desirable and feminine.

He helped the naked girl to her feet, putting his arms around her and drawing her chilled body against his own.

'This is going to sound pretty rough, Roz. I know you're probably not up to playing again tonight. But if you don't get back to the table soon, you'll be disqualified.'

Her slender body was trembling in his arms. Ignoring the two men beside him, Carter pulled off the hood and gazed down into her flushed face for a moment. The blue eyes were wide and unnaturally bright. There were even tiny beads of blood showing on her lower lip where she must have bitten into it at some point during her captivity. But it was difficult to gauge how well she was coping with whatever had been done to her. She did not seem particularly distressed or in pain. Quite the opposite, he thought with surprise, noting the fresh marks across her breasts as she pulled away from the support of his body.

'You OK to walk then?'

Roz managed a hesitant nod. 'Of course.'

'What's the matter?'

'They . . . took my clothes.'

He gathered the skimpy garments together and handed them back to her while she dressed, her movements quick but shaky. 'Those two are Paula's brothers,' she started to say as if needing to explain the situation to him, then slumped weakly against the wall of the van. Her voice became thin. 'I'm sorry. Can you carry me?'

Lifting her easily in his arms, Carter carried her back towards the warehouse, hearing the van door slam shut behind them within seconds and the engine roar into life. So the two men who had taken her prisoner tonight were Paula's brothers, no doubt attempting to protect their sister and ensure she won the tournament. That nasty little bitch would stop at nothing to keep herself at the top. He wanted to punish Paula for doing this to his star player, though he knew that this rivalry – both on and off the table – was simply another facet of the game. The open conflict between the two players was what drew the punters back to watch their matches, time and time again – though it had taken on a peculiarly vicious twist tonight.

They had reached the back entrance to the warehouse and Roz stirred in his arms, putting her hands flat against his chest.

'Put me down now,' she said. 'I can walk the rest of the way. The others mustn't see me like this.'

Carter frowned down into her pale face, unwilling to let her go. She weighed so little in his arms, it was almost like carrying a child. And although the punters would go crazy if she did not make an appearance tonight, he was not convinced that Roz was in any fit state to play her match or cope with their sexual attention afterwards. His jaw hardened as he glanced down at her slim body. It was hard not to keep imagining what those two men had done to her in the darkened back of their van. He had seen more than enough when he opened the door. It had been burnt into his retinas for ever. She had been there just as he expected. Naked and hooded, down on all fours, her pale skin flushed and shaking as she waited for them to use her. She must have only just climaxed. Mere seconds before he had thrown open the door to the van. Carter was certain of that now. There could be no other explanation for those trembling limbs and over-bright eyes, or the rich musky scent of her sex as he gathered her into his arms.

Jealously, Carter wondered what it would take for him to make her respond in the same way. Then he suddenly realised the dangerous path he was taking and stopped himself before it was too late. He was her manager, not her lover. The scent of her sex must have gone to his head, he thought grimly. He had to shake this obsession and the sooner the better for both of them.

'You're expected at the table straight away,' he reminded her.

'I need my cue.'

He let her slide gently to the ground. 'You still look a bit shaken. Are you sure you're up to this?'

'I'm a player, aren't I?'

Lauren was lying face down in the tattooist's chair, her mouth slightly open and her eyes closed. She looked so vulnerable in that position, Roz thought sympathetically, her backside angled awkwardly in the air and her breasts pressed down into the plastic cover. Their hands were touching now, the other

210

girl's fingers beginning to tighten as the pain intensified. The tattooist was a woman in her early forties,
slender and dark-haired, frowning in concentration as
she bent forward over the pale smooth globes of
Lauren's bottom.

'Come on, say something. How much does it hurt?'
Roz asked her curiously.

Lauren did not manage to reply for a few minutes,
brows knitted together as she fought to keep her
breathing even. 'Worse than the whip, I suppose,' she
whispered in the end. 'But not as bad as the cane.
Across the palm of the hand, that is.'

'So you can handle it?'

'I can if you can.'

Roz nodded slowly, understanding. 'But where
should I . . .?'

'Only your bottom or one of your breasts. That's
what we agreed before we came in, remember?'

'Left breast, then.'

'Great choice, kid. I can't wait to see Carter's face
when he sees it.' Lauren had started to perspire, her
skin was shiny with it. Every now and then her face
would twitch, as if a muscle had gone into spasm and
she could not control it. But it was obvious she did
not want to think about the pain, trying to distract
herself by keeping up this stilted conversation with
Roz. Though she was still smiling, upper lip trembling and beaded with perspiration, her grip felt like an
iron vice. 'So which one are you going to choose? The
pretty little rose we looked at, or the dragon?'

'I'm still not sure.'

'Have the rose design, sweetie. It's small and it'll
hurt less.'

'But the dragon's sexier.'

'True.' Lauren winced as the needle bit into her
flesh, her face paler than before. 'Christ, this hurts.'

Roz watched her. 'Perhaps I'll have the rose after all.'

'Coward!'

It was dark inside the small backstreet tattooist's shop, the low slanting ceiling immediately above them covered with a vast assembly of designs and photographs of past triumphs: young girls hoisting up their skirts to show a neat snake or Celtic knot on their upper thighs or buttocks, men flexing muscular forearms almost blue with decades of tattoos. The tiny room smelt of musty ink and stale sweat. Though that was not surprising, really, considering the way Lauren's forehead was running with perspiration as her breathing became more shallow. Behind them a bead curtain swayed and rattled uneasily in the draught from the open shop door onto the street.

The fat balding man at the front entrance must be watching the television, Roz thought, trying not to imagine how it would feel to strip off her top and lie down in this reclining chair herself. She could hear an occasional drone of voices and applause mingling with the insistent buzz of the tattooist's tool. The shop was not much to look at from the outside, but it had been such a relief to come inside and discover that the tattooist was a woman. The man on the front till had glanced at them oddly as they came through, pointing the way without any comment other than a grunt and a nod, but clearly intrigued by the way the two girls were dressed. It had been impossible to find any normal street outfits in the penthouse, so they were both walking about in tiny PVC skirts and high heels, their sequinned tops embarrassingly designed to reveal more than they concealed. Lauren had giggled as they left the building, saying they must look like prostitutes. But it did not seem quite so funny now, two young women clinging together in

212

this small tattooist's shop with no watchful minders around them, no Carter on hand to protect them.

'OK, that's it,' the tattooist muttered, fiddling with the needle. 'You can get up now.'

Lauren could barely speak. 'Th . . . thanks.'

'Now it's your friend's turn,' the woman said, nodding across at Roz. Her grey eyes were peculiarly intense as she straightened up, as if trying to assess how well Roz would cope with the pain of a tattoo on the breast. No doubt the woman thought from their conversation that she was a complete coward. 'You want the little rose then?'

Some stupid stab of pride made Roz shake her head, pointing up at the crimson dragon on the ceiling above them.

'I've changed my mind. That one, please.'

'Expensive, the dragon. It'll hurt quite a bit more too.'

Roz looked at her. 'Can you do it?'

'Of course.'

'Then just do it,' she said shortly, yanking off her sequinned top and nudging Lauren out of the chair. 'I don't care about the pain. And I'll pay whatever it costs.'

The bloody woman was right though. The dragon tattoo did end up hurting more than she cared to admit. But she gritted her teeth to avoid looking like a fool, concentrating on the ceiling designs instead and the light chatter of Lauren sitting beside her and nursing the sore site of her new tattoo. Then she made the mistake of glancing down at the needle, buzzing and vibrating against the tender skin of her breast, and a wave of nausea made her gasp and clutch at the arms of the chair. The lights seemed to flicker above her. Lauren put a hand on her arm, asking something. Her voice sounded terribly far away, almost as though she were under water, and Roz realised with sudden horror that she was about to faint. That was why the world had dimmed so much. With a supreme effort of will, she fought her way back to consciousness and managed a reply.

'What . . . what did you say?'

'I was talking about that nasty bitch Paula.' Lauren bent even closer, her voice low and conspiratorial in her ear. 'Don't you have any plans yet to punish her for what she did?'

'It wasn't so terrible.'

'You can't mean that. Two strangers in the back of a van, no one to stop them hurting you . . .'

'Carter found me in time, didn't he?'

'But what if he hadn't? Something awful could have happened.' She paused, staring at Roz. 'What on earth's the matter? You did take my advice, didn't you? You're not falling in love with Carter?'

Roz felt heat rise slowly in her cheeks and suddenly could not answer her friend, looking down at the floor instead.

'You drive me crazy,' Lauren exploded. 'OK, so the man came to rescue you like a knight in shining armour. But don't fool yourself into thinking that means he cares about you. As far as he's concerned, you're just another player.'

'No.'

'The best player on the tour, agreed. But that only makes you valuable, not special. If Carter bothered to storm in there to rescue you the other night, it was only to save his own reputation. He's paid to look after us, remember? McNaughton would have sacked him on the spot if anything had happened to you.'

Roz closed her eyes for a moment, desperate to escape from the hard truth behind her friend's advice. The tattooist's tool continued to sting and drag at her pale skin like an army of red ants. But at least the lights had stopped flickering overhead and she guessed that meant the worst part was over. She was not going to disgrace herself by fainting after all. That was one good thing. She felt slightly stunned though, as if someone had hit her while she was not looking. Her mouth was horribly dry too, she could not swallow properly and she kept craving water.

Then she heard the rattle of the bead curtain and knew the fat man had come into the small back room. He was standing over them both, gazing down with unashamed interest at her bare breasts. She had seen the way he looked at them when they walked in, teetering on their high heels and with those tiny PVC skirts scarcely covering their thongs. Prostitutes – that was what he was thinking.

The buzzing stopped at last and the dark-haired tattooist laid aside her tool, straightening her back with a weary sigh. The man was still there. His small pudgy eyes crawled across her naked breasts and he licked his lips, giving her a sickly smile.

'This one's on the house.'

'No thanks.'

His fingers fiddled with the zip on his greasy trousers. The hideous bulge there was only too obvious.

'You don't understand, love. That dragon's one of our best designs. It's going to cost you a packet. But I'm sure we can forget about the fee if you're not in any hurry to leave.'

'I'd rather pay, if you don't mind,' she replied tartly. 'I came in here because I wanted a tattoo across my tits, not your spunk.'

They paid the bill without any trouble and left the shop, walking further into town together arm in arm and still giggling at the expression on his face. Roz adjusted the soft gauze pad the tattooist had secured over her left breast, wincing a little at the pain. But at least the weather had improved while they had been in the tattooist's chair and the sun felt warm on their bare legs, their high heels clicking noisily over the pavement. Several men in the street turned to stare after them with lust in their eyes. One even gave a low whistle as they passed but the two girls ignored him.

'I don't want to go back yet,' Roz said, dragging her friend into an expensive-looking Chinese restaurant. 'Let's have lunch instead.'

'Carter will kill us!'

Undeterred by that possibility, she asked the waiter for a table in a quiet alcove, sliding in opposite Lauren with a determined smile on her face. They had a few more hours of freedom before it got dark and she intended to enjoy herself fully.

'So what? It's nearly the end of the season and I'm sick of obeying orders. After all these back-to-back tournaments, we must have earned a little time out from the tour. Let's just do what we want for a change and really let our hair down!'

'You're crazy.'

'Maybe I am. What are you going to eat?'

Lauren stared across at her as the waiter approached to take their order, biting her lip irresolutely. Both of them had now caught the delicious smell of Chinese food wafting from the kitchens. It had been such a long time since either of them had eaten anything but salads or those low-fat meals piled high with roast vegetables that were served to the players every day on tour.

'I can't believe I'm actually agreeing to this. Char Sui Chow Mein? With spare ribs and water chestnuts.'

Roz nodded. 'I'll have Sweet and Sour Chicken with special fried rice, please. And a large bowl of prawn crackers.'

'And maybe a glass of rice wine.'

'Make that a bottle. Oh, and we'd like some Chinese tea while we wait for the food.'

Once the waiter had disappeared, Lauren sank her head into her hands and moaned with delight. 'Chinese tea too.'

Roz laughed at her friend's reaction, allowing one of her high heels to fall to the carpet and slipping her bare foot up Lauren's thigh. The other girl's skin felt pleasantly warm and smooth. She remembered how Lauren had looked in that tattooist's chair, her exposed bottom stuck up in the air and her face flushed with a combination of pain and pleasure as the vibrating tool did its work.

Slowly, watching the girl's expression change from one of amusement to breathless anticipation, her toes manoeuvred their way into the moist deep cleft between her thighs and found the tiny lace thong which covered her sex. Having that tattoo done must have excited Lauren, in spite of her noisy complaints; the lace thong was soaking and easily pushed aside.

Using only the soft pad of her big toe, Roz felt around cautiously for the protruding nub which was her friend's clitoris. Then she began to massage it with slow deliberate movements, careful not to scratch her or press too hard.

'You like that?'

There was a pinkish tint in Lauren's cheeks. 'Stop it.'

'Why?'

'Because people are watching us.'

'Good.'

Lauren squirmed in her seat, gasping and scratching at the tablecloth as the strange clitoral massage started to take effect. 'Please don't. Oh God, stop it. I'm going to come . . .'

Lauren's high-pitched cries echoed noisily across the restaurant, causing other diners to turn in their direction and even the busy waiters, arms laden with dishes, to stare curiously at their alcove seat. A group of dark-suited businessmen at a nearby table smiled and watched Lauren with unconcealed lust as she writhed about like a young child needing the toilet and almost knocked over a jug of iced water in her ecstasy. Judging that her friend had taken enough stimulation for the moment, Roz withdrew her foot and slipped it casually back into her high heel as if nothing had happened.

Lauren's cheeks flushed with sudden embarrassment as the orgasm subsided and she realised how much noise she had made. She reached across the table and stabbed Roz with one of her chopsticks, her tone accusing. 'That wasn't funny, you bitch.'

'It wasn't meant to be.'

Their food arrived in a beautiful array of steaming aromatic bowls and silence fell for a while between them. It tasted utterly delicious and was far more appetising than their usual lunchtime diet of lettuce and raw vegetables with a few scattered prawns. But as she reached the end of her meal, Roz became aware that they were still being watched. She stopped eating and laid down her chopsticks on the ornate little block provided, dropping her voice to a whisper.

'Hey, Lauren. Have a peek behind you.'

The other girl popped a last piece of succulent roast pork in her mouth and turned her head. The two waiters who had been hovering near the table during most of their meal were looking at them both, their smiles interested. She glanced back at Roz, her eyebrows raised. 'Do they want what I think they want?'

'Probably.'

'But we couldn't. Not in such a public place.'

'You're not up for it?'

'I didn't say that,' Lauren hissed. 'But it's imposs-ible.'

Roz shrugged, finishing her glass of wine. 'How about downstairs in the toilets?'

'Classy.'

'Which waiter do you prefer?'

Lauren looked back over her shoulder at the two waiters, her eyes narrowing speculatively. She licked her lips before answering. 'The younger one, I think. With the nice eyes.'

'And the big bulge in his trousers,' Roz finished drily.

They both giggled, then Lauren stood up and disappeared down the stairs towards the ladies' toilets. A few seconds later, no doubt responding to a suggestive look or smile as she passed, the younger of the two waiters muttered something to his companion and hurriedly followed her down the winding staircase.

The other waiter stayed where he was, continuing to stare at Roz without any sign of embarrassment. He folded his arms across his chest and fixed his eyes on her cleavage in the low-cut sequinned top, his expression unreadable. A much older man, probably in his late forties, his body was thick-set but still muscular enough to promise an interesting time down in the ladies' toilets. And it was clear that the waiter was thinking along similar lines himself; his trousers too had tightened over a prominent bulge now, the dark fabric shiny where it was being stretched. Perhaps she had not done so badly, allowing Lauren to pick the younger and probably less experienced man. This one did not look the sort who would need any encouragement to take control of the situation, she thought, which was precisely what she needed right now: a firm hand, preferably on her backside.

Roz shifted provocatively in her seat, leaning back to cross her legs so that her upper thighs and possibly even a glimpse of her thong would be on full view to the waiter, and felt the soreness of her new dragon tattoo as it rubbed against the thin material of her top. She wondered how Carter would react when he saw her tattoo. Perhaps with a genuine explosion of temper this time, she thought to herself, and had to restrain a smile. It was notoriously hard to get any reaction out of the tour manager, no matter what the players did to annoy him. But slipping away from the penthouse without permission and coming back with a sprawling red dragon tattooed across her left breast might prove too much even for his self-control.

When Lauren finally returned, the brunette settled back into her seat with a smile, wiping her sticky face with a napkin.

'Good, was he?'

Lauren nodded, a satisfied look in her eyes. 'He pulled out at the last minute and came in my face. Fast and messy, the bastard. Just the way I like it.'

'Hung?'

'Like the proverbial donkey.'

They both laughed, then Roz stood up and sauntered across to the stairs in her strappy high heels.

'My turn, sweetheart. Back soon.'

Standing in the doorway to the ladies' toilets, Roz heard someone descend the staircase behind her and glanced back to see a dark shape enter the corridor at the far end. It was the older waiter, on his way towards her. The swing door with its greasy porthole banged shut behind him. Her heart started thumping erratically and she was suddenly unsure whether she wanted to go through with this. But it was a little late now to back out. This man would not accept a change of heart without some demand for recompense, so she might as well take a deep breath and let him do what he wanted.

He came close but said nothing, looking down over her body with a blank expression on his face. They stood in the doorway in silence for a moment. She could hear his breathing, steady at first but beginning to shallow out as his hand stroked along her bare shoulder and down below the flimsy material of her top to locate her nipple. She removed the blood-stained pad to reveal a tattooed dragon clawing at her breast, and guessed from his smile that he was impressed.

Without any comment, the waiter pushed her through the narrow doorway and into one of the toilet cubicles. Once the door was locked behind them, there was hardly any room to move. He positioned her like a human doll on the toilet seat, head forced back against the cistern and her legs straddling the ceramic bowl, then reached down to squeeze her breasts for a moment. With quiet satisfaction, he watched her face contort in pain as the freshly-tattooed skin burnt and stung. She had not been mistaken about his air of casual cruelty. This was a man who preferred to be in control.

Standing astride her body with his legs apart, the waiter unzipped his tight black trousers and released his penis. It was thick and sturdy, nestling in dark hair and growing ever more erect as he fingered the head. This was not going to be a lengthy encounter, she thought. He pointed it towards her face, grasping her hair in one hand and feeding himself into her mouth.

'Suck,' he said bluntly.

Her lips stretched submissively around his penis, tasting the thick male flesh with a growing sense of excitement. This was exactly what she needed; no audience avidly watching her every move but silent, one-on-one, anonymous sex with a stranger. It might feel cheap and mechanical but at least there was no pretence here. The waiter wanted something from her and she was happy to oblige. It was nothing like the sex they expected from her at tournaments and exhibitions. Without the usual crowd of minders and onlookers to keep her from harm, these sordid minutes in a basement toilet cubicle felt infinitely more real to her.

The waiter began to thrust deeper into her throat and Roz had no choice but to submit, head tilting back to accept more of his penis. The cistern felt cold on her neck and shoulders.

Her unused sex ached with its emptiness, oozing fluid along her thighs and into the toilet bowl beneath. She could smell her own musky arousal and longed to touch herself, bring herself to orgasm while this stranger fucked her throat, but her hands were busy cupping his balls and slipping inside his trousers to stroke the narrow hairy crevice of his buttocks. From his strangled moan, Roz guessed it must be a sensitive area for the waiter. She did not want to disappoint. One of her fingers located the tight opening to his anus and pushed its way inside, feeling his whole body jerk against hers in reaction. He moved even closer with a loud groan, smothering her face with his body, pushing himself right up to the hilt in her throat.

Roz fought to pull away, suddenly needing oxygen, but his hands would not release her hair. She had a sudden whorish vision of herself, sitting astride a toilet seat and sucking this stranger's penis into the back of her throat, cheeks bloated with his girth and her lungs struggling for air. It was so disgusting. She was both excited and horrified by her behaviour. Her hands tried to push him away but the waiter continued to thrust, ignoring her protests. He seemed intent on using her until he was satisfied, penis ramming her throat and his balls slapping stickily against her chin in a stream of saliva.

At last he came, exploding into her mouth with a hoarse grunt, and held himself there until the last thick pulses of spunk had slipped down her throat and he could carefully withdraw.

He took a few sheets of toilet paper from the roll and methodically cleaned his penis before tucking it back into his black trousers. It was obvious that he did not want to get himself dirty before going back into the restaurant. She was still gasping like a landed fish, leaning back against the cold cistern to support herself. The waiter had not looked at her properly before, not as though she were a real person. Now he glanced down at her spunk-covered lips, her naked breasts with the burning dragon tattoo and her wide-spread thighs, the tiny PVC skirt having ridden up almost to her waist.

'Thank you.'

On that remark, still oddly expressionless, the waiter unlocked the cubicle door and left her there to satisfy herself.

Roz closed her eyes for a long moment, listening to his quiet tread retreating up the staircase. Her chest was still heaving as she dragged air into her lungs and thought about what she had just allowed to happen. She had come such a long way from that first evening on the tour, her outraged shock at the way the other players behaved, her sense of superiority. Now she was one of them, she realised: a shameless wet-cunted slut who had willingly taken a complete stranger into a toilet cubicle, sucked him to orgasm and swallowed every drop of his ejaculation. It was still there now, the thick taste of his spunk on her tongue, acrid yet somehow deeply satisfying. She had not refused. She had not pushed the waiter away. Instead, she had opened her mouth and submissively accepted what he put there.

With those dirty thoughts wheeling endlessly in her head, Roz reached down between her thighs and brought herself to a silent sweat-drenched orgasm.

Thirteen

'Where the hell do you think you've been?'

Carter confronted Roz immediately as the lift doors opened on her surprised face. He had been alerted by the desk staff in the lobby that the two girls were on their way up. Her cheeks flushed suddenly as she realised they would not be able to sneak back in without being noticed, and that instinctive sign of guilt made him even angrier than before. What was she trying to hide? From the way her hand hovered in mid-air, it was clear her first instinct had been to close the doors again and press the button to return to the ground floor. But Lauren must have nudged her from behind, because she stumbled out instead into the plush decor of the penthouse suite, followed closely by the other girl. Neither of them could raise their eyes to his face.

'I'm sorry. We just wanted some time off –'

'You'll get plenty of time off at the end of the season,' Carter interrupted harshly. 'Which is not for another fortnight.'

'We weren't doing anything wrong,' she continued defensively, smoothing her dishevelled hair. 'Some window-shopping. Had lunch in a nice restaurant. And got a . . .'

'Got a what?'

Her momentary hesitation made him suspicious. What else had these two girls done while they were out of his sight, apart from disobey orders? Dressed like that, in the same revealing outfits they wore for exhibition matches and the sex that inevitably followed, they must have been a magnet for every red-blooded male in town. Jealousy was eating away at him inside, his whole body was rigid with it. Her eyes locked with his and she smiled as if able to read his thoughts. Slowly and deliberately, Roz pulled down the straps on her top one by one and allowed the shimmering material to fall almost to her waist so that he could see the dragon tattooed across her left breast.

'A tattoo done,' she whispered.

Carter looked at the exotic red dragon in silence for a moment, then lifted his eyes to her face.

'Have you gone insane? Did you get permission for that?'

'No.'

'Do you have any idea what sort of punishment you deserve?' His voice was shaking with rage. 'You leave the penthouse for hours without telling anyone where you're going, then expect to waltz back in here like some common whore with a tattoo across your tits.'

'It's only –'

'Get down on your knees!'

Roz stared at him without moving, clearly surprised by his anger. Perhaps the girl thought he was joking, or perhaps she did not take him seriously enough to be worried. But if she harboured any illusions that she could control him, Carter thought wildly, she was in for a shock. He might be a fool sometimes where she was concerned, too emotionally tied up with one of his own players to do his job

226

properly. But he was no puppet whose strings she could jerk whenever it suited her.

Her lack of response made him lose his temper. He grasped the blonde by the shoulders and forced her down to the floor. She yelped as his fingers crushed her pale skin, leaving red pincer marks which would no doubt later become bruises. Then his eyes flashed to Lauren's face, making the dark-haired girl jump nervously.

'Now what about you? You went with her on this stupid escapade. Do you have any tattoos you need to show me?'

Lauren gave a frightened little nod and turned slightly, lifting her skirt and dragging the lace thong to one side to reveal a beautiful Celtic design tattooed on the rounded fleshy skin of her bottom. Her hands trembled as she lowered the skirt and faced him again.

He pointed to the floor. 'You too.'

'I'm sorry.'

'Shut up,' Carter said tersely. 'Follow me and stay on your knees. Which is where you should have been all season. I've been too lenient with both of you. This is where it stops.'

He led them along the corridor towards his own personal suite of rooms, uncaring how their knees must be rubbing painfully against the carpet as they struggled to keep up with his pace. Carter was not yet entirely sure what level of punishment should be meted out to these two – and especially to Roz, whose continuing disobedience both angered and excited him – but it was going to hurt.

Their impromptu disappearance from the building had reflected badly on him as tour manager. And that was not his imagination; the minders and the other girls were beginning to look sideways at him, even whispering behind his back as he passed. No doubt they thought he was going soft towards the end of the season, allowing players to sneak out without permission whenever they liked. Next thing he knew, more of them would be taking advantage like that. Then McNaughton would get to hear of it and it would be *adios* to the tour. He would be replaced swiftly and without any opportunity given for explanation. However much he might find Roz attractive and wish to protect her, that must not be allowed to happen.

Once inside his suite, he ordered Lauren to remove her skirt and bend over in the centre of the room. She obviously knew what was coming next from the strained imploring look she threw Roz before taking up the required position, legs held slightly apart for balance and her bare bottom raised obediently in the air. It took him another few minutes to locate a particularly lethal white cane which he kept for this sort of special occasion. Then he was back by her side, yanking the almost non-existent thong she was wearing down far enough to allow him access to the fleshier parts of her bottom.

The slim white cane swished through the air at a satisfying speed. Once, twice it came down, and then the third time he altered direction at the last second without bothering to warn the girl and struck right across the site of her new tattoo with vicious accuracy.

Lauren cried out at the sudden pain, shuddering and instinctively clutching her bottom with both hands.

'Come on, you know better than to do that. Don't make this any worse for yourself. Now put your hands down and grasp your ankles,' he said levelly enough, though his breathing had quickened considerably at the sight of the cane biting into her pale buttocks. And it increased his pleasure to know that Roz was kneeling a few feet away, watching the proceedings with a look of mute horror on her face. No doubt she was only too aware that her own turn would be coming soon.

The girl's face was flushed. 'Please . . .'

'Do you want me to double the number of strokes?'

'No, sir.'

'Then shut up and do what you're told.'

Carter allowed himself a little smile as she obeyed, hands slipping down to grasp her ankles and only the merest whimper escaping her lips when he raised the cane for a second time. But he knew how much pain she must be suffering and did not bring it down again with quite so much emphasis. Even though she had broken the rules and needed to be punished, there was no point incapacitating the girl. There were still a few matches left before the end of the season, he reminded himself, and Lauren was one of their better players. Personal contribution to the tour was something a manager was expected to take into consideration when administering punishments like these. So he restricted himself to only six hard strokes of the cane and tried to avoid contacting the more sensitive area around her tattoo, which, he was forced to admit, did look rather sexy on the rounded curve of her bottom.

'Now you,' he instructed Roz, pointing to the same spot where Lauren had stood. 'Remove your clothes. Then stand up straight with your hands raised behind your head.'

Roz obeyed him without argument, adopting the position with her legs apart and her high naked breasts thrusting towards him. Her face was paler than usual, but apart from that the player showed no obvious sign of fear. He stood silently in front of her for a moment, flexing the cane in his hand while he examined the dragon tattoo on her left breast, keeping his face deliberately blank even though his heart had begun to race at the thought of the caning ahead. The tattoo gave her an exotic and powerful look which she had lacked before. No doubt McNaughton would be furious that his star player had been tattooed without his express permission, but it seemed unlikely that he would stay angry for long. Not once he had seen this curious shift in her appearance. For it was not so much that Roz had improved her looks, he thought, as discovered a different version of herself; as though she had scratched at her skin until the dragon tattoo showed underneath, a mark she had always secretly possessed and which was now to be proudly displayed to the world. But none of that meant she could escape her punishment.

'Why on earth did you do it?' he could not resist asking her, half angry, half curious to know what had possessed her to behave so recklessly.

'I just wanted a tattoo.'

'Even though you knew you would be punished?'

'Yes, sir.'

He hesitated, his mouth suddenly dry. Standing obedient and naked in front of him like this, her body was truly magnificent. The marks of previous beatings showed pale on her skin from breast to belly and, as he wandered casually around to the other side, along her spine and criss-crossing her buttocks too. His fingers itched to add fresh lines across them, especially over her breasts where the scarlet dragon clawed at her left nipple and breathed fire down towards her navel. His eyes dropped automatically to the smooth shaven triangle between her thighs, the full and pouting lips which hid her sex. Carter had seen those lips parted and soaked with sperm many times since she joined the tour, yet never had the pleasure of entering there himself. Roz was such a consummate player, perhaps the best he had ever seen. But as far as he was concerned it was nothing but a cruel and frustrating game that she played.

'Six strokes,' he said unevenly, standing back and taking aim at her exposed breasts.

Though her piercing cry provided him with a certain amount of satisfaction, his eyes still flew to her face as soon as the cane had landed, trying to gauge her ability to cope with the pain. But much to his surprise, after that initial spasm had passed, she reacted to the cane almost as though she were sexually aroused: her pupils dilated, her nipples stiffened to taut peaks, and a slight hint of moisture began to ooze from between her sex lips.

Carter took aim once more and stared in disbelief as her pained grimace at the impact turned into a howl which soon gave way to a sudden heated writhing of her body. Finally, her lips parted on a low soulful groan and she thrust her breasts even further towards him, her blue eyes half-closed as she waited for the next blow to fall. The girl was genuinely excited. Both cane strokes had caught her firmly on the left breast, straight across the site of her brand-new tattoo, and the pain there must be intense. Any of the other girls undergoing such a gruelling physical punishment would have begged him to stop by now or else fainted at his feet. Yet Roz appeared to be excited.

He had never seen such powers of endurance from a player before. His admiration for her strength grew, lending a new dynamic to the remaining four strokes of the cane. Each blow was a challenge, a question he was asking with his eyes and wrist and shoulder. Her answers became increasingly breathless, a fine sheen breaking out on her forehead and her eyes wide open now, only her high-pitched cries revealing the extent of her arousal. It was like watching an animal in the act of mating, her entire body taken over as it raced towards the inevitable end.

'Enough?' he gasped at the sixth stroke.

'Please . . .'

Carter brought the slim white cane down across her left breast for a seventh and final time, watching the girl jerk and moan in helpless reaction, then threw aside the cane. He was erect himself, his trousers uncomfortably tight as his fingers parted her glistening sex lips and located the fleshy swollen bud of her clitoris. It took only a few rubs to bring his best player to orgasm, her body covered with sweat and moving with him rather than against him, head thrown back as she screamed aloud at the height of her climax.

Then her body went limp and Roz sagged forward into his arms, eyes closed in a dead faint.

When she finally came back to consciousness, the room was darker and she was lying on a sofa with her head supported by cushions. The blinds had been lowered on the floor-to-ceiling windows but Roz could tell it was evening outside. Looking down at herself, she realised she was naked and that her small breasts ached and stung in a pleasant manner. The cane marks across them cut deep, criss-crossing the scarlet dragon with its outstretched claws. Slowly, she began to recall what had happened to her: Carter's sudden implacable anger, the punishment he had administered to them both, her fierce uncontrollable orgasm, and then nothing but darkness. Something had clicked on in her brain as he beat her, she remembered that. She had been terrified and excited at the same time, wanting him to stop but secretly burning for him to go on, finish it, harder and harder, push her to the absolute limit. Now, rather like a marionette whose strings had been cut, her whole body felt loose and relaxed in a way she had never experienced before, her mind floating free and her limbs too heavy to move.

Drowsily, she turned on her side to locate the source of a series of muffled grunts and sighs to her right.

It was Carter, still on his feet with Lauren kneeling before him, his penis deep in her throat. His shaft was slick with saliva as it withdrew from the girl's mouth and then ploughed back inside. She could see the man's face, it was tense and excited, a mask of desire. His fingers were tangled in her long dark hair, urging her on, and he was grunting under his breath now as his orgasm approached.

Instinctively, her fingers slipped between her thighs and sank into the heated flesh, still tingling and buzzing from the violent orgasm she had experienced when Carter touched her. It was wet down there, far too slippery for her to get the right friction, so she had to rub in a wide circular motion using her open palm. There was a curious irony to this situation, she thought, becoming so aroused by watching her best friend perform fellatio on the man she wanted to be her lover. But being on the tour for the past few months had changed her, turned her into a sexual creature, willing to put aside her personal feelings and take pleasure wherever it was offered.

Her dry lips parted and Roz gave a helpless little moan, letting her head fall back against the cushions as she watched. The other girl was touching herself too, she realised with a fleeting smile. One hand worked feverishly between Lauren's thighs as she swallowed Carter's penis, head tilted back to accommodate his full length, the other hand skilfully manipulating his scrotum. Yet it was obvious that she too was on the verge of orgasm. Her body was trembling in a familiar manner, the cane-marked skin of her buttocks flushed dark pink and her little tattoo there jiggling as she strained to keep control.

Carter had noticed that she was awake. Without altering the rhythm of his thrusts into Lauren's mouth, his eyes met hers with an unfathomable look.

'You fainted. Feeling any better?'

She nodded.

His gaze slipped to the hand working between her thighs and he smiled drily. 'So I can see. Enjoying yourself there?'

'Y . . . yes.'

'Would you like to watch me fuck her in the arse?' His voice was teasing, not serious at all, though she suspected that he might actually do it given the right circumstances.

Roz looked back at him, her eyes cloudy with desire, fingers still working restlessly in and out of her sex as she allowed herself to imagine that scenario: Lauren down on hands and knees, Carter kneeling behind her, the long cry as he entered the narrow channel of her anus. Her own body began to shake and she knew with a sudden heated burst of desire that she wanted to be the one he chose for his final pleasure. To be the one pushed down like an animal on all fours, mounted and anally penetrated by the tour manager. She was breathless and eager for it, her whole body ached at the prospect.

'No,' she whispered, making her message abundantly clear as she wriggled sideways on the sofa and presented him with the bare upturned cheeks of her bottom.

'Don't tempt me.'

'Fuck me in the arse, Carter.'

His voice hardened. 'Stop it. You're just asking for trouble.'

'Am I going to get it?'

There was an odd pause. Then he must have withdrawn his penis from Lauren's mouth because she heard his footsteps seconds later, crossing the room towards her. She had expected him to refuse as usual, to point out that it was against all the rules, but he was clearly as frustrated as she was by the restrictions of the tour. Impatient hands took hold of her body, lifting and rearranging her to his satisfaction, her thighs angled further apart and her buttocks raised even higher. Then there was the protesting creak and smell of leather as Carter pushed her head right down into the cushions and positioned himself at the entrance to her anus. His penis felt huge and for the first time she was frightened, unsure how much it was going to hurt.

'You're sure this is what you want?' he asked briefly.

'Is it what you want?'

'Yes.'

Roz exhaled and deliberately tried to push out with her muscles to make the initial penetration easier for him. For a moment it felt as though she was going to mess herself, her cheeks flushing as she realised he must be able to see every detail of her hairless puckered opening, but she no longer cared what he thought.

'Then put it in me.'

She had barely given her assent when he was lubricating her hole with his spit and guiding himself into that tiny entrance. She cried aloud at the intrusion and squirmed helplessly on the leather cushions. But she did not try to pull away. This was what Carter wanted from her and she was determined to go through with it. Besides, pain or no pain, it was something she had wanted for a long time too. He bent forwards over her body and let gravity do the work, pushing his full length inside her while her anus stung and burnt.

'Does that hurt?'

'Yes,' she groaned into the sofa. 'Don't stop. Keep moving.'

'Like this?'

His hands dropped to her hips and he began to work himself more forcefully in and out of her bottom, the narrow entrance stretching to accommodate his penis with every new thrust.

'H . . . harder.'

The power of his thrusts increased. She was so excited, her empty sex gaped invitingly and she could feel her own fluid trickling down her inner thighs. His scrotum slapped against her with each strong forwards swing and above the harsh sound of his breathing she could hear the slurp of her own anus as it opened and closed on his penis like a valve. The lewdness of it rose in her throat like a bubble, this sensation of her rectum being filled, utterly bloated to the point of bursting, and the knowledge that he must be able to see everything down there.

In this position, nothing was hidden, nothing was sacred. So there was shame mixed in with the excitement, prickling under her skin and leaving a trail of heat between her thighs.

'Is this what you wanted? My cock in your arse?' His voice was hard and urgent. He repeated it several times like a mantra, jerking her back and forth on his penis. 'Say it.'

'It's what I wanted,' she breathed.

'Properly.'

'Your cock in my arse. Right up my filthy arsehole.'

Carter groaned loudly at her response. His hands tightened on her hips and he thrust into her anus so powerfully it made the breath catch in her throat and her legs tremble. It hurt like crazy at first and took all her will-power not to beg him to stop. She bit down into her lip and tried to endure the agony, even though it felt at times as though she were being sawn in half. The thrusts were so rough and brutal, pushing deep inside the narrow channel of her anus. After a while the rhythm became easier though, when he had stretched her wide enough that she could move with him, jerking her hips back and forth with his penis. Then he stopped without any warning. For one disappointing moment, Roz thought he had come and that would be the end of it. But to her relief he was still fully erect as he withdrew and adjusted her position, pulling her down from the sofa so that she was kneeling on all fours instead.

Poised above her buttocks once more, Carter took her hand and placed it between her thighs. 'Touch yourself.'

She obeyed without demur, her fingers immediately finding the tense peak of her clitoris and tugging at it while he pushed himself back inside. It should have been easy. Her sex felt hot and tight. His thrusts were no longer painful and she could even hear herself panting under the exciting weight of his body. But touching herself suddenly felt wrong and Roz could not seem to bring herself to a climax. Tonight she wanted to lie back and have someone else do it to her. She wanted to become an object – nameless, faceless, something to be worked on like a machine, each part taken to pieces and oiled.

'I can't,' she said simply.

His hands stilled on her hips. 'Can't or won't?'

'I need . . .'

Carter turned his head and summoned Lauren from the other side of the room where she was still on her knees, watching them.

He could not have made a better choice. Lauren's expert fingers slid into Roz's sex like a knife into a sheath, twisting open afterwards to put maximum pressure on the hot flesh inside, and Roz felt her mind spin dizzyingly, so close to orgasm now that her legs were shaking. Their damp naked bodies pressed against each other in a brief embrace, part reassurance, part erotic kiss. In an odd moment of lucidity, she realised the dark-haired girl still smelt of his body, that hint of masculinity oddly overlaying her more delicate feminine scent.

Then the man behind them abruptly sunk himself back into the burning crevice between her buttocks and Roz gasped, beginning to forget everything she had ever known about pain as the pleasure inside her corkscrewed to an almost unbearable extent. Each urgent thrust took her further away from herself. She could not remember how long she had been waiting to experience this intensity. An eternity, perhaps. Perhaps Carter had been waiting for this too. She might have caught it in his eyes sometimes, a strange echo of what she felt too, those fierce desires that kept her wet at night, but concealed before she could really be sure.

It was not being concealed any more though. His very rigidity told Roz what she needed to know, the way his hands grasped her hips as he thrust, the odd little grunts in the back of his throat as he struggled not to climax. She squeezed her sore muscles around his shaft, allowing the burning wave of pain to pass through her, and heard Carter groan somewhere above her.

He did not stop thrusting but his knees nudged against the inside of her legs, pushing them wider apart. She could feel his body tremble as he ran his hands along her spine and knew that he was right there with her, lost in the maelstrom. His hands reached for her small breasts – swollen with excitement, hanging down as she swayed with the rhythm of his thrusts – and pinched them cruelly.

'Please . . .' Her voice betrayed her need, stammering and breathless. 'Please . . .'

Lauren said nothing but gave her an odd brief smile. She seemed able to read her condition perfectly. So close now, so close. Their mouths met in a frantic kiss, tongues dancing against each other. Then the other girl withdrew her fingers from Roz's sex and began to stroke her clitoris instead, flicking at it casually, circling the sticky peak with finger and thumb a few times before squeezing it hard.

Roz felt the heat rise in her cheeks, moaning without inhibition as her orgasm approached. She was teetering on the edge just as Carter was, both too tense to let go, her mind reeling with what they were doing together, best friend fingering her sex so deliciously and this man, her own manager, hunched like some male animal on her back. Suddenly he shifted position, dragging her closer and ramming himself deep into her anus with a hoarse series of grunts. It had happened. The impossible had happened. He was coming inside her at last. As his penis finally began to twitch and pump, flooding her rectum with a warm mass of sperm, Carter's shuddering groan of satisfaction seemed to provide exactly the trigger she had been waiting for.

Roz felt the familiar reddish-darkness of ecstasy swamp her vision and arched into spasm herself, screaming his name.

Fourteen

McNaughton put down the phone and glanced across the desk at Carter, unsmiling. The older man looked more formidable than ever in his dark-striped business suit and Carter could not help feeling a little uneasy as he watched his boss pick up a sheaf of papers and flick impatiently through them before speaking. There was something about this man's long and deliberate silences that made the hairs rise on the back of his neck. Waiting to be informed why he had been summoned to the main office like this, less than an hour before the last and most important match of the season was due to start, Carter drummed his fingers nervously on the chair arm.

'Word has come to my ears that you have not been following correct procedure,' McNaughton murmured at last. He slid open the top drawer of his desk, placed the papers inside and locked the drawer afterwards, pocketing the key before looking across at him.

'Sir?'

'That new player you brought in. Blonde thing.'

'Roz.'

McNaughton nodded thoughtfully, leaning back in his swivel chair and watching him from under hooded eyelids.

'I believe you've been flouting my rules of non-contact and indulging yourself with this girl.' There was a sudden sharp note in the older man's voice. 'Is that true?'

Carter hesitated. It was a real temptation to say no, though he knew there was absolutely no point lying to this man. He had probably been caught on film by one of those damned closed circuit cameras that constantly monitored the penthouse. Unless Paula or one of her spiteful sidekicks had come running to McNaughton with this story in the hope of getting him kicked off the tour. Whichever was the true explanation, it seemed to Carter that trying to deny what had happened would only make his situation worse. He straightened in his chair and met the older man's eyes without flinching.

'Yes, sir.'

'You fucked this girl in the arse?'

'Yes, sir.'

'I think you'd better explain yourself.'

'I did it . . . ' Not sure how to defend his actions without sounding weak, Carter felt his fingers tighten on the chair arm as he struggled for the right words. 'Because I wanted to, sir.'

McNaughton threw down the pen he had been playing with and rose from his desk with an unreadable expression on his face. He strolled across the room to his drinks cabinet and poured himself a small glass of whisky, loosening his tie as he turned to offer the bottle to Carter who refused, shaking his head stiffly. The tournament would be starting soon and he was still working. Besides, he was in no mood for a drink. His body felt tense and ready for a fight, waiting to be told that he had lost his job or been demoted for a season. But his boss merely shrugged and gazed out across the evening glow of the city skyline, sipping at his glass as he stood beside the floor-to-ceiling windows.

'She is eminently fuckable, of course. But that is no excuse for disobeying me and losing control like that.'

'No, sir.'

'You're the tour manager, Carter. That means you ought to be setting an example to the other male members of staff, not letting them think they can get away with fucking the players whenever they choose.' McNaughton glanced at him, his eyes intense. 'You realise I will have to punish you for this?'

'Yes, sir.'

McNaughton threw back the last of the whisky and put down his empty glass next to Carter.

'I've been offered a chance to take the tour out to America next year. There's serious money involved if we can get the girls trained to a high enough standard.'

'That's excellent news, sir.'

'Yes,' the boss agreed. 'But we can only take our four best players and the training they will require is quite rigorous. It's the last match of the season tonight and most of the girls will be leaving next week. That only gives us a few days to teach them a different routine. I'm sure Paula and the others will cope perfectly well. But this new player of yours may need extra time to complete the training.'

'I see.'

'However,' McNaughton continued smoothly, 'I think a satisfactory solution to both matters would be achieved if my punishment were to involve you training this new girl during the off-season. Unpaid and on your own terms, of course. What do you think?'

Carter stared at his boss, taken aback. It was hardly the sort of punishment he had been anticipating.

'I . . . don't know what to say, sir.'

The telephone on the desk began to ring and McNaughton crossed to pick it up, his voice suddenly impatient.

'You're a damn good manager. Count yourself bloody lucky you've still got a job.' He put his hand on the phone, gesturing Carter to leave the office before he picked up. 'Go on, get back to the players. I'll talk to you later tonight after the tournament has finished. We can discuss the finer details then.'

Heading back through the maze of corridors towards the players' preparation suite, Carter felt dazed but ecstatic at how that much-dreaded interview had panned out. He could scarcely believe his luck. Not only was he still in charge of the tour, McNaughton had basically ordered him to spend the next few months with Roz. It could not have worked out better if he had planned it himself. Though it was still a surprise, after expecting the sack or a demotion at least. Maybe the boss valued his skills as a manager more than Carter had ever realised. Or maybe he just needed his best player in perfect condition for this proposed tour of America.

But whatever McNaughton's reasons for that decision, it meant Carter was going to enjoy the off-season more than ever this year, setting Roz such a harsh training programme that it would involve her sexual submission on a daily basis. His penis stiffened in his trousers at the prospect. The slender blonde had come a long way since she had first joined the tour but there was still plenty of emotional and physical distance for her to cover before she was trained to his satisfaction. And with no minders looking over their shoulders, and no closed circuit cameras watching their every move, it would be an effortless shift from manager to master, able to bring

Roz to orgasm or sate himself inside her body whenever he chose.

The girls had been bathed, waxed and oiled before their very last tournament of the season, all eight of them standing or lying naked in the players' preparation suite as he strolled in without knocking.

'Everyone ready?'

Lauren came up to him, her smile conspiratorial. She put a hand lightly on his arm and whispered in his ear. 'Paula was given the job of waxing Roz tonight. But I don't think she did it very well. This may be our chance to get even with the bitch.'

He found Roz stretched out in a corner, in the loving process of oiling her pool cue with linseed oil. The blonde happened to glance up as he approached and their eyes met briefly. For one crazy moment, Carter wished he could tell her what had happened between himself and McNaughton, but this was not the right time or place. They still had one last tournament to play before the season was over and they were both free of restraints for a few months. So he ordered Roz abruptly to her feet and made her bend right over in the middle of the room until she was curved like a hairpin and her naked buttocks were on full show.

'I need to check you've been thoroughly waxed,' he said loudly, making sure the other players heard him. 'Grasp your ankles with both hands and hold that position.'

He kicked her legs further apart, ignoring her soft hiss of protest. Smooth and pale, though still showing a few bruises from her canings, the firm globes of her backside shone from their recent oiling. Contrary to what Lauren had told him, her thighs seemed waxed to perfection and the protruding mound of her sex was as nude as the day she had been born. Even the pouting slit that concealed her vagina, a notoriously difficult area to wax, had been faultlessly stripped of hairs.

His hands lingered over those swollen lips, disappointed that he had no reason to punish Paula for a poor waxing job, and felt Roz begin to tremble with anticipation under his touch. Her capacity for pleasure seemed endless, he thought with admiration. He had barely touched the player and she was already aroused enough to be shaking beneath him. If they had been alone together, he would have slipped two or three fingers inside her moist slit up to the knuckle and worked the little blonde to orgasm. But they were under close observation here, and besides, there was still one area of her body he had not checked.

Carter parted her buttocks with ease and leant forward to examine that cleft in detail, enjoying the sweet nutty scent of her anus as it opened slightly beneath his probing fingers. Then he paused, frowning as he came across something thin and wiry still attached to her skin close to that dark puckered opening.

'What's this?' He straightened, summoning Paula with an angry snap of his fingers. 'I've found a hair.'

Paula stared up at him, her face flushed as she tried to struggle into a rubber skirt two sizes too small for her hips.

'That's impossible!'

'Have a look for yourself,' he shrugged.

Reluctantly, the girl peered into that warm smooth cleft between Roz's buttocks and gasped in horror as she too saw the hair.

'Please, I don't understand how I could have missed that one. I waxed her so thoroughly.'

Carter smiled, taking great pleasure in grasping Paula by the hair and pushing her close to the blonde's raised buttocks. 'We don't have time to debate the issue. You know the punishment for shoddy work, Paula. Just get on with it.'

'But it's only one hair!'

'Oh, stop squealing and do what you're told.'

He forced her head right down into the oiled skin until her mouth was level with Roz's puckered opening.

'You remember the rules? No fingers or tweezers allowed this time. Use your teeth to remove the hair and then give her anus a good licking to check the area's clean.'

He watched as the crouching girl struggled to remove a single hair with nothing but her teeth, failing miserably several times before she finally managed to seize and drag it out of the skin.

She dropped the hair obediently into Carter's outstretched palm and then returned to finish her punishment, tongue flashing out to lick and wriggle into the tight bud of her rival's anus. Paula's groans of humiliation, oddly muffled as she continued to clean the other girl's buttocks with her tongue, were a source of great satisfaction to Carter. Perhaps next time she would not be so quick to fall out of favour with him by treating Roz so badly. It had been an excellent choice of Lauren's to thoroughly embarrass the girl in front of her peers. Nor would she be able to run off to the boss and claim unfair treatment. Carter was not meant to mark the players immediately before a tournament but this sort of punishment would be perfectly acceptable to McNaughton.

'That's enough,' he said abruptly, pushing her to her knees and releasing his penis from his trousers.

Watching her lick the blonde's arse had made him uncomfortably stiff and he needed some quick relief before the tournament began. It was not entirely against the rules to do this, he told himself, so long as he did not enter the girl fully.

Carter masturbated himself with smooth unhurried strokes, holding Paula by the hair and directing his penis straight into her face. Simply the thought of spunking in her face should have been enough to get him to orgasm, but it was not long before his eyes slid sideways to admire the smooth oily buttocks of the girl he was to spend the next few months tormenting. He allowed his mind to wander, reminding himself how he would take every opportunity to slip between those firm cheeks and shoot his come deep inside her rectum, or teach her how to take his full length inside her sex after strapping her down to a pool table and caning the hot little bitch until she climaxed, and within less than a minute he felt his orgasm begin to rise inexorably inside.

He glanced back at the player in front of him, pretty little Paula with her large dusky-pink nipples and smooth belly, down on her knees like a good girl for once, that ridiculous rubber skirt stuck halfway up her thighs and her despairing gaze fixed on the thick purplish tip of his penis as he worked his hand back and forward, faster and faster, until he thought his balls would burst with the sheer tension of it and then they did, rather suddenly. His hand convulsed around the rigid tip and he felt his balls burst right into her upturned face.

Paula cried out in humiliated anguish as long salty streams of his spunk hit her in the eyes, nose and mouth, trickling down her chin to make a slimy channel between her breasts. It was a fantastic sight and his eyes closed on a groan of pleasure.

'You look filthy. Use your hands to wipe your face clean,' Carter ordered the girl, his voice still a little breathless as he tucked his sticky penis back into his trousers and zipped himself up. 'That's good. Now put your fingers up inside yourself. Go on, push them right up inside. I want to watch you fuck yourself.'

Paula's eyes were brimming with resentful tears but she obeyed him nevertheless, her embarrassed glance shifting momentarily to the other players as they stood watching the scene.

That particular punishment had been designed to humiliate the girl in front of her friends and it had worked. Paula's face was darkly flushed and she had bitten into her lip until it showed blood. Not that she was unaroused by the way he had treated her. That was obvious from the ease with which her sperm-covered fingers disappeared up into her nude slit and began working back and forth as instructed. She gave a few sharp little gasps, clearly enjoying the sensation. Then her eyes closed and it was not long before her whole body began to writhe and buck as Paula approached orgasm, finger-fucking herself with total abandon in front of the amazed players.

'That's one hell of a performance from Paula. It looks like you'll have a real fight on your hands for the trophy,' he commented wryly, turning to look at Roz as the blonde straightened, her cheeks flushed from holding that unnatural position for so long.

'I don't care. I'm still going to beat her tonight,' Roz said in a low voice, though her eyes narrowed as she followed the other girl's orgasm through to the last sobbing gasp. For a moment, her hand strayed to the prominent mound of her own sex and fingered the moist hairless lips there. 'Even if it takes everything I've got.'

The overhead lights were dazzling. Roz could feel sweat slipping down her back under the tight rubber outfit and pooling in the cleft between her buttocks.

Her heart was thudding. The audience, mainly middle-aged men in smart executive suits, waited in silence as she stared blindly down the table at the black. It was angled so tightly into the jaws of the far left-hand pocket that she was afraid if she caught it badly, the ball might simply bounce out with the impact and leave Paula a chance at the title. She had two choices here: to pot this black and win the tournament, or leave it somewhere so tempting that Paula would have no choice but to play a risky pot and hopefully miss. It was by no means an easy decision to make.

So how reliable was her game tonight? Roz paused to ask herself, chalking her cue as she stood at the head of the pool table. Brilliant enough to sink this last ball or dodgy enough to leave Paula in with a chance at the title?

Her opponent was playing in a smooth and confident manner. Roz had seen her on better form in the past, it was true, but that was no reason to assume the girl would automatically miss a difficult pressure shot. In fact, Paula might even raise her game in response and take this tournament with one good pot.

She glanced across the rows of male faces until she located Carter, leaning against the wall at the back of the room with his arms folded across his chest. Their eyes met for a few seconds and the tour manager smiled. He looked so calm and centred that she felt her heart rate begin to slow immediately, reminding herself that Carter believed in her as a player, believed that she was good enough to win this tournament in spite of Paula's experience on the tour. And if she wanted to do herself justice as a player tonight, in front of all these wealthy and powerful-looking men who had come to watch the grand finale of the season, she would have to believe in herself too.

Roz narrowed her eyes with utmost determination and bent to the shot, legs slightly apart and her cue arm deadly straight.

Within seconds the game was over. The last ball slammed into the pocket exactly as she had hoped it would and there was a great roar of approval from the watching men.

Then the front row rushed forward and she felt several pairs of male hands lifting her high onto the baize. For a moment she balanced there precariously on her hands and knees, not sure of her next move. Somebody removed her strappy black heels and she saw them borne away triumphantly into the crowd, like some sort of trophy or souvenir. Breathless and still dazed by the overhead lights, Roz could only stare out at that sea of expensive suits and wonder what they had planned for her. The men pressed closer to the table, hands reaching out to touch and stroke her, their eyes filled with lust and admiration, though none of that frightened her any more. It excited her to see how much she had aroused these men with her game.

Her heart had began to beat against her chest like a trapped bird. She had no idea what had happened to Paula. Her rival seemed to have been swallowed up by the crowd of male admirers, though she could hear faint cries from a distance and guessed that Paula too must be receiving some sort of attention from these men. But there was no time to wonder how their treatment might differ as winner and runner-up.

The tight rubber outfit was slowly unpeeled from her body. Several of the men exclaimed in admiration when they saw her tattoo, the vivid crimson dragon clawing at her nipple. Then Roz felt their hands tug her down until she was stretched out in a starfish position, face down on the hard surface of the pool table.

'Could we have a generous round of applause, gentlemen, for our new Player of the Year? The beautiful Roz!'

The noise was deafening: men all around her started clapping, whistling, stamping their feet or drumming their hands on the edge of the pool table. But she could sense a change in the atmosphere. Those male hands which had been stroking her so suggestively suddenly retreated, leaving Roz free to feel cool air on her body as she lay there, stripped naked and with her cheek pressed into the baize.

It had been Carter's voice she had heard, rising above the general hubbub and inciting the audience to applause. Now she felt his hand trailing along her spine and over her buttocks, sliding down one leg until he reached the ankle. Her skin tingled beneath his touch, her heart beginning to race once more as she wondered how major a role he was going to play in tonight's post-tournament proceedings. Then his fingers tightened around her ankle and she felt the cool familiar weight of a manacle, securing her to the table. Carter fastened a manacle around her other ankle too, clipping its chain so tightly to the edge of the table pocket that she could only move an inch in any direction, then straightened up to secure both her wrists in the same manner.

'I won't pretend tonight will be easy,' he whispered, close to her ear so that nobody else could hear. 'Because it won't. But you won. That's what you have to remember. You're a great player now.'

'Am I?'

Carter stroked her hair. 'The best, sweetheart.'

She smiled secretly to herself, eyes closing as she laid her head back down on the baize and waited for the inevitable pain to begin. Her entire body felt flooded with sweetness and warmth. Whatever happened to her now, Roz did not care. She had won tonight, she was a player. The best player on the tour. It would all be worthwhile.

Beside her she could hear Carter's voice changing, hardening to a steely note as he called the audience to attention and instructed them as to the rules of their own game: firstly, one stroke of the cane from each man present across either her thighs and buttocks, then another stroke across her breasts, belly or the front of her thighs after she had been turned to lie on her back. Had they understood? Their noisy assent was like the baying of hounds. It sounded cruel and harsh. Yet she said nothing in her defence, even letting her tongue slip gently over her lips in an anticipation of the exquisite torture to come.

When the first stroke descended and the cane was passed on to the next man, she did cry out. But it was as much with pleasure as pain, her skin breaking into a fine sweat as she took another stroke across her thighs and the next right across the fleshy part of her buttocks. Roz did not know how many men were present. It was several dozen at least. Each blow snatched her breath away, then stung rather like bad nettle rash or a series of wasp stings, and eventually faded to a dull ache soon blotted out by yet another sharp blow and sting. With the right rhythm though, she was able to forget after a while that she was being caned. Her body jerked and gasped to their satisfaction after every mark of the cane was delivered, unable to rise more than an inch from the baize, but her head was swimming too much with the heat and the lights to be able to register each individual stroke as painful.

When they unfastened the manacles and rolled her onto her back, Roz began to feel a familiar buzz of excitement between her legs. Her eyes searched the room as the men repositioned her, seeing the other players kneeling in rows just beyond the pool table. The girls had been stripped down to their lace thongs, each one sucking fervently on a penis, heads bobbing up and down in unison while McNaughton stood behind them with a whip in his hand. Whenever any girl paused, even if only for a few seconds, the flailing whip would snake around her breasts or the curve of her thighs, making her shriek with pain and hurriedly return to the task of fellating the executive in front of her.

It felt strange to be apart from the other players for once, elevated on this pool table where she could be observed by everyone in the room during her beating. It was as though winning this final tournament had set her above the others, made her special. Roz found the thought a little uncomfortable at first, then began to find enjoyment in it. That was what she had desired most when she joined the tour, after all: to be special, to be the best. She caught a final glimpse of her friend Lauren, mouth straining to accommodate a particularly thick and rugged-looking penis, then found herself staring up at the lights as she was manacled into position on her back.

The cane came down almost immediately across her tattooed breasts and she yelped at the impact, feeling her nipples stiffen and her belly clench in a tight knot of arousal. The balding man in glasses who had struck her lowered the cane, watching the flush deepen on her face and chest, then handed it to the man behind him and stepped aside. The next one to come forward was in his late fifties, taller and rather sallow-skinned, possibly of Italian or French descent. He caught her across the nipples again, eyes drawn to the crimson dragon tattoo, and gave a satisfied grunt as her body jerked upwards in agonised reaction. Then he too passed the cane to the next man in line.

Roz turned her head to look up at the newcomer, her eyes silently imploring him not to strike her in the same place. It was a mistake. He chose her belly instead of her tattooed breast, but with such a harsh diagonal swipe that it made her cry out and writhe in her bonds. Before moving aside, he pushed a couple of fingers deep into her sex and brought them out again covered in clear sticky fluid.

'Look at that,' he muttered to the men behind him and held up his hand, his eyes glazed with lust. 'It's obvious what she needs.'

She lost track of the number of men who caned her after that, or deliberately sucked on her bruised and aching nipples, or penetrated her sex with their rough fingers to demonstrate her arousal. Their faces became a blur of pain and mounting excitement, her head spinning under the hot lights as she opened and closed her mouth on high-pitched cries like a baby or a cat in the night. Part of her wanted the relative safety of Carter's face looming above her, his hand wielding the cane across the tender flesh of breasts, belly and thighs. But another part, the wild and animalistic core of her being, needed to see how far these men could take her before she broke.

When the room went oddly dark at one point, her eyes flickered open again on Carter's face. She was half-sitting, half-lying in his arms, still on the pool table. He had unfastened the cruel manacles and was sponging her temples with something cool. She glanced around herself in a daze and realised that the other players and McNaughton seemed to have vanished. The men were still waiting in silence for her though, their faces lean with hunger.

'Can you carry on?' he asked, realising she was awake.

She nodded mutely.

Carter swung her round onto her hands and knees. The pool table felt uncomfortably hard and damp beneath her. Then the tour manager disappeared without saying another word, his eyes unreadable as ever, and the crowd of men swarmed around the table again as if that brief interruption had never happened. Yet it was clearly time to take things one step further.

Roz was lifted into the air while a fat man shuffled into position beneath her. Then several pairs of hands lowered her back onto his erect penis, their hoarse shouts urging each other on. She gasped and moaned with red-faced embarrassment as his penis slid up easily inside her wet sex. Then a heavy-set man in a grey pinstriped suit lumbered up onto the table behind her. She heard him unzip his trousers, then felt the warmth of a snub-nosed penis fumbling between her buttocks. So she was expected to accommodate two men at once. It would be difficult and a little painful but certainly not impossible. Bending forward, she let her chest brush against the fat man so the newcomer could penetrate her more easily. With a raw-edged cry and a grimace, Roz took his thick penis up her anal passage and did not even struggle when her head was dragged up, her mouth prised open and she felt yet another anonymous penis pushed into a moist opening.

It was a lewd and shameful act. Three men at once. Her legs began to shake and she felt herself jerk uncontrollably into orgasm.

The man in her anus came first. Her scarcely used passage must have been too tight for him to make it last. His hands gripped her hips and he lunged forward, grunting and shoving his full length into her rectum as he shot his load. The heavy-set man withdrew soon after he had finished coming, slapping her on the backside as if she was a horse he had enjoyed riding. But that was not the worst of it. Her face flushed scarlet as the spunk oozed out after his slippery penis with an embarrassingly loud squelching noise and she felt it begin to trickle down her thighs like the remains of cold porridge.

The fat man seized her buttocks and pulled Roz closer, jabbing into her sex with a fierce rhythm. His face was screwed up though as he battled against his approaching orgasm, coming inside her belly with a series of loud groans that left his cheeks quivering and his breathing laboured. She felt his fluids mingling with hers at the apex of her thighs, sticky and abundant from her own excitement. But he did not pull out, clearly aware that the man in her throat was also about to come and not wishing to break his concentration. So she remained where she was for another few minutes, prostrate on his fat belly with her breasts crushed into his chest, while the man straddling her face pumped into her harder and harder.

His hips jerked one last time, ramming his penis so violently against her tonsils that tears sprang to her eyes, and she took his sperm down her throat in a hot torrent. Then the man withdrew, still releasing a few spurts of come that spattered against her nose and even hit her stickily in the eye as he reared up, trailing a thin viscous streamer of sperm from the slit in his penis.

Her sex and back passage ached intolerably from their intrusion and her battered throat felt like sandpaper. Then, as though summoned by some magical act, the crowd around the pool table parted and there was Carter again.

She slid her arms about his neck in mute entreaty and the tour manager lifted her away from the stained and sodden baize, placing her gently on the carpet only a few feet away. Roz had thought she wanted to be taken away from this place. But he must have seen the frustrated desire in her eyes because his fingers told a different story. Reaching between her thighs, he located the tense flesh of her clitoris and rubbed it until she cried aloud in abandon, head thrown back as she came to orgasm yet again.

'You're beautiful,' Carter whispered in her ear as she floated back to earth. 'Every time I see you fucked like that, completely lost in your private world, I want it to happen again and again.'

'I'm a slut.'

He shook his head. 'You're a player.'

'I shouldn't be here.'

'Stop talking and listen to me for once. You'll be staying with me after the tour finishes,' he said quietly. 'For some extra training before next season. It's all been arranged by McNaughton.'

Roz stared, her heart racing. 'I don't understand –'

'I'll explain it properly tomorrow. But for tonight, remember your duty as a player and finish this in style.'

At that moment one of the minders pushed through the crowd, bearing a large silver trophy on a red cushion. The inscription along the bottom read: *Player of the Year*. The cushion and trophy were placed respectfully on the floor near the pool table. As if responding to some prearranged signal, those men in the audience who had not yet come gathered around it in a sort of rough circle. They unzipped their suit trousers, grasped their penises and began to masturbate above the trophy in a feverish absorbed silence.

Watching in astonishment, Roz was still bewildered by what Carter had told her. But even the incredible knowledge that she would be going home with the tour manager after the season finished was not enough to stop her feeling horny. If anything, it only served to increase her desire. So she would be staying with Carter until the next season; training with Carter; sleeping with Carter; fucking Carter. Her used sex ached at the thought and her nipples stiffened inexorably. She watched the last remaining men masturbate, unable to tear her eyes away from their jerking hands and rigid straining shafts, her own fingers slipping between her thighs so she could masturbate with them.

It did not take long before the first man came with a hoarse groan, spattering his thick white come across the trophy and cushion. Another man followed suit seconds later, this time successfully directing most of his spunk into the trophy. Then three or four men came at about the same time; their ejaculate pulsed into the trophy in several generous bursts, adding another inch or so to the white fluid inside. Other men in the outer circle were beginning to come, hands clutching their penises as they stepped forward to make sure their come entered the silver trophy. The groans and cries of their pleasure filled the room and Roz pushed a couple of fingers up into her sopping sex to relieve the tension.

By now the trophy was swimming with spunk, its elegantly curved silver sides spattered and dripping onto the red cushion beneath. Less than a minute later, the last man still masturbating exploded in a thick white arc of sperm which coated the inside of the trophy in glorious slime. The audience shouted in approval and stamped their feet, leaving Roz shivering as she guessed what must be coming next.

Carter bent to lift the silver trophy on high, turning to offer it to her as she rose to her feet.

'Please accept our congratulations. You are our new Player of the Year. And as the tour manager, I'm proud to present you with this beautiful silver trophy filled with the spunk of your grateful admirers.' He held it ceremoniously to her lips, raising his voice so that even the men at the back of the room could hear. 'Your reward for being the greatest player of them all.'

Their eyes clashed for a moment over the rim of the spunk-filled trophy, then Roz dipped her head obediently and drank.

Nexus

NEXUS BACKLIST

This information is correct at time of printing. For up-to-date information, please visit our website at www.nexus-books.co.uk

All books are priced at £6.99 unless another price is given.

- - - - - ✂ -

Please send me the books I have ticked above.

Name   ....

Address   ....

               ....

               ....

               .... Post code....................

Send to: **Virgin Books Cash Sales, Thames Wharf Studios, Rainville Road, London W6 9HA**

US customers: for prices and details of how to order books for delivery by mail, call 1-800-343-4499.

Please enclose a cheque or postal order, made payable to **Nexus Books Ltd**, to the value of the books you have ordered plus postage and packing costs as follows:
   UK and BFPO – £1.00 for the first book, 50p for each subsequent book.
   Overseas (including Republic of Ireland) – £2.00 for the first book, £1.00 for each subsequent book.

If you would prefer to pay by VISA, ACCESS/MASTERCARD, AMEX, DINERS CLUB or SWITCH, please write your card number and expiry date here:

....

Please allow up to 28 days for delivery.

Signature ....

Our privacy policy

We will not disclose information you supply us to any other parties. We will not disclose any information which identifies you personally to any person without your express consent.

From time to time we may send out information about **Nexus** books and special offers. Please tick here if you do *not* wish to receive Nexus information.   ☐

- - - - - - ✂ -